First Love

SHEEJA JOSE

FINGERPRINT!

Published by
FiNGERPRINT!
An imprint of Prakash Books India Pvt. Ltd.

113/A, Darya Ganj, New Delhi-110 002,
Tel: (011) 2324 7062 – 65, Fax: (011) 2324 6975
Email: info@prakashbooks.com/sales@prakashbooks.com

facebook www.facebook.com/fingerprintpublishing
twitter www.twitter.com/FingerprintP
www.fingerprintpublishing.com

ISBN: 978 93 8905 317 3

Processed & printed in India

To

Mohan Nadaar, Merliyn Joseph, Arijit Biswas
Shridhar Raghavan, Navneet Choujar,
Mahesh Inani & Ashok

Memories are many and random,
so are the names.

The feeling that can be named is not love,
The love that can be heard is not said,
The said that can be unheard is not real,
The real that can be repeated is not the first love.

—SJ

CHAPTER 1

Pain @ Love

May 15, 2016

I had a lucky life in many ways, hard in some ways, and unpredictable in most ways. The irony was that happiness and sadness gave me the same feeling—pain.

It all started on that evening when, struck by lightning, thrown out of my own body, choking on dreams that swashed against a reality which seemed to break every single bone in my body and numb my senses by emptying my soul, I learned that something called love did exist in this world. I was in love. It made my life suck, yet I longed for this magical thing to take me on its wings up to the rainbows, the stars, the moon, and the sun. But instead of flying, I fell deep into an abyss only to lie there shattered, cracked, and dead.

I flew about our kitchen like a pigeon feather that had trespassed through the window. It was going to be a romantic night, after all. Now, here we are, celebrating our wonderful ninety-one days of togetherness. I blushed as I thought of him. I must have blushed even in my sleep. This is no exaggeration.

All these years I dreamed of being his girl; he was always mine. But the years crawled by pathetically. Finally, when it happened, it was nothing short of magical—the sensation of my first kiss, the first sexual experience, and my very first orgasm, they would remain with me forever. It was like nothing ever existed in this universe except for him. Ever since then, I was 'tearless', 'grumpless', 'bitchyless', 'dreamless', and 'aimless' because he was my smile, courage, happiness, trust, dream, destination, faith, hope, and ultimately, my life in this life and in the lives yet to come.

The clock on the kitchen wall struck five. The dinner menu had only two items—chicken cooked in coconut milk and lavishly sprinkled with cashew nuts and steamed rice. Well, he hated rice. He hated coconut milk too. But when you cook for the first time for your guy, you might as well forget his favourites and cook what you know best.

My mother watched me, hiding herself behind the door.

'Mom! You are making me nervous.'

'Let me help you. I can be your assistant.'

I didn't want to give away my glorious entry to his stomach and heart to someone else. I started cutting the chicken.

'No, thank you. Which movie you are going for?'

'Not decided yet.'

Of course it wasn't pre-planned. My mom was thoughtful enough to give us some privacy. Incidentally, her friends were my friends' mothers and they all lived in the same building. For every child, their parents are the best. I can't vouch for my father anymore, but I can guarantee that of my mom. She is the best.

'I don't want to see you crying when I get back.'

'Mom, stop being a pessimist!'

'You've got only two weeks, Angel. Don't forget that.'

My frowned look conveyed my answer. She didn't argue, but gave me a kiss on my cheek, a reluctant one. Then she took the car keys and left. I have this special skill of upsetting her and I have always excelled at it, but she has mastered the knack of ignoring such things over time.

I put on some music and got back to cooking. I forgot how I used to hate the kitchen and the idea of being in it; I forgot how much I had hurt my mom and myself; I forgot I had to shower before he arrived, but I didn't forget to take out that last bottle of scotch which my mom had saved for such special occasions. What could be more exceptional than this? I hadn't taken her permission though. But I knew she wouldn't have said no.

I reached the last lap of my cooking adventure. The chicken curry smelt good; it would taste good as well. I put the coconut milk into the boiling chicken. I watched as the white milk disappeared into the red gravy and became one with it. Red . . . it was as if I had just witnessed the birth of our universe. What a lesson! All the ingredients have to disappear to become one with each other to taste the best, like me and—My phone rang before I could explore my new theory further. I blushed. Of course, it was him.

'I was just thinking about you!' I squealed out in excitement.

'Listen, I won't be able to make it. I am so . . .'

Sorry? No. That is not enough. You quashed my enthusiasm.

'What the hell are you talking about?'

'Shruti is back.' He ignored my anger.

'So?'

'She is back, Tina.'

'I heard it, Adi. So what? Did you forget that you guys broke up? You always get amnesia when it comes to your break-ups.' Adi always showed this bloody zen-like detachment whenever I tried to say something valid.

'What the f—' I stopped because I couldn't breathe. Shit. Is this a relapse? I no longer have asthma, but when I land myself in such screwed-up situations, my throat just closes up.

'We are going out for dinner.'

'You are supposed to be having dinner with me here. I am cooking for us.' I ruined the surprise. But I couldn't care less about a doomed surprise if Adi wasn't even going to be here. I wanted my boyfriend to have dinner here, with me, not anywhere else, not with Shruti, not with anyone else in this galaxy.

'Tina, can't you just stop this drama?'

'Why do you always do this, Adi?' Tears streamed down my face.

'Do what?'

'Ditch me for that bitch?' Adi was speechless. I guess he was furious to hear his current girlfriend call his ex-girlfriend a bitch. At this point, I was confused—who was the current girlfriend and who was the ex-girlfriend? It seemed like I had become the "ex" even before he updated his Facebook relationship status with a photograph of us. I deserved this much as Adi had flaunted every girlfriend on his homepage in the past.

'You need to grow up. When did I say we are—'

'When you had "that thing" with me ninety-one days ago, why didn't you tell me you were just fucking me?'

'Tina, you are complicating things unnecessarily . . .'

'Oh really? Unnecessarily, huh?! I should have known . . .'

I wanted to throw the chicken and the rice out of the window, but I tossed my phone instead, not out of the window, but onto the kitchen slab. *Why does this shit always happen to me?* I sat there and cried. It wasn't the first time I had cried for Adi. It wouldn't be the last time either. However, every time it felt like the first time, and every time, I wished for it to be the last time. *Who cares about what I wish for!*

When my eyes refused to shed any tears, I flung myself into the bathtub, into the cold water with my T-shirt and shorts still on. If this tub could speak, it would have told me, 'Come on, Tina, I am so tired of seeing you howling all the time. Get another boy and get a fucking life.' And then I heard the doorbell. Was it Mom already? How the hell did she make these mind-boggling predictions about me every single time?

I got out and opened the door, still wailing as if I had opened the gates of hell. It was him, Adi, giving me a "you are such an asshole" look. I didn't bang the door on his face. I could never do that. That's my curse, that's his blessing, and that's the Chinese puzzle others have failed to decode. The wet tee hugged my braless, toned body. But he didn't give a damn about it. How could he ignore a beautiful set of fully-developed breasts, even if they were smaller than his girlfriend's? Adi pushed me a little to find his way in. I closed the door and followed him.

'Why are you crying like a child? For God's sake, Tina, we are seventeen.' He made it sound like we were in our late seventies. I was so angry that I felt like smashing his head and wanted to scream at him, kick his ass, then hug him and say, 'Please don't leave me! All I want in this life is you.' But I just stared at him and wondered how he could be so handsome! His stubble had grown greener than yesterday, his dimples appeared even when he got angry, he had slightly long, shiny hair, and he had gotten a pimple on his right cheek, near his nose, in the hours since we had said goodnight last evening. I was pretty sure he would be six feet tall before he turned eighteen. After all these years, Adi could calm my breath and senses. I loved it.

And I hated it.

I thought Adi would say, 'Don't be stupid. You know that I love you. Let's have dinner together.' Instead, he screamed.

'What makes you think that we had something? We are just friends. Why can't you dry your hair for God's sake? You will get a cold.'

This is what made him so different from any other boy who ever walked this earth. This bloody asshole had half of the Messiah and half of the devil in him. Just when the nasty devil disappeared, the caring Jesus would thrust out. Then I would forget my wrath and the fight. This time, however, I didn't give a shit about Jesus and went behind the devil like an exorcist who had failed in her previous attempts.

'Do you sleep around with your friends, Adi?'

'Why do you have to get stuck on that? If I wasn't there that night, you would have slept with all those guys in that car. It was you who started it. I am not some saint. If you jump on me and kiss me, what am I supposed to do?'

'You know I haven't kissed anyone except you. If you remember, it was you who kissed me first, not the other way round . . .' How could he forget that divine kiss that had happened under the stars on that full moon night? Asshole!

'Are we living in the Stone Age? Tina, we are friends and we will remain so. How can you be so stupid? Do you ever think about anyone but yourself?'

'I am not beautiful like your Shruti or Riha or Sia or Lina or Windy or Rupa or Amy or Neena or Cathy or Lida or Meena or any of the other bloody girls you've dated. I am not rich like you or them either. Then why did you make me feel like you cared for me? Why did you come to me when you were troubled? Why are you always there for me? Why did you tell me that you love me when you made love to me?' I hugged him. 'Adi, you know that I love you more than any of those bimbos do. You like spending time with me. We fight but we patch up, we laugh, we do stupid things together. We don't need to pretend to be someone else when we are together. That's because we are made for each other. You know that I can die for you. What do you like in all these other girls that I don't have? Just that they are more beautiful than me? Is that all that's important in life? Why do you break my heart again and again?'

I was on my knees now, my arms wrapped around Adi's legs. I know I shouldn't have behaved like this. But I would've done anything—shamelessly, lovingly, cunningly—to save my love. Everything is fair when someone threatens to snatch away your reason to be alive.

I used to believe love is to be smelt, to be felt, to be there between two people even when they are not around. Love is not to be discussed, dissected, argued, compared, bargained, or begged for.

However, my theories always boomerang. This time, I wanted to open my mouth and tell Adi how much he meant to me. I wasn't ashamed of it. If you love someone truly, you shouldn't think about what you should or shouldn't do. You shouldn't worry about his or the world's opinion of you.

'Tina, you are embarrassing yourself.' Adi pulled himself away from me. I lay still on the marble floor, face down, my tears happily making a pond below my chin.

'No guy wants a girl who would die for him. At least, I'd prefer someone who can live for herself. Nobody wants someone who lives only in daydreams. I want a girl who has some dreams for herself too. You have become so pathetic, Tina. I am bored of all your tactics. I pity you. You are one of those who hate the rich and the famous but think we are the best to get laid with, to date, marry, and have kids with just so they can upgrade themselves from the general compartment to the first class. Otherwise, they hate people who fly business class, have chauffer-driven, high-end cars and diamonds to match the colours of their clothes every day. They want every bloody rich man to become a beggar on the street. They hate everyone who has worked hard for a life filled with luxuries. You are just one of those bloody whining pigs who hate everything that's better than the shitty life they have. You suck. I tolerated you until now because I keep my word no matter what happens, but I'm done.'

My jaw dropped. All in one go I wished to be deaf, mute, and dead. No girl on this planet wants to hear that she sucks, that too from someone she adores. Was he lying? No, he wasn't. His face had turned red, his eyes had narrowed, and he was looking away. How could he be so mean?

'You turned out to be a little bitch who cries every now and then. I am tired of it, Tina. Get the fuck out of my life and get a life for yourself. You need it.'

'So I am a bitch now! Look into my eyes and tell me that I never meant anything to you and when we made love whatever you said was just another lie. Look at me and tell me, you asshole . . .' My voice cracked. Adi and I used the word "asshole"' with a bittersweet effect. The meaning changed as per the situation.

'I was drunk, if you remember. Then you kissed me. I kissed you back. We kissed. What do you expect me to do? And when did I say that we are in a relationship? I am looking into your eyes and telling you—go, get a life. Get it?' Adi stared at me, making me feel as if he had just walked into my eyes and then walked right out of my mind, robbing me of all my senses. I stood frozen. For me, the night I had spent with him had been the happiest in my life. I had even written about it in my diary:

Such a divine night! I felt like I was floating in the air. I saw a world a million light years away. It was full of bright stars, shining comets, golden moons, and Adi was in the centre of it all. He was smiling at me. My heart thumped and I was pulled towards him. We exploded and became one. Just one. It's like he lives in me now, in my cells, in my memories, in my thoughts, in my future, in my death, and in every one of my births. I want to believe in reincarnation so that in every birth I can be with him, be the wind and the rain, be the flower and the fragrance, be the stone, the tree, the dust, be time itself, just so he is in me and I am in him wherever, whatever, and whoever we are . . . I wish I could freeze this night, this very moment, and be with him forever. Nothing would have mattered anymore. He gifted me a world, one where I have no more tears, no more pain, no more screwed-up days. All I have is love, love, and love . . . Thank you, Adi. Everything I went through was worth hearing how much you love me . . .

I still remember these lines without missing a comma or a full stop or the emotions I had felt when I was with Adi that night and when I was writing about it later on. It was me. My thoughts. My dreams. My reality. I have thought about that night a trillion times ever since. It always gives me goosebumps, makes me wet, and forces me to long for him. Now, I can no longer differentiate between my emotions. Everything feels like a stab in the heart. I believe pain is the only surviving emotion in a person's life. When I was happy, my body ached in love. When I saw myself losing him, my body ached in pain. Love means pain. Pain means love. Mankind should understand this fact rather than break their heads over the relativity theory or the Big Bang or how to be happy or successful.

Now, as I cry like an idiot, I want to remember his confession no matter how awful it was. This way, I would be less miserable and would end up hating him, if not forgetting him altogether. But instead of getting my heart back in place, his nauseating words crushed it, turned it into blood and water that vaporised, as if trying to escape me. Because I felt nothing—no love, no pain, no joy, no sadness. I had nothing—no wishes, no dreams, no hopes. Nothing except a silver lining of collapsed truths. I never knew Adi hated me so much.

All I had done was love him for years and continued loving him, thinking that one day, if the law of attraction—we get what we truly and persistently wish for—was right, he would reciprocate the undying love I have had for him ever since the first time my eyes fell on him.

I stood speechless. Memories stormed into my heart and head. I forgot Adi was in my home, helping himself from our last bottle of the scotch. I wanted to break it. It wasn't a special occasion anymore but a bloody one.

But why the hell am I freezing?

'How much more do you want me to insult you for you to get on with your life? Why are you not ashamed at all?'

'I am not ashamed, Adi, because loving someone is not a crime. Loving someone irrespective of the rules of the world is not tantamount to being crazy, despite what you may think. Loving someone more than your own life is not a punishment or a curse. It's a choice one makes because everything else appears meaningless without that person. I am not perfect. I don't want to be perfect. But the love I have for you is perfect. Without making any calculations to upgrade myself to first class, I started loving you when you weren't what you are now. I would have loved you in the same way even if you were not the person you have become now. You don't know how to love someone without any reason, logic, or rules. That's why you change your girlfriends as often as you change your underwear. I pity you because you don't know the pain of being in love. You don't know the happiness love brings into one's life. You have never seen the colours of love. You have never seen a rainbow in sunshine. You have never seen stars in the day. You have never heard the music from heaven. You have never seen the wind dancing or the sun crying. You have never heard the birds talk to you. You have never felt the waves when they bring back your sutured heart. You have never been in love. What's the point of having the world at your feet when you have a rusted heart? You are completely incomplete. That's what sucks. And I never want to see your face again.'

I saw Adi's eyes widen. He was the one who had held the apple of wisdom in his hands and we had all looked up to him. But now, I was the enlightened one in life. It hadn't been easy. I had died many times to live. Was it worth it? My mom says every experience in our life helps us to become a better person. Maybe one day, I will be a better human rather than being as silly as I have always been. That would happen the day I embrace life, when I learn not to run away from it.

I walked towards the front door to escape the hatred venting out from Adi's eyes.

'Where's Rachel Aunty?' Adi asked.

'Mom will be back at nine.' I went out and closed the door, leaving behind the boy who made me feel complete even while making me feel incomplete.

I took the lift down. Why couldn't I go back and scream at him and call him names that he would never forget in his life? Why couldn't I go and slap him for telling me he had just fucked me? Why couldn't I ask him to get the fuck out of my home? Why couldn't I tell him that he is the worst human being I have ever seen, like Shruti had once said? Why couldn't I tell him that I hated him more than I loved him?

I must be a coward like he said.

When the lift reached the lobby, I realised that the more I wanted to hate him, the more I loved him and hated myself. Adi might come down to get me.

I waited in the lobby.

Fifteen minutes passed by. I was still staring at the lift.

This was the same lift that had changed my life for the good, the bad, and the ugly.

CHAPTER 2

The Boy Who Fell from the Sky

2012

A lot happened in 2012. The Mayans had predicted an apocalypse in 2012, and that helped many mint money out of our everlasting love to live or rather out of our fear of death. It didn't make much of a difference in our lives, except that we—friends from the building and the school—debated the plausibility of an apocalypse, screamed and fought, and called the other side idiots.

2012 also witnessed other important events in this galaxy. There are some major ones that are registered on my memory palate, in no particular order. Memories hardly toe the line of exact time frames.

I was in the eighth grade when the world was getting ready for doomsday. Around the same time, I went through many tragedies in my own life. Ugly pimples ornamented my face. I abhorred the hormonal changes coming about in me—the nastiest being that my girlfriends' breasts had started to grow enough to show through their uniform shirts and invite special attention from boys. My best friend, Dia, had started wearing a bra before she had even turned twelve. My boobs, on the other hand, were in no hurry to blossom and chose to remain small, which didn't please me. I would stand in front of the mirror for a considerable time every morning, wondering how I could coax them to come out faster and bigger. Almost at the same time, our girls' gang also figured out the forbidden fruit hidden in our panties. Dia became our guru and we started taking our anatomy more seriously than anyone would have expected us to. Sometimes, I passed the time thinking how it would be to be kissed and loved in bed by a boy.

Three months before December 2012, a thin trickle of blood between my legs marked my transformation from a girl to a woman, much to the pleasure of my mom, her friends, and my friends. I had learned by then why nobody liked this cruelty bestowed upon us girls. The creator must have hated girls and wanted us to suffer. We discussed our changing bodies and the unfairness of it all during lunch breaks at school. There were days when the boys would run about playing cricket and we had no choice but to just sit and watch them. The boys weren't curious. The menstrual cycle, PMS, kissing, sex, delivery, breastfeeding, they knew it all better than us girls.

'Chill . . . Do you have PMS?' they would ask. Indeed, they were nicer to us on our grumpy days.

My mom wasn't worried about the delayed appearance of my womanhood. At the end of the day, she was a trained doctor who had chosen to be a homemaker following my birth. Basically, I had put the brakes on what could have been a flourishing career in medicine. But once a doctor, always a doctor. She shared a few packets of sanitary pads with me and gave me an hour-long lecture about the female and male reproductive systems. Clearly she had forgotten that it was an era of Google and YouTube!

'Mom, come on! Dia and Rakhi have already kissed boys. I think they have also had sex. Everybody knows everything in 2012.'

'Angel, having periods doesn't mean you get a license to have sex. You all are still kids. It's natural to have curiosity about sex and get attracted to boys, but—'

'Mom, I am the only one in my class who doesn't have a boyfriend!'

'You should have a boyfriend. Nothing wrong in that.'

'Then you will say I shouldn't kiss him. Dia broke up with Veer because he didn't let her have sex with him. She is dating Jeevs now. Please don't tell her I told you, she will kill me.'

'I won't. But I want to hear about your life from you and not anyone else.'

'This year, I am going to fall in love. Some people think I am dating Krish. But how can I date my best friend? I kind of liked Veer, but Dia proposed to him. I think I should find a boy from the senior class, like Jyoti . . .'

'Big plans, huh? Angel, there are no calculations and reasons when it comes to falling in love. Most of the time it will break all your bones, but you will learn to walk. It will hurt you, but it will also make you a stronger and a better person if you are sensible enough to learn from it. Otherwise, it will only harm you.'

'I want to break my bones. It will be fun.' The question was who would break them? Whatever, I was excited about the idea of falling in love. I wish now I had known what I was wishing for! Sometimes, our wishes do get granted.

My mom had gifted me a diary on my twelfth birthday, and had asked me to write down my thoughts, whatever they may be. Being a lazy bum, I didn't write every day. I had a 'MY WISH

LIST' section in it though, where I wrote my wishes and then struck them out as and when they got fulfilled. I added one more wish to the list that day:

5-Fall in love and break all my bones. Where are you? Come fast and help me to break them. ☺

Okay, now back to other major events in 2012.

PSY released the song 'Gangnam Style' and soon it became the most watched video in the history of the Internet. We danced to its tunes during our sleepovers, imitated him, shook our asses until they pained, making our contribution to his success and wealth, and got scolded by our parents in the bargain.

Usain Bolt's "triple-double" at the Olympics made him a star. The world watched him carefully; otherwise he would have been missed, like a lightning flash.

The Syrians continued fighting and killing more people. Why the hell on earth had nobody stopped them? I blamed Obama while my friends said, 'Who the fuck cares?'

Barrack Obama was elected for a second term as the US President. I didn't like it. I wasn't being racist. Killings are killings, even if it's all done in the name of a war.

Queen Elizabeth II celebrated sixty years of her ascension to the throne. The effect of "long live the queen" chants—what else could it be?! I preferred kings and queens only in stories, unless I was the princess.

The movie *Hunger Games* hit the theatres. Hiyaa . . . I am a big fan.

Whitney Houston died ☹. My dad had loved her.

Neil Armstrong finally left this earth. I still believe they didn't actually go to the moon the first time round. On a clear full moon night, I could have made a considerably solid argument to prove my point, which would have terrified even a NASA guy. My interest in the outer space is all thanks to Dad; he made me love the cosmos.

Rajesh Khanna died. My mom cried. I hadn't seen his movies. Since then, though, every Sunday we watched one of his movies. I fell in love with him too, and wrote in my wish list:

6-My boyfriend should have Rajesh Khanna's cute smile.

Ajmal Kasab was hanged to death. All the news channels and the newspapers missed the glory of debate and speculation as they came to know about it after the hanging. It was, probably, one of media's biggest misses in getting a scoop on time.

Shah Rukh Khan won the IPL. I didn't care who played for the Kolkata Knight Riders, I loved watching Shah Rukh more than watching the game itself. I added another wish that night. After all, wishes needn't be small.

7-Getting a birthday wish from Shah Rukh Khan. I wouldn't mind a gift also ☺☺. What would I tell him then? I have to wait ☹.

Sachin Tendulkar announced his retirement from one-day international cricket. India cried. My friends Krish and Rahul didn't eat for a day. I polished off their lunches and evening snacks.

We saw Venus visiting the sun. A rare astronomical event that would be repeated again only in 2117. I thanked YouTube and watched Venus move like a black spot across the sun.

The *Curiosity Rover* sent by NASA landed on Mars successfully. I watched some idiots' conspiracy theory about there being pyramids on Mars on YouTube. There were such brainless conspirators.

But the most important thing in 2012 was yet to happen—the death of the world on December 21, 2012. But the world didn't end, once again proving that those Mayans had been a bunch of idiots. It disappointed many. We had expected something like a tsunami or an earthquake, or the Everest falling off from its crest . . . but nothing. While people continued with their speculations, something happened in our building,

Daffodils. For me, this would be the most important event to have occurred in 2012, and in my entire life.

December 21, 2012, four p.m. A boy fell from the sky and landed right inside our building lift. It ended my world, if not the world outside.

And I, Tina, five feet five inches tall, born thirteen years ago, almost died that day, before my wishes got fulfilled and without even a chance to write my last wish:

RIP Tina, you are the most awesome human being to have ever lived on this planet.

CHAPTER 3

The Hangover

May 15, 2016

I used to love the idea of time machines.

I enjoyed those science-fiction movies where the hero travelled to outer space to fight aliens and bring glory to the human race. What if aliens were real? When I was seven, my dad told me that we have an indefinite number of galaxies and universes. There are an astonishing two trillion galaxies in the universe that have been counted so far by the Hubble Space Telescope based on images collected over twenty years, and that number is only increasing day by day. Would these galaxies ever collide because the universes are all supposed to be expanding? It was fun to think about what would happen if we could travel at the speed of light.

But I didn't need a time machine to travel back in time and start over from when I'd met Adi for the first time in my building lift. Then, in my imagination, I erased all the imperfections in our love story. It demanded exorbitant amount of creativity and emotions to redo everything, right from installing love in Adi's heart to making him fall madly in love with me. But this was my hobby. No, this was my life. And I've learnt it's possible to create parallel worlds as per one's wishes.

'Are you crying again?' Mom sat next to me on the lobby sofa. She had just returned from the movie and was appalled to see me in pieces once again. 'You will fall sick.' She tucked my hair behind my ears.

'Mom, it's like someone has cut open my ribs, taken out my heart, and set it on fire. Adi told me he spent time with me because of his promise and that he was drunk that night . . . Mom, how can he say that now?' Even through my tears, I saw the shock in her eyes.

'Do you remember what I told you? Falling in love can make you or break you . . . You got admission in IMG Academy, one of the best tennis academies in the world. You should be grateful for that. Focus on that, instead of all this. Trust me, Angel, you will find love again. It's great to love someone, but it's important to be loved as well . . .'

'Nobody can make me feel the way he does . . .'

'I am so tired of seeing your non-existent love story. Four years is not a short time to understand what love is. You are not a kid now.'

'You always take Adi's side and blame me.'

'I can't blame him, Angel. It was you who was and is in love with him. I know how it feels to be rejected and ignored, but you have to deal with it. Come on, let's go home.'

'The more I try to forget him, the more I love him . . . Can we go and watch the stars instead? When I go to Florida, I may not get the chance to do so.' She looked at me, amazed.

'Really? You won't change your mind about Florida when you wake up in the morning, right?'

'I promise.' But she didn't believe me.

I didn't believe myself either.

'I am not pressurising you to be a national-level player. But I want you to start living. You can drop it if you don't enjoy playing over there, but not because a boy has control over your life. That's not fair, neither to you nor to him. We all have the right to be happy and we must strive to be our best.'

Everything had gone wrong, but I had Mom. It made me feel better.

'Let's go and watch the stars after dinner. I am eager to have your chicken.'

Mom and Krish used to accompany me to gaze at stars during my childhood. Adi had taken over that honour in the recent past. Eventually, he had started to like those twinkling eyes up in the sky, but not me.

I opened the door to our house. Mom let out a shriek. She had stepped on Adi who lay on the floor like a corpse.

'Adi! Are you okay?' She turned Adi towards her. There was vomit on the floor around him along with an empty scotch bottle. Mom gave me a so-not-cool look. I shrugged innocently, but was secretly thrilled to see the half-finished plate of chicken and rice on the dining table. How would I know if he had liked it? He might say he was so drunk that he would have eaten it even if it were a stone. Anyway, like a dutiful wife, I helped remove his shoes and socks while Mom removed his stained shirt.

A splash of cold water brought Adi back to his senses.

'Where am I?'

'You are in hell, Adi. What were you up to?'

Adi looked at my mom as if he was seeing an angel in hell. I stood next to her with a smile on my face so he could see me too. But he ignored me or pretended that I had been dead for a long time.

My mom dried Adi's hair. I wish I could've done it. She loved him more than me. Well, not exactly, but she loved him dearly. He could make anyone fall for him, even a pole or a stone. If I had returned home before my mom, I would've had the golden opportunity to tend to him. I hardly got any chance to indulge Adi while he had stood by me like a rock in my most embarrassing and horrible moments. Of course, that was all in the past.

Mom left the room for a couple of minutes and brought back Dad's shirt and track pants.

I looked at her. Unbelievable!

'Don't give me that look . . . I gave away the rest,' she told me before I could say anything.

'Mom, let me help him.' I gave her a pleading look.

'I am going to heat some dinner.' She handed me the clothes and went to the kitchen.

I led Adi to the bathroom. He blinked his eyes, as if trying to feel the world around him. He didn't like the bathtub. He didn't like the person standing next to the bathtub.

'Get out.' He snatched the clothes from my hand.

'Adi, you are in my home, in my bathtub. And it's not like I haven't seen you naked before. So shut the fuck up and let me help you.' He showed me the middle finger and tried to button up Dad's shirt, but he kept missing them.

'Don't touch me.' Adi ignored my help, wrapped himself in a towel, and stepped out of the bathtub.

'We can fight when you are okay. Until then, truce.' I blew into his ear but he moved away from me and slipped. He was about to fall and break his bones, but I caught him just in time. It wasn't like any of those romantic scenes in the movies. It could have been if Adi had some interest in me, but he didn't. I buttoned up his shirt.

'At least this shirt had a bigger cause!' He ignored my statement or maybe he didn't hear it or wasn't bothered about it.

'I want to sleep.'

'You can sleep in my room.'

'I want to go home. If I see your face, I won't get any sleep.' What's wrong with him?

'Adi, I am the one who is hurt here. I'm trying to be nice to you for the sake of all the time we have spent together. I wanted to put your head into this water in the bathtub and make you plead for forgiveness for what you did to me today. I didn't do it, but that doesn't mean I am not angry or heartbroken.'

'Your heart is made of a torn balloon, Tina.' He gave me a smile, a vicious one and walked towards the hall. I followed him like his shadow. I wanted to help him to settle on the sofa. But he ignored me.

'Angel, ask Minu to send someone to get Adi.' Mom shouted from the kitchen.

'Let him sleep here, Mom. Please. His dad will kill him.'

I buttered her up. She knew it was her daughter who wanted Adi here and that his father's wrath was a mere excuse.

'Tina, if you don't respect yourself, don't expect others to respect you.' She called me Tina only when she was awfully upset with me. I wanted to ask her something. But not tonight. She read my mind as always. 'I took years to learn this.'

I wanted to hug her and tell her that I love her. Instead, I said, 'You told me falling in love requires no calculations and reasons. I love him without worrying about who loves the other more. I promise you, I am going to Florida. Can Adi sleep in my room?' It was a weird request for a teenage daughter to make of her mother. 'Nothing will happen . . . I promise . . . For old times' sake . . .'

Both Adi and I had had sleepovers at each other's houses and somehow our parents had never made a fuss about it. And my mom knew anyway. We shared secrets. I told her about everything, including my first kiss and the first time I had sex.

Mom didn't answer. But she didn't say no either. She seemed confused upon seeing how fast I could make U-turns when it was about Adi.

'You know you'll get hurt . . .' I got her suggestion.

'For God's sake Mom, we had a million chances, but we did it only once. Don't embarrass me . . . I am seventeen and I've had sex just once!' She appeared to be at a loss of words, or perhaps she was trying to choose the most appropriate ones.

'Don't lock the door.' Finally, it came out.

I helped Adi lie down on my bed and closed the door, but didn't lock it. It would've been awkward for Mom to see how I stared at Adi after he fell asleep, especially after I had decided to move on after all these years of madness and tears. I would have loved for Adi to see me change. I hardly got such exciting opportunities with him. This time, I blew into his eyes. He didn't even blink, and looked as good as dead. I changed into my pyjamas and tee without a bra. Nothing fishy, no one sleeps wearing one. Adi's warmth ran over me even before I hit the bed.

My phone beeped just then. A message from Minu.

Adi with you? Idiot isn't answering.

Yup. He's here!

Where?

H☺me.

His gf is eating my head, yaar ☹☹☹. Is he coming home tonight?

I doubt it.☹

Grr . . . Use a condom. Won't get lucky all the time. How is he dating you and Shruti at the same time? Asshole!!

Not me☹☹

WTF?? ☹☹☹ You ok??? See you tomorrow?

Yup. K. Hugs.

Love you, hon.

We ended our quick chat. Had Minu not been Adi's sister, she too would have joined the "Gang War of Girls" for Adi. Minu could be right, it was all so confusing—who was dating whom and when and for how long? Was I ready to quit? No. How could I just let go of my first and last love? Even if the world tried to stop me, I won't quit. Winners never quit.

Sitting there, I watched over Adi like the angel from all those childhood stories I had heard from my mom.

Adi turned towards me. I slowly pulled open his eyelids.

'Can you see me? Huh? Just blink if you can.' He didn't blink. 'Don't act like you are in a coma.' I held Adi's hand and continued sitting there on the bed beside him. The calmness soothed me and made me forget about the tears and the anger.

How do I learn to hate him? What is it about him that makes me act so stupidly every single day? He has everything a girl can dream of. When God moulded him with such great perfection, he sent me down to earth with a curse, 'You will die in love. You will never live in love.' I had a choice now to challenge God and walk away. But I never did. I wanted to keep God as sadistic as he wanted to be.

I stared at Adi, overwhelmed. He opened his eyes, looking exactly like a zombie in the horror movies.

'What the fuck are you doing?' he asked.

'I . . . I . . . I thought you couldn't sleep . . .'

'Stop thinking about me, Tina . . . Get some sleep.' He turned away, dragging his feet towards the wall and away from me. Idiot. Looks like my tear glands' remote rested on Adi's mouth. When he had kissed me, I had cried. When he had said he loved me, I had cried. When he had said he hated me, I had cried. I had two choices—being miserable or learning to walk again. It was time to be sensible. I picked up my diary—not the one I had when I was thirteen—and wrote under my wish list.

I am going to the tennis academy.

I will learn to live without Adi.

These two weeks, I will be a better person.

At last I started to show some courage to collect my broken bones and heart, to stand up and walk again. To live again.

God, please help me. I can't do this alone. My mom would have helped me to sail through; still, I wanted the Gods to be a little kinder for the sake of living up to their name and for the sake of our human belief in them. Why couldn't they tell me, 'Tina, we are tired of your tears. Fuck off and get a life with Adi . . .?' Don't they have a heart and emotions? Why do they want me to be unhappy and feel like a loser?

I heard not the Gods, but Adi snoring. I had never heard him snore before.

Then I heard him laugh in his sleep. Only this time, it wasn't funny.

CHAPTER 4

As Good As You Give

2012

Adi didn't laugh then. He didn't even smile. He was a snobbish, arrogant little devil, who appeared in our lift, wearing a red T-shirt and a pair of blue jeans. As the lift came down and the door opened, I looked at this dashing boy, believing that he had fallen from the sky. His white shoes were shining. He smelled great. His rosy cheeks reminded me of apples from the Kashmir valley. His hair had the same tinge as the copper flower vase at my home. He was as tall as me, which made me guess he too must be thirteen or perhaps a year younger, since boys grew tall much faster than girls did.

'This place smells like shit, Dad,' I heard him say. Contrary to what his nostrils told him, that day our lift had been thoroughly cleaned. Next to the boy stood a tall man, who appeared to be his father. The man's hands were hairy, and he was dressed in a white shirt, white trousers, and white shoes. He looked like a human angel. I noticed a girl dressed in equally flamboyant clothes, most likely a year younger than the boy, standing next to the man. He held her close.

Who could they be? That too on doomsday! A smile erupted on my face, but I wasn't even aware of it. The boy turned around and gave me a look filled with disdain, as if he had heard my thoughts. I saw his blue eyes, no, green eyes, no . . . I couldn't tell for sure except that they weren't black.

At that very moment, something bizarre happened to me for the first time. It could be what they call getting struck by lightning. I lowered my head and tiptoed backwards into the lift until the cold steel chained me. I felt like a part of me had leapt out of my body, floated in the air around the boy, flew up, hit the roof, then came down to the floor just in front of him, and stood still, looking at him. I held on tightly to the wall, fearing I might drift away in colours I had never seen before, colours that now waved in and out of me, that wrapped me and the boy up, threw us up into the clouds, rainbows, stars, the moon, and the sun. I sweated and I shivered. What the hell? Is the world really going to end? The girl looked at me with a wide smile on her face.

'She is not our class.' The boy turned her head away from me. She heard it. I heard it. She nodded and looked at me as if I had just turned into an alien. I wanted to pull out her beautiful eyes. Was there fear in them now or was it sympathy? Also, I wanted to hit the boy for demeaning me like that. Their father's presence, however, intimidated me. It was better to ignore them.

The lift opened just then and I came back to the present. The man walked ahead. The boy helped the girl get out of the lift and then he turned to me with the same weird look on his face that had left me breathless and senseless before. Still, I saw something else. Very discreetly, I moved my left foot towards his shoes and stepped on his open shoelace. We all heard a thud, followed by a scream from the girl. The boy fell in the lobby, face down, hurt enough to learn not to act too smart in my building.

I stepped out of the lift and stood a little away, waiting for the drama to unfold while preparing to run, if needed.

'You never tie your laces properly,' the boy's father said and walked away. I swallowed my laughter. The boy ignored his father and was consoled by his sister. He held her hand and limped behind. Why did she cry and he didn't? It bothered me. But the boy didn't look at me. He is a chicken. My chest swelled with pride. I won. I smiled. Nobody had the right to poke fun at us in our building. Period.

The aliens got into their white Mercedes and left.

Who cares? Holy hell! The boy again glared at me until their car disappeared out of the gate. It was as if his eyes were saying, 'You wait and watch.'

I felt unwell. I lost the enthusiasm to play cricket with my friends and debate about the flopped doomsday. I was their captain and without me they wouldn't have started a game. But the boy who fell from the sky hung above my head and below my feet. His eyes had pierced through me and sat in my heart without my permission; my nose couldn't get over his smell. I started sweating.

I walked back towards the lift and pressed the button for the seventh floor. As the lift took me up, I cried looking at the spot where the boy had stood barely a minute ago.

I got out of the lift and entered our home. My mom was surprised to see me back so soon, and that too in tears. I sobbed until she reached the end of her patience.

'He said it smelled like shit.'

'Who?'

'I don't know. This boy in our lift; he was with his sister and his father. I have never seen them here before.' I described the filthy rich family.

'Are you crying for that?' Was I? I don't know. She had heard about them from Sarojini Aunty—the benefits of being friends with the building secretary. The kids' father, Mohan Kapoor, was a movie producer. His movies had all flopped recently. He had lost a lot of money, and that's why he had rented a flat in Daffodils on the eighth floor. Before that they had apparently been staying in a bungalow right next to Amitabh Bacchan's, arguably a bigger one.

'These kids will take time to adjust.'

'He is not a kid, Mom.' I didn't like her being concerned about them.

'Angel, go and play. Don't be silly over these petty things. Your dad would be disappointed to hear this.' Do I care? No. Not anymore.

'I made the boy fall flat on his face. Dad would be proud.'

'You really think he would be?'

'Yes, he would . . . He should.'

'Then let me tell you, he wouldn't. They have only lost their business. That boy can still get up and beat you. Then don't come crying to me. You should try and make friends with them instead of being nasty.'

I went down to play, thinking that perhaps Mom was right and that I could have been nicer, though I was happy to know that the boy and his family had to stay in the same shit smelling building as me—only if they were lucky enough to be able to continue paying the rent for their flat.

We had a three-bedroom flat which my mom had decorated in white and grey, with a lot of plants and flowers to add colour. My dad worked in the Indian Army as a doctor. My mom could also work if she chose to, but she didn't. She had also inherited some of her parents' property in Delhi. I felt good, I was sure that I was richer than that boy. That's what I wanted to believe.

I must say something more about my father. I call him "ex-father", at least in my head. Marriages often end, but divorce brings a lot of changes into one's life, including words like ex-husband, ex-wife . . . It happened in my life when I was seven years old. I was lucky, I didn't witness any ugly fights for alimony or custody. If you have a mother like the one I have, you will also end up hearing philosophical tidbits like, "a father is always a father", "we have to see the positive side of things", "either we can sulk or learn to be happy", "only a relationship status changes, love never changes", "divorce doesn't change a father-daughter equation", "your father will always be there for you", "we love you" etc., etc. Of course, she was good at it. My father was also there, mainly through calls and on my birthdays. He never stopped loving me. But learning to live without him made a dent in my heart. I didn't wait for his calls any more. I didn't ask him to tell me about galaxies any more. If he did, I listened. If he didn't, I didn't bother. Did I miss him? The answer could be a yes and a no. But I know my mom cried when I wasn't around. Time heals everything. And I had my mom. She had her Angel. We were no less of a family without a man at our dining table. We were happy.

I ran to my friends to break the news about the new boy and girl in our building and how their father's flop movies had made them poor.

I called out to my friends. But they didn't run to me like they had in the past. They stood in a circle, nodding their heads the way we do in front of our teachers. Then they took their positions on the field to play cricket. How could they do that without their captain—me? My jaw dropped. He—the one who had called me classless, the one who had said our lift smelled like shit, the one whom I had made fall down—had snatched away my captainship! My friends, including my besties—Krish, Rahul, and Dia—had turned a blind eye and were royally ignoring me. I hadn't anticipated this tragic turn of events.

'Yes, Captain Aditya Kapoor . . .' Oh, so that's his name! Krish bowled and Captain Aditya swung his bat up in the air like Sachin Tendulkar. The ball rocketed up in the air, right towards me, and landed exactly on my head. I fell down.

I didn't scream, I didn't cry, I didn't see the grin in his eyes. I was unconscious. However, before everything turned black, I heard a laugh which would give me nightmares for many more days, weeks, and months. It was him—Aditya, the devil. And so, I witnessed doomsday. Not the world's, but my own.

Slowly, the darkness and the laughter gave way to those colours that I had seen inside the lift. They danced around me, covered me, and entered me, leaving me breathless. It couldn't have been my asthma or I might have just died.

I was lucky, my mom told me later. The cricket ball didn't kill me as Dr. Shyam—Sarojini Aunty's husband and my doctor since the day I was born—was right there. Mom always chose not to treat me herself for emotional reasons. Half an hour later, I woke up in Sarojini Aunty's ground floor flat. Even if Shyam Uncle hadn't been there, I wouldn't have died. Some people are born to die easily while others are not. I belonged to the second group. The reason for my misery would be Aditya, the stranger who appeared in our lift and in my life.

And he was just about to turn my life upside down. I didn't know then how.

CHAPTER 5

The Guilty Passion

May 16, 2016

As I remembered my first encounter with Adi, he raised my heartbeat even as he slept in my bed. My dreams and I were partners in crime. The night couldn't have been better. I snuggled my head onto his chest, heard the rhythm of his heartbeat, felt his breath, and became content. The air around us shed tears. Soon we would be separated by the seven seas between us. Would he cross them to see me? No. He wasn't the prince who fought fiery dragons to save his princess. I fought my own demons—should I leave him or love him?

'God, prove to me that you are alive and listening. Prove my love for Adi is true and nothing can replace it. Give me one sign that somewhere in his heart I am alive. Please, give me a chance before I go away,' I said out loud. I wanted my sound waves to travel in space and reach the Gods to convey the pain of love, the hope of love, and the fear of losing love.

Nothing happened. I waited and waited, repeating the same request.

And then, Adi turned towards me and put his hand around me. His nose touched mine, his breath travelled into my lungs, my every cell. A divine shiver ran through me, reminding me of the orgasm I had had when I was with him that night three months ago. I controlled my heavy breaths, careful not to wake him up. What a marvellous feeling! I felt the earth under my feet, stars crowned me, clouds draped themselves around me, rainbows shone on my neck; I turned into a princess and a girl in love.

I gently kissed Adi on his lips. We blazed in the colours of love. It might sound gross to kiss a drunk boy when he was asleep, a boy who had ended up in my bed just because Mom had trusted me enough to leave him with me, but I just couldn't stop myself. Who knew if I'd ever get this chance again! Still, I moved away from him then, leaving a part of me with him.

'Adi, do you even know when I fell in love with you? The very first day when I saw you in that lift. You smelt so divine and I stared at your shining shoes, thinking you must have fallen from the sky. Then, you turned towards me. Instead of your eyes, I saw the stars. There I stood, lost in time. Ever since then, I haven't had a day without you inside my head and my mind. How can someone fall in love with another person so madly? At seventeen, I feel the same flood of emotions whenever you are around me. It is like the first ray of sun every day, the first bloom of a delicate rose, the first rain, the first snowfall, the first feather of a mockingbird . . . Whenever you look at me, I become breathless and I drown. Whenever you ignore me, I become breathless again; I drown and die inside. All these years, you have been the only one to have existed in my world, not my mom who lives for me and not my dad who made me believe that he loved me. My days have started and ended with you. When I sleep, I dream of you. Your girlfriends make me miserable and our fights break my heart. Why do you always ignore me and never love me back? What should I do to get a bit of you that's only mine? You are my day. You are my night. You are my dream. You are my life. You are my death too. I want to love you until the day I die, more and more until my love for you rips off my ribs, cuts out my heart, and stops my breath. But I know I shouldn't. I am trying to live without you. The thought sucks . . . but I have to . . .' I stopped. I would never have the courage to say all this to his face, especially after today's debacle.

Adi moved in his sleep and his legs came to rest on top of me. Their weight held me to him, like a promise that he would never leave me. Or at least that's what I wanted to believe. I heard the faint sounds of the morning *namaz* coming from the nearby mosque before I drifted off to sleep, tucked under Adi's arms and legs.

If I could see myself in my sleep, I would have realised that I had been smiling all night in Adi's arms.

I heard a knock on the door. Time stops only in your sleep. The moment you open your eyes, it runs ahead of you. Adi's hands and legs were still around me. My body had gone numb from his weight over me, but it was cute.

Mom pushed open the door, and then she closed it immediately. I missed her reaction at finding us sleeping together.

It wasn't the first time Adi had slept in my bed. Mom had once talked about Adi and said, 'It's good to dream about having the sun in your hands. But you forget that you will burn to ashes before you even get there . . .' And I had said, 'Mom, I can die for him.' But this time I would say, 'Mom, these are my last few days of guilty passion. I will be gone. He will be gone. It'll all be a memory . . . A worthy memory in this worthless life on this worthy planet.'

CHAPTER 6

Game of Friends

2012

The news of my alleged death spread faster than wildfire. My disloyal friends had barbarously advertised how Aditya's sixer had killed me. They added an "almost" just before five exclamation marks at the end. Aditya dethroned me in popularity with Bolt's speed. He became the Sachin Tendulkar of our building, while whoever saw my face would ask, 'Are you okay, Tina? Oh, you look so pale!'

Aditya's parents visited me at home to apologise for their son's brutality. His sister, Minu, carried an expensive cake which I hogged once they left. I didn't speak to them even after my mom cajoled me to be nice to them. She and his mother, Neelam, however, spoke and laughed like childhood friends who had just been reunited. How could she do that? I, her daughter, the victim, had lost my captaincy to Aditya, along with my popularity and my pride. My so-called friends had let me down and were hanging out with him. I had gone from being an all-important star to a nobody in a matter of minutes. And it was just the beginning of a bloody war.

Whenever I used the lift after that, I felt scared, nervous, anxious, and curious, among other things. I hoped to meet Aditya, so he could apologise and end the cold war between us. I loved cricket. But I didn't want to play under Aditya like an enemy. However, I failed to spot either him or his sister after the incident.

'Could it be that he left because he feared me?' My mom just laughed at my suggestion. Aditya and his family, she told me, had gone to Australia for an outdoor movie shoot. That was good. But there was something else that wasn't good. My dad didn't visit us for Christmas even though he had promised to be there this year. But you can't expect too much from an ex-father!

Krish's birthday fell on December 28. I was three months older than him and we had been inseparable since our playschool days. We had promised to be friends forever. A few months ago, he had told me what our classmates thought of us. 'Our classmates ask me if you are my girlfriend . . .'

'Krish, you are stupid. Girlfriends and boyfriends happen in high school.'

'I will wait then.' However, I never fell in love with Krish nor did he ever confess his love for me.

On Krish's birthday, I went to his house with a new set of his favourite Batman comics. Throughout the party, Dia animatedly spoke to his cousins from Delhi, while Jeevs tried hard to get some time alone with her. She used to have a crush on Krish before she started dating Veer. After Veer, she started dating Jeevs, and then fell in love with Karan, the cricket captain from the tenth grade, while still being with Jeevs. Love can make someone crazy. Dia ended up in the swimming pool just to be around Karan.

I hated water, especially in swimming pools.

'Everyone pees in the pool. Why would you take their piss in your mouth for this boy?'

'Anything for my love. Tina, you don't know what we can do for love. If Karan says yes, I will ditch Jeevs that very second.' We all looked up to Dia for many things. She proudly carried the unconquerable crown of "Miss The First" amongst us—the first one who had masturbated, the first one who had gotten the chums, the first one who had worn a bra, the first one who had kissed a boy, the first one who had displayed her breasts to a boy, and soon, she would be the first one who had sex too.

Dia kissed a boy when she was in the fifth standard. 'It's like living a dream. You do not even realise it's real,' she told me after her one of kissing adventures, this time, it was with a seventh standard student, under the table after the class got over.

She let another boy play with her breasts by the end of the semester. 'It's fun, you get a tickling sensation when they suck on it. You should try it,' she said. By the last semester of the session, she had had something she referred to as "half-sex". She wasn't too impressed by the boy's little tool. 'Tina, I think what we saw on YouTube doesn't make much sense. I thought all these boys carry an elephant's trunk down there. Man, it's so small, you need to search for it.' And she had had "proper sex" for the first time with Karan in the back of his car, just a week ago. 'Fuck, this is awesome. I am speechless. This guy knew all the right moves. I texted him, asking if he will date me but he hasn't responded yet.' We also waited with her, but in vain. Karan chose to use his cars for more than dating. In short, Dia was our flirt guru, kissing guru, porn clips guru, and sex guru.

I was meeting everyone for the first time at Krish's house after my so-called death and resurrection. The missing devil, Aditya, made me happier. I gave Krish a big hug and handed over my gift. But he didn't show any excitement either over my presence or the Batman comics I had got for him. That was unusual.

'I got a real Batman.' He took me to his room. And there it was, a Batman figurine standing taller than Krish! Some of our friends touched the Batman figurine. 'My Batman talks too.' Proud owner Krish pinched Batman's right nipple.

'Thank you, Mr. Krish. I wish you a supercool time with your friends.' Krish's Batman spoke like Shah Rukh Khan! It was so cool.

'Where did you get it from?' No excitement. Pure curiosity and hidden jealousy.

'Adi got it for me.' My face fell. Did he just call him Adi?

'You told me you had invited only our friends. He is not our friend, Krish.' Krish gave me a look, a disgusting one.

'Tina, never say that again, ever. He is my best friend, okay?'

'Krish, you can't have two best friends. I am your best friend.'

'You were, but Adi is the one from now on.'

I hated this Adi even more. Now, he had hijacked my best friend also. Day by day, Adi was making my life uglier. The bigger shock, however, was yet to come. Soon, it arrived in form of this Adi and made my jaw drop to the ground. He sat like a crowned prince amongst all the aunties and uncles at the party. Minu sat next to him, smiling. Everyone, including Krish's parents, were busy with Adi who was being treated like the eighth wonder of the world, while I was being ignored. An irritated me stood behind the door and watched him like a hawk.

'Shah Rukh is a family friend and his son is my pal.'

'Shah Rukh Khan's first hit movie was produced by Adi's father.' One of the uncles at the party ran a quick Google search on his BlackBerry and read out the names of ten other hit movies made by Adi's father. They didn't talk about the flops though.

'How is Shah Rukh Khan in real life?' The overenthusiasm of an aunty!

'He is cool, chilled out. He taught me how to play cricket when I was a kid.' Oh, he didn't say Shah Rukh Khan taught him to walk and poop also. Adi showed everyone some photos on his phone of him with his "pal" Shah Rukh Khan. The aunties and uncles exclaimed and blushed, as if Shah Rukh was present there, amidst them in person. Aditya smiled. I stood mesmerised. His smile was like Rajesh Khanna's! I had never seen him smile before.

Again, something jumped out of me. I perspired.

'You are cuter than Shah Rukh. When will you become a hero?' someone asked. Adi answered, 'Everyone, including Shah Rukh, says so. So it's kind of a huge responsibility.' Bloody hell! He was acting as if he was about to become the president! 'When I turn nineteen, my dad will launch me.' Was he some rocket that needed to be launched? The aunties adored him and pulled his red cheeks. The uncles loved his conviction and confidence.

'What happened to your bungalow in Juhu?' an old aunty finally asked Adi. I wanted to kiss her feet. You are screwed, man!

'It is getting renovated. It will take a year or more. Dad wanted it to be like the Buckingham Palace.' Adi didn't bat his eyelids. Those around him looked at each other and then nodded their heads. What the hell? Did they even know what the Buckingham Palace was?

I laughed. I laughed until everyone turned to me.

'His dad has rented a flat here. I will give you a Buckingham Palace clay model for your birthday.' Adi didn't react. Neither did his audience, except for Krish.

'Tina, I have seen his bungalow. It's bigger than our entire building.' Krish became Laxman to Adi, his Ram, and protected his new-found liar best friend. I waited for the aunties and uncles to ask me more. But they only seemed to care about Shah Rukh Khan and Deepika Padukone and Kajol. Adi continued building up his cinematic life with all the drama and suspense possible. Everyone, except me, believed him. That wasn't cool at all!

Rahul, who came in late, joined us. Though he was a year older than Dia, Krish, and I, and not our classmate, he was a good friend and part of our gang. He didn't show much interest in my revolt against the new villain at the party. 'Tina, I have seen the pictures in Adi's phone. Man, Shah Rukh, Salman, and Amir are his pals. Ranbir and Ranveer look like his *chuddy* buddies, man.' My chuddy buddies had forsaken me for a good storyteller.

At dinner, some of the elders at the party cared to show some concern towards me.

'Tina, are you okay? You always fall sick . . .' I smiled politely, but all I wanted to do was kick their asses.

My eyes followed the hero of the night, no, the villain of the night and of my life. Adi took care of his sister, made sure she ate, and all my friends, including Dia, rallied around him.

'Tina, I am going to date Adi. Look how cute he is! You know, yesterday in the lift, we spoke a lot. And oh, my God, his smile . . . I had an orgasm right there. I am not kidding. I swear I got wet. I want your support and your romantic WhatsApp messages. Your lines always work their charm on my boys.'

'For you, every boy is your boyfriend and everything is an orgasm. Dia, he is a liar. What's wrong with you, yaar?'

'I don't care even if he is a serial killer! I am going to propose to him before someone steals him.'

'He must be already dating like five girls. All movie people are like that. They change girlfriends before they store a girl's number in their phones.' Dia stopped eating.

'Tina, are you helping me or discouraging me? Let's ask him if he is dating anyone.'

'I don't like him. You go.'

'Okay, pray for me.' She turned, but then stopped in her tracks. Adi stood a foot away from Dia and two feet away from me.

'Dia, come on, let's go. We have a great surprise tonight.' That was Adi and he ignored me. Dia blushed. He was gone. Dia was gone. Everyone was gone except me.

After an early dinner, it was decided that the children's gang would be shifting base to the Daffodils' terrace. It had a play zone which we accessed only on vacations, birthdays, and festivals.

I walked towards the terrace, bummed out and nervous.

A ghost would have gotten more attention than me at the party. Overlooked and being a nobody wasn't my style. Now, my past resembled a lacerated dream. The throne set down by my friends pierced me. I wanted to win back my friends, restore my command, and bring back my lost glory.

I had no clue how to do that, or go about the Game of Friends.

CHAPTER 7

The Unsaid

May 16, 2016

'What the fuck?' Adi jolted up with such force that I could have fallen off the bed. I pretended to be asleep. By now, I had imagined us getting married, going for our honeymoon, and having three kids.

'Oh shit . . .' Adi's second reaction was a little softer. He took his hands off me, although his leg still rested on me. I felt his eyes on my face. I tried not to open my eyes, not to smile. Then his head came back onto the pillow, he turned to me, and moved closer. This time, he put his arm around me. I heard his thundering heartbeats, and felt his breath on my face.

You asshole, I know you love me. Your tongue and eyes can lie, but not your heart. I wanted to say as much to him, to the world, and above all, to Shruti. I desperately wanted to look at Adi, but I suppressed my desire. The most beautiful things in this world are meant to be felt. I felt a peck on my forehead. Oh, my! I pressed my feet harder into the bed to make sure I was not dreaming. The peck felt real, Adi seemed real, the touch of his lips felt real. Then the previous night's insults and fight ripped into this illusion. I wouldn't mind dying in the lap of all the colours of love, in Adi's arms, right then, right there, or anytime. I heard a knock on the door again. My mom was being a spoilsport in my already non-existent love life. Adi got up in a hurry, while I continued my sleeping act.

'Good morning, Aunty.'

'Good morning, Adi. Did you sleep well?' Of course, he did. He snored like a jet plane. 'Minu called. Your dad is trying to reach you. I spoke to him, but you should call him.'

'Did you say . . .'

'No . . . Go and freshen up. I will fix some breakfast for you . . .' Mom left, leaving Adi to make the call and me to sleep. The benefit of holidays. Our class twelfth result would be out in a week, but none of us were bothered. My friends and I had decided not to wait for the results to fix our life plans.

I sneaked a peek at Adi. He muttered something and put the bed sheet over me. He stayed there a little while longer, placed a pillow under my head, and then gave me a lingering peck on my cheek, which could have easily turned into to a kiss. I know how much I struggled not to kiss him back. The moment Adi hurried out of the room, I jumped up and down on the bed like a spring ball saying, 'Thank you, thank you, thank you—'. I stopped dead. Adi came back into the room to pick up his phone and looked at me, spooked.

'What the hell are you doing?'

'I . . . just woke up.'

'I am not blind. Why were you jumping like crazy?'

'Oh . . . this?' I jumped again to cover my awkwardness. 'This is the way I get up every day . . . Kind of an exercise . . . Huh . . . Saying thanks to God for a new day.' Adi looked confused, but didn't question me and went out of the room. I dreaded seeing him once he had checked the messages on his phone. I had read those annoying twenty-seven messages from Shruti. Bad habit for sure. One can't play by the rules in matters of the heart. Her fifty-nine missed calls had made his phone vibrate through the night and had tested my patience until I turned the damn phone off.

Adi didn't come back. I followed him out like a little cat. Cats always show such attitude of doing a favour whenever they do anything, except eating. The breakfast on the table looked delicious. I brushed as fast as I could.

Adi took his washed clothes which, of course, I had cleaned, and disappeared into the bathroom. He came out faster than me after a quick shower. Mom dried his hair, while Adi glanced through his messages. I expected an earthquake after Adi saw the number of missed calls, but he just helped himself to some breakfast instead. I beamed. Mom looked at me as if she was seeing a monkey in her kitchen.

'Adi, I didn't expect you to drink again. Angel told me that you had stopped.'

'Aunty, I don't know what happened yesterday . . . I am sorry . . .' So innocent, huh? 'Tina didn't drink after that.'

The "that" he had just mentioned was my "first night" with him. Mom put a spoonful of sugar into Adi's coffee and two in mine.

'Adi, I have something to tell you,' Mom stated dramatically.

'Mom . . . What?' Though she never needed my permission to talk to Adi, being his unofficial girlfriend for the longest time, I had all the right to hear what she had to say and approve it before she dug up something related to us.

'Angel, I want you to keep quiet.' Her voice froze me.

'Aunty . . . Nothing happened . . . I was asleep . . .'

Adi rarely fumbled, but this time he did.

'Mom . . . Please don't bring this up. I promised you . . .'

'Okay, then why can't you tell Adi about it?'

'Mom, the same way I couldn't tell him a lot of things . . .'

'When will you learn, Tina?' She called me Tina and I sensed her anger. Maybe it was time I told him about going away.

'Adi, I am going to Florida in two weeks . . . to IMG Academy . . .' I fiddled with the spoon in my cup. 'I didn't want to go until yesterday night, when I realised I should . . .' Adi's attention remained focussed on the omelette in front of him. I wanted to hit him on the head and say *I am going away because of you.*

'What great news! We should celebrate.' Finally, he spoke.

'It's for two years.' I wanted to tell him, *you will be missing me for a long time. Just say don't go and I won't.*

'Wow! You told me Williams and many other world champions are from the same academy . . .' I had expected to see shock, sadness, guilt, an imploring look, and a few tears in his eyes, but I saw nothing. Bloody nothing. He just ate his breakfast as if it was his last wish to eat that omelette before being hanged to death. He didn't give a damn about me or the two years of my life that I would have to spend in a place that was completely new and unknown to me. I dropped the spoon on the table and got up. He didn't stop me or even look at me.

'Adi, you know that I love you. You are a part of our family. All these years, I have tried to wake Tina up from her daydreaming. I explained, begged, pleaded, threatened . . . I did everything a mother would do. It's not that I don't understand her. She says she can't see you as a friend, and you say you don't love her . . .' Mom's eyes turned red, not in anger but in pain. She loved me, she loved him.

'Mom, please stop.' She ignored me.

'Tina can't be a kid forever, a kid who believes in time travelling and in the fantasy world that she makes up somewhere amongst the stars. She has to go to college, travel, see the world, and do something in life which makes her happy. It would be a shame if she never gets to know what it is to feel loved. That will happen only when she understands that dreams and real life are different. She may cry, break her head, write twenty more poems, quit her training, and stop playing, but at the end of all this, she will learn to live and see you as a friend. Until she gets used to the fact that she must live without you, Adi, please stop meeting her. Help me and help her. It's a harsh request, but it's the only way left . . .'

My coffee turned salty with my tears. Adi hugged my mom and she planted a kiss on his cheek. They didn't say anything more. Adi's eyes turned moist, something I had never seen before. Mom held him, as if she wanted his forgiveness. Then she went into her room. Her heart broke whenever mine pained, she felt pain when I got hurt, her soul cried when I wept. I sat back on my chair and looked at Adi. He got up and hugged me from behind. Good, I didn't need to see his teary eyes or look at him for the last time. I had wanted these two weeks to be memorable. But the inevitable end came quicker than expected.

Adi's chin touched my head.

'Tina, I never ever wanted to hurt you . . .'

'Then stop me from going . . . Tell me once, from your heart, that you love me.' I didn't want to let him go until I had tried, and failed, in all possible ways. Hope is the biggest cancer. Adi said nothing and I said, 'Thank you, Adi, I understand . . .' This was the eulogy of my love, my first love, and possibly my last love too. When my eyes created a fountain on my face, Adi said, 'You are our rockstar.'

I wanted to disappear in him. When we hugged, my forehead touched his lips. He couldn't have avoided kissing my forehead anyway.

'Tina, when you learn to live without me, I will come back.'

'Why would I need you if I can learn to live without you?' He looked into my eyes, the same look that he had had in the lift, years ago. The colours of love engulfed me. Then he was gone. We wouldn't be talking anymore, or seeing each other anymore. I watched my prince, my devil, my angel, my life walk out of our home and out of my life. He didn't turn around, I didn't move.

Why do I feel that everything is turning upside down? Why does my heart threaten to leap out of me? Why does love give pain rather than happiness? Why does love play hide-and-seek? Why does one's heart reject another's so mercilessly?

The silent cries are more painful. It killed me, my dreams, my hopes, and my future. And it slaughtered my soul, now and then.

Who watches over me now? The angels or the devils?

CHAPTER 8

I Saw the ~~Devil~~ Devils

2012

The last full moon of the year transformed the sky. Beside it, the stars put up a spectacular show for us. Krish's birthday party exploded with fun games. I had always loved theses kind of nights—the moon, the stars, my friends, our terrace parties—but not this time.

Adi's euphoria and his magic—yes, he claimed that he had X-ray vision—filled the air and suffocated me. He stood on a table, threw his hands up in the air, whistled, got everyone's undivided attention, and dazzled us more than the stars and the moon.

'Minu has a hairband in her skirt's pocket.' Adi's first prediction turned out to be correct. Rahul questioned the magic, saying that since Minu was Adi's sister, he probably knew that already.

'Okay, Rahul, you've got twenty rupees in your pocket.'

'No, I have fifty rupees.' Rahul sounded confident.

'Anybody wants to confirm it?' Krish, Aditya's new assistant-cum-best friend, promptly went and checked Rahul's pocket and pulled out a twenty-rupee note. Everyone clapped for the magician, who took a bow.

'I thought it was a fifty.' Rahul looked baffled.

'Dia has a clip in her right pocket.'

'What colour?' Rahul asked again.

'Red.' Dia had this "Miss Universe" expression on her face. She screamed, jumped, and cheered, as if Adi had just kissed her. She pinched me, 'Tina, if he can see what's in my pocket, I am sure he can see what's beneath my tee. I told you I will find my soulmate when I am thirteen. I know it's him. Tina, you are a lucky girl.'

''Why am I lucky if you've found your soulmate?'

'You stupid girl! I will tell you how orgasms with a soulmate feel for real.' I wanted to put that bloody red clip on her lips. Whenever Dia liked a boy, she always got him. For the first time, I thought that was not fair. At the same time, I couldn't figure out the trick behind Adi's magic. He must have checked things beforehand to fool us.

'Someone here is without underwear,' Adi shouted. Silence fell on the terrace. My breath stopped. How the hell could he say something like that?

'Who is it? Adi, come on!' Jeevs, Rahul, and Krish cheered him.

'I will tell you guys the name of this person only if you all promise to stop talking to the person.'

'Adi, we promise. Who's it?' Dia shouted.

'All of you have to promise me,' Adi raised his hand in the air to take the oath. Minu tried to stop him.

'We will not talk to the person who is not wearing an underwear.'

Everyone repeated the words after Aditya.

I looked at the full moon and the shimmering stars instead of taking the oath. Could they see us, at least me?

'Krish and Dia will check and confirm it.' Adi's wish became a command, and everyone agreed to do whatever this narcissist pig told them to.

'The one without the underwear is Tina!' Aditya announced my name as if I had won a national championship. All heads turned toward me and I fixed my gaze on my feet.

I wanted to run.

Krish and Dia approached me dramatically. I tried to stop them. How could my friends raise my skirt and check whether I was wearing panties or not? I put up a struggle. Dia held my hand. Minu tried to stop her brother again.

'Krish, we are friends. Don't do this.'

But Krish didn't heed my pleas. He forgot how we had stood by each other through all the years. I fell to the ground, trying to save my ass. Krish raised my skirt and uncovered my butt, without any underwear to cover it. I lay there in tears, in the cold, my bum shining under the moonlight. My heart dried up. I realised the pain of silent tears for the first time. It killed me, it killed my soul. The devil's angels carried Adi on their shoulders and did their victory march around me.

I got up and ran down like a maniac.

When Mom opened the door, I just ran to my room, locked myself inside, and sobbed. My worried mom begged me to talk to her and open the door. Finally, when I refused to open the door, she made her way up to the terrace to find out what had happened from my friends. Krish told her about Adi's X-ray vision and his prediction about how Tina was not wearing any underwear. But these assholes didn't tell her that they had actually exposed my ass. My mom told Aditya and Minu that I had not worn underwear because of my allergy and skin rashes. She also told him that I had asthma. The rest of them knew.

'Sorry, Aunty.' Aditya worked his charm on my mother.

My mom smiled and patted his shoulder and came back home. I was sure that Aditya must have winked as soon as Mom's back was turned. When Mom had come back into my room, she wanted to put some Neosporin powder on my rashes. But I didn't let her; I had also worn my panties.

'Angel, you have to help me help you get well. We are almost there. You haven't had any rashes for months. Don't you like that? If you keep getting upset like this, those kids will only make you cry all the time. I thought you were smart enough to handle them.'

'Mom, Aditya told the others to not talk to me. All my friends are his friends now. He told them he will take them to meet Shah Rukh Khan . . .' I cried my heart out.

'When I was a kid, I had no friends . . . I used to stammer and the kids in my school and in my neighbourhood would imitate me. Embarrassed, I finally stopped talking to them altogether. Then one day, my mother came to know about it. She told me, "You don't need to pay attention to other people's opinions. This will help you in two ways: first, they will get tired of teasing you and will eventually just stop, and second, you will learn to not quit in life."'

It was such an inspiring story. But could I be like my mom? I wasn't sure. But then, even though we can't see the Gods, we believe in them. I decided not to quit.

'Can I sleep with you today?'

'Only if you let me apply the medicine.' I removed my panties. Mom has been doing this for me for a long time, but now, for the first time, I somehow felt ashamed.

'You can do it yourself from tomorrow onwards.' I agreed.

I hugged Mom and went to sleep. I felt protected. No Adi,

no Krish, no Dia could harm me or strip me or laugh at me. However, I woke up in the middle of the night feeling like I was standing naked in front of Adi.

'Baby, you've got a cute, big ass . . .' He pulled my butt cheeks and then laughed, and laughed, and laughed. And I cried. Mom got up and consoled me.

Tomorrow wasn't guaranteed for anyone, except me. It will be made of Adi's wicked grins, of the laughter of my mean ex-friends, of the taste of my tears, the colour of my blood, the laughter of the devils, and the heart-wrenching prayers of my mother.

CHAPTER 9

The Undone

May 16, 2016

My brain shredded itself into bits inside my skull.

I stood numb in the vacuum left by my heart which had gone with Adi. Then I fell on the floor and cried aloud. This time, my screams stemmed from my pain and my hatred. The memories paralysed me. The world I had created for us had crashed like a sandcastle. I didn't want to remember anything, feel anything. I didn't want to experience either love or rejection anymore. Neither did I want the kisses, the orgasms, or the following heartbreaks.

'Time heals everything . . .' Mom turned into a philosopher as she let me cry.

'I don't want to be like you, Mom. You are so stony-hearted. How could you just let him go?' I wasn't talking about Adi now.

'I didn't let him go. Your dad chose to leave us ten years ago. Do you think fighting with him would have gotten him back or made us happy? No. You can't fight and force someone to love you. First, there has to be love there. You are still fighting with emptiness. Are you happy? You've started to believe your pain, your insecurities, your being jealous over Adi are your happiness. They are not, Angel. You have to trust me and believe me. I am sorry I let go of your dad without a fight. I am sorry he isn't here for you . . . But there is a life beyond all this. And I will be there for you, always, whatever happens.'

My dad was the person who had taught me to stand up for my rights. Then one day, he took away our right to have him in our lives. And it happened on my seventh birthday. Dad and Mom made sure I had a memorable birthday. But my dad alone made sure that I had a never-to-be-forgotten night of my life. Because that was the night he chose to confess to Mom about there being a new woman in his life. That same night, he also promised her that he would always be there for me, his daughter, as he handed her the divorce papers. I wanted to scream. I wanted to cry. I wanted to stop him. But I stood dazed, hidden behind the door, and watched my mom signing the divorce papers without a question, without a fight, as if she had been waiting for this moment for a long time. It seemed to me like she had known it all along. That night, in my room, I looked at the birthday present Dad had given me—a telescope. I looked through it and saw the shining stars. I saw the moon so close it felt as if I could touch it. Then everything became a blur. I was sobbing. I was sobbing for my mom, for my dad, and for myself.

The next day, at the breakfast table, Dad tried to tell me about the divorce. My mom had asked Dad to inform me about the divorce. He hadn't been expecting to have to look into my eyes and tell me, 'Your dad is an asshole. I have let you both down.' Dad looked at Mom to find an excuse. But she was firm, 'I don't want to lie to Angel. She should know, and I am here to help you . . .' She wanted him to take responsibility for his actions. And she wanted me to know the truth and live in reality. But I didn't hear what my dad was telling me. I was lost in the sky, with the stars and the moon. I saw him leaving the house after waiting for some response from me, maybe a hug. But I had nothing to say, except that something somewhere inside of me pained. As I heard the door close, I thought that it would be the last time I would meet my father. I looked at the door for some more time. Then, I felt my mom hug me. She was smiling, and telling me, 'Angel, Dad loves you. Mom loves you. Just that sometimes we grown-ups grow apart.' I hugged her back. I knew we would never grow apart. My mother would never leave me. I would never leave her. I said, 'I love you, Mom.'

After that morning, we never spoke of it. But my dad wasn't my hero any more. My mom was.

I looked at my hero mom. She was right. I didn't want to ditch the universal law of attraction—you get what you wish for.

'Angel, you will find love again. Love is not only the pain you always talk about. It is also the smile you radiate with, the goodness you share when you live in love. All that you have been doing to win over Adi has just been making you miserable. Sometimes, we fall in love with a person who may never love us back. That's okay. We can't blame them or ourselves. This is the way life is. But you can't stop living because of this. Let me help you, Angel . . .'

'Mom, you wanted to know what the colours of love I talk about are . . . It's black now, Mom. Just black.' Her face turned pale.

'Thank you for finally telling me. I'll wait to know what the colours of love are when you smile as well. Do you want me to stay with you?'

I wanted to be alone. I lay there in my bed, blank and black. Sometime back, I had been sleeping in Adi's arms for real. I could still smell him, feel him. I hated myself. I hated Adi. I hated Mom. I hated my fucking Dad.

'I hate you . . . I hate you, fucking Adi, I hate you, Dad . . . No, ex-dad . . . You all go to hell . . .' I began throwing all the photo frames that had been kept neatly arranged in my showcase.

'You want something more to throw?' Mom walked into my room.

'What?' I was about to throw a trophy I had won in a tennis match.

Mom took me to Dad's study room.

I had never gone into that room ever since the day my dad had left. It had his memories—books, photos from our family trips, his well-maintained bar, his study table, a sofa, and his guitar. He had wooed my mom by flaunting his pathetic guitar skills.

'Are you ready?' She closed the door behind her. What does she want to do? Does she expect me to clean it now? It wasn't so cool to ask a daughter to clean her ex-dad's room when her first love had literally become her first lost love.

'Mom . . . Do you understand I am heartbroken now? Don't be so mean . . .'

She picked up a framed family photograph and threw it towards the wall and screamed.

It fell to the ground, in pieces.

'I hate you . . .' Saying that, she turned to her ex-husband's bar, picked up his favourite French wine, and threw it on the spotless white wall which he had so adored.

I stood there, puzzled. Mom gave me some scotch bottles.

'Come on, Tina, let's do it.'

'Are we breaking all these? These are expensive, Mom.'

Mom just flung the bottles one after the other with surprising ease, as if we were playing cricket. I inaugurated my breaking spree with a scream louder than hers.

'Fuck you all.' Mom didn't let me use the "f" word normally. Today, however, she didn't stop me.

'Fuck you all,' she squealed too. 'Angel, keep one bottle aside. We will save it for a special occasion.'

I couldn't believe what was happening and just stared at Mom as she continued breaking things with great joy. Then we both shouted, abused, broke yet more things, laughed, cried, and abused some more, until we had destroyed everything in the room—Dad's books, his guitar, his shoes, paintings, drinks, CD collections, and photos. I went to my room and got the gifts I had received from Adi, along with some of the things that I had saved—not all though. Sometime later, the beautiful study room looked even more beautiful with different colours splashed on the wall, and every fucking thing in the room on the floor, turning it into a junkyard. We sat in one corner of the room to save ourselves from the broken pieces and stared at the mess. What a great feeling! A storm just ran out of me, my tears stopped.

'Thank you, Mom.' I hugged her. She brushed my hair.

I thanked the Gods for sending her into my life.

Without her, I would've been dead by now, not by cutting my wrist, but by jumping off the balcony that I could see from where I was sitting.

Now, I lay on my bed, filled with a new-found peace. I fell asleep.

Still, everything looked black. Black. Just bloody black.

CHAPTER 10

~~Love~~ Hate Your Enemies

2012-13

I had made many mistakes.

The worst one was trusting my friends. The morning after the merciless display of my bum, I woke up suffering from scary bouts of sneezing, a running nose, and swollen eyes. The cold and the embarrassment of the night before brought on another asthma attack, the first one since last year. For now though, it was enough to keep me safe at home.

Shyam Uncle visited me. He advised me to use a steroid inhaler for a week. Nobody likes to pump medicines into their body. But when you feel breathless, you desperately need air to stay alive. I waited for my friends to come and visit me as they had done in the past. They, especially Krish, Dia, and Rahul, liked to play chess with me whenever I fell sick. But they never came to see me that day.

'Mom, they are really not talking to me.'

'Do you want me to talk to them?'

My memories were my worst enemy. I drifted off to the past.

Once, when I was eleven, Mom and I were visiting Dad in Dehradun. He had been posted there. It was the first time we went to meet him after their "no-fight divorce" four years ago. My mom wanted to keep him in my life as much as she could and she wanted me to spend some time with him.

During that trip, we were staying in a beautiful hotel from where we could see the picturesque landscape all around us. I loved the place, though I wasn't enjoying what was happening around me. That first day, we visited Dad in his quarters and that was where I met Akash, a three-year-old boy. I hated him the moment I saw him, though I knew, without any introductions, that he was my stepbrother. This was what they might call a "blood connection". His mother was on call in the army camp nearby. As Mom and Dad spoke at length about my asthma and his job and my studies in the garden, I pushed Akash hard enough to land him in the hospital with a fractured right arm. My parents decided to take me to the hospital to let me make amends for my "satanic" ways. I asked Mom to accompany me, but Dad stopped her.

'Kids should sort out their differences. The moment we get involved it becomes more than the kids' problem.' Nobody could beat my parents in their one-liners of wisdom.

I stared at Akash. Smileys decorated his plaster cast. His smile looked so familiar. I felt icy. Looking at that three-year-old boy, I wondered how I could sort out my issues with him. He didn't know what his dad, who was my dad too, had done to us. I stood there for a while and then left the room. I wanted to say sorry to him, but I didn't. I just told my parents that we understood each other now. They were happy.

As I recalled this, I decided it was better not to involve my mother in my mess. I should know how to deal with it myself.

In the coming days, I watched my friends playing from the balcony. I focused only on Aditya who smashed balls like Sachin. The evenings passed. Adi remained with me in my thoughts. Always. Even when I took a leak, or crapped, or watched a movie, ate food, listened to music, tried to sleep, or when I woke up, Adi boogied around me like my own breath. My hatred for Adi was so strong that I thought about him constantly. Well, I started to call him Adi in my thoughts.

Our school reopened after our Christmas vacation.

I had never hated going to school except that morning. Though I had saved my frontal nudity from my friends, they could still tell the others at school about my naked ass. Who would care about my rashes or my allergy?

When my father heard about what had happened, he telephoned and asked me not to behave like a kid. Come on, I am the bloody victim here. They were friends who were supposed to stand with me through good times and bad, not leave me when I needed them the most. Why do I need friends who do not know what a friend truly stands for? I wanted to show them all the middle finger.

'Friends and families are supposed to stand by each other, whatever the situation. If they don't, it's worth leaving them,' I told my dad before I put the phone down. It was meant for him, who had left his wife and his daughter for another woman, and for those friends who had let me down.

I sounded like Aristotle over the phone, yet I was as scared as a mouse. I faked a stomach ache, but it failed to grab enough maternal sympathy to keep me at home. Mom put the inhaler in my school bag, and said, 'Fear is an illusion. It's just in our head. If you want to keep it, it will stay. If you ignore it, it will leave you.'

'It's easy to say, Mom. It wasn't your bum.' I picked up my bag.

'Let me come down with you.' That gave me extra confidence to face my friends. I didn't see Krish at my door before the clock chimed nine.

Rahul and Dia were waiting outside the gate as always.

How stupid was I? They were my friends and were waiting for me.

My mom had said the same thing too. I kissed her and hastened towards them. They waved, but not at me. I turned back and saw Adi and Minu in our school uniform, walking down along with Krish. My friends greeted the three musketeers and ignored me. My mom looked concerned, but she didn't say anything.

I got onto the bus when it arrived. Did I have any other option? Adi sat next to Krish. I used to sit there, until now. I found an empty seat at the back. Why was this boy and his sister in our school bus, wearing our school uniform?

My stomach cramped, this time for real.

Meanwhile, Adi turned the bus into a circus. Some of the kids wanted to see his magic again. Students who were not from our building befriended him too. Dia eyed him like she was in a dream.

'Today, everyone is wearing underwear,' Adi announced, using his X-ray vision. The disappointment in the bus was palpable. 'Krish, do you want to check?'

Krish dramatically walked towards me. I held my bag in my lap and tucked my skirt under my thighs.

He stood in front of me like a bull ready to charge. The students cheered. I closed my eyes. *Fear is just an illusion.* I opened my eyes. Krish was no illusion. I took my bag and hit him hard on the head. He lost his balance, but his so-called best friend Adi caught him. Krish charged at me. I picked up my bag to hit him again.

'Heroes don't beat up silly girls.' Adi pulled Krish away. I held on to the seat, trying to stop myself from shivering. My rashes burnt me. I may have pissed a little in my underwear.

I never wanted to see Adi's face again. But my eyes refused to obey my command. I got glimpses of his eyes, his forehead, his lips, his dimples, and his hair as students around him burst into laughter. And when I saw these bits and parts of him, my heart skipped a beat.

The bus stopped inside our school—St. Michael's High School. I wanted to wake up from this nightmare. Since the night of my ass display, things were getting worse by the second. I realised then that their bullying won't stop. It sucked!

I was the last one to get down from it. I was reciting a prayer to Mother Mary to save me from these little devils and I didn't see it coming—a foot in a spotless white shoe. I tripped and fell on the rocky ground with a thud. It hurt, my skin bruised and blood gushed out of my knee. The darkness smiled at me deviously. I was falling. Down. Down. Down. I couldn't scream for help, I was paralysed with fear. The sick feeling in my stomach and heart exploded. I tried to get up. I saw Adi wiping off the dust from his shoes. Then he gave me that same "lift look" and walked away. Instead of getting up, I lay there on the ground, unsure of what to do next.

I wanted to scream at him, but I couldn't. So I didn't.

I wanted to throw a stone at him. I could, but I didn't.

I thought I was lying in a grave, my grave covered in the mud and the darkness, instead of lying on the school ground. I was alive, despite that I couldn't move my body.

I hated Mom for telling me the world survived on Jesus' principles and Gandhi's ideas—love your enemies.

This world was not for Jesus or Gandhi anymore. The rights and wrongs do not matter anymore. Adi was the one who started the cold war. He had labelled me as "not their class". I was ready to ignore that and take the blame of starting the war by making him trip and fall. But the moment he had thrown that cricket ball at my head and knocked me unconscious—as good as dead—we had been even. Still, he had schemed to expose my private parts, had taken away all my friends, and my right to play cricket. He had captured my seat on the bus and had made me fall again. The score was one to five now! Even though I was hurt, I managed to walk into my class amidst the laughter and hush-hush of my classmates.

Krish, the backstabber did it again. He unmasked my "bum story" before the rest of the students. Nobody bothered about my stained uniform or my bruises. I just thanked God that Lucifer Adi wasn't in our class. That was the best moment I had had ever since he had appeared in our lift.

Kaya, the girl next to me, stopped laughing, and asked, 'You really got a black mole on your right bum?'

Did I? What the fuck! Did I have eyes at the back of my head to see my bum?

Dia and Krish were talking animatedly. I guess Adi and I were the hot topics right then.

Miss Rose, our English teacher who was always right on time, gifted me five extra minutes in purgatory. When she appeared, I wished I was dead. Adi stood next to her and "dimpled" out his charm. The girls gasped, Dia had another orgasm, and my heart skipped a beat.

Miss Rose introduced Adi as the new student to join our class. Aditya smiled and raised his hand like a movie star, like his so-called friend Shah Rukh Khan.

'Guys, I am going to steal your heart.' He crossed his heart. What a cheesy line! All the buffoons clapped except me.

'Tina, what happened to you?' Why would Miss Rose care if I didn't clap? Oh! She was asking about my dirty uniform.

'I slipped.'

The lie sounded better than the embarrassing truth.

Adi soon became a hero not only in my class, but also in the entire school. The girls passed through the corridor outside our classroom more times than ever before. Dia and Krish became popular because of their proximity to Adi. The teachers adored him, especially our principal, who even suggested that he would be grateful if Adi could pull some strings and get either Shah Rukh Khan or Ranbir Kapoor to attend our annual day. You only had to name a hero or heroine, and Adi would whip out his phone to show you his selfies with them. He became the most popular kid in school in a matter of days. And I became a fossil under him. Wherever I turned, I saw him—in the school building, in the playground, canteen, and even outside the washroom corridor. My friends became my ex-friends, the school resembled Tihar Jail, I disliked coming back home, I interacted less with Mom, and I avoided Dad's phone calls. I spent more and more time inside my locked room, thinking and writing about Adi and how he was wrecking my happy life.

Days passed and my miseries rocketed when Miss Rose summoned me to her office. She wanted to know what was wrong with me. But I decided to keep my mouth shut. Her intermittent interrogation ran on and on for some days until I met my mom in the principal's office, sitting next to Miss Rose.

'Dr. Rachel, I think she needs both parents beside her. She is obviously going through a hard time. It's a crucial age. I don't need to tell you that.' Miss Rose didn't beat around the bush. Mom promised her she would take care of it and Miss Rose sent me back to my class. They always excluded us—the students—from the key parts of their discussions. I had to wait on tenterhooks until I was home to know what the results of this meeting were.

That evening, Mom asked for my diary.

'It is personal, Mom.' I didn't give it to her.

'Angel, as we grow up, at some point or the other, we all feel like we are not good enough. But that feeling will go away. You should know your Dad and I love you. I always want to be your friend first, and then your mom. You do not eat well or play outside with your friends anymore. You have lost weight. You failed your class tests . . . You have to tell me what's bothering you.' I hadn't slept in her lap since Adi had entered my life. He had not only spoiled my relationship with my friends, but also with my parents. I kept quiet.

'Let's restart your tennis coaching. What do you think?'

I used to love playing tennis much more than my studies and I had won many trophies until I entered the seventh standard. Mom wanted me to concentrate on my studies in high school, so she stopped my coaching. Now, she started it again and my days after school became brighter. I could see the disappointment in the devil's gang on seeing me in my white skirt and tee, with my toned legs showing. Above all, Mom would come to pick me up after the coaching every day. I must say, we got back to our old ways. We spoke more and smiled more.

My spying from my bedroom window gave me a clear idea of Adi's schedule. He played in the garden till six p.m. Later, he attended cricket practice and came back at half-past seven. After I started my tennis coaching, I missed seeing Adi play as I came back home around eight p.m. But I couldn't stop myself from looking for him wherever I was. And one day, we met him in the garden. He was coming back from his coaching later than usual that day.

'Hi, Aunty!'

Can you believe this? Aditya was walking straight towards us with a great smile on his face, as if we were the best of friends.

'Hi, Aditya. How are you?' Mom responded with equal enthusiasm.

'I'm good, Aunty. Just on my way home. Krish will be at my house to do homework soon.'

It looked like he was just making conversation, but I knew what he really meant. My friend was his friend now; he was so happy to rub it in my face. Man, he was a born actor. A liar. A pig. An asshole. Adi looked straight into my eyes. Fuck. It was the same look and I had the same feeling. I held my mom's hand like a toddler.

'Good. I believe you all are friends now. Tina seems to be happier as well.'

'"These fucking bitchy friends are not worth being friends with." That's what Tina had said then. I told her that survival has a tinge of adventure attached, better than just existing. She said she loves adventure. Yes, all okay now.' Adi stopped.

How he lies his ass off! We never had this conversation.

'How can you use that kind of language, Angel? Why don't you go with Adi and meet your friends?'

How could she believe Adi over me? Who was her child here?

That night, I wrote in the diary.

How shameless this Adi pig is. How could he just look at me and lie? My mom also hates me. Survival has a tinge of adventure attached, and that's better than just existing. Where did he copy this line from? I want someone to treat his sister the same way he treats me. Then he will understand how it feels. God, either kill me or kill him. Or make his dad's movies hit again and take him away from my school and my building.

PS: He was right. Those fucking bitches, including him, are not worthy of being my friends. From today onwards, I don't give a shit about them. I am done with them.

My new-found happiness would end soon, faster than it had come, leaving me in a worse situation than I had ever been in.

CHAPTER 11

Burial of a Heart

May 16, 2016

I woke up at lunchtime.

I had had a great nap after that breaking spree with Mom.

'Let's go for a movie,' my mom suggested while we ate my favourite pasta for lunch. But Mr. Khan, my coach, wouldn't be kind enough to let me go for a movie just because I had gotten enlightened about my stupid past. Hitting the balls would keep me away from Adi.

I had developed a habit of flipping sides when it was about Adi. Before my nap, I was bawling because I couldn't be with him, and now I wanted to stay away from him.

Fuck you, Adi. What do you think, I can't live without you? You are just a strand of hair on my pillow. Goodbye. That's what I had thought before I went to sleep.

Then when I woke up, however, I wanted to phone him! He was my addiction.

I left my phone with Mom, fearing I might give in to the temptation. She kept it without asking any questions. We could easily read each other's mind. I took the car keys, but Mom stopped me as I didn't have a driving license yet. Adi had been driving ever since he had turned sixteen though.

'I am not expecting to pick you up from Juhu.' She meant Adi's bungalow in Juhu.

The first two years that Adi and his family had lived at Daffodils, Adi's father's movies had been hits. But when two of his movies flopped back-to-back in 2015, Neelam Aunty panicked and asked him to stop making movies. He wasn't ready to quit. Instead, he started doubting that perhaps his luck had run out in Daffodils and shifted the family back to their "Buckingham" bungalow in Juhu. Surprisingly, the movies he released after moving back to their bungalow became money-spinners. Nobody had any idea how his houses brought him luck and also took it back from him from time to time, neither did he.

It was not only us girls, but everyone else who missed Adi and his family at Daffodils. They had been nice to everyone, and had shared in others' sadness and happiness.

I don't have time to think about Adi right now. I am late for practice. Being even ten minutes late for practice was a crime according to my coach. Mr. Khan and Rohit, my tennis partner, were waiting for me when I got to the stadium.

'All well? I see some fire in there,' Rohit asked me.

'All well.' I knew he didn't believe me.

I played a broken and dead game, much like my heart. My coach warned me twice before finally throwing me out of the court. He rarely lost his temper, but when he did, apologies never worked.

‘There is no tomorrow in sports.’ My coach stormed out.

‘There is no tomorrow in our lives too,’ Rohit whispered a moment later, and winked. ‘Do you want to go for a coffee? You and I haven’t gone out for some time now. You are going to be an adult soon, so a drink maybe?’ he tried to cheer me up.

‘It’s finally over between Adi and me.’

‘Oh, you guys end it and then patch up every second day. He dates every good-looking girl there is. I still can’t figure out what a fucked-up equation you two have.’ He had witnessed some of our so-called fucked up equations. That’s not pleasant for any normal guy. Rohit was normal. Adi wasn’t. I wasn’t.

All this Adi business was giving me a headache. I felt like seeing Ajit Uncle. He might have some good advice. So I took a taxi to Versova and stopped in front of his bungalow. The new security guard stared at me from behind the half-opened gate.

‘Is Ajit Uncle there?’

‘No, Sir is not here.’ He frowned at me.

‘Let me wait inside.’

‘He will be back tomorrow.’

I decided to call him up later and left.

Not wanting to head home just yet, I decided to take a walk on the beach. The Versova beach looked relatively empty.

Yes, this is where I’d bury my broken heart.

I walked into the sea and closed my eyes. I could clearly picture dipping my bloodstained hands in the water. The last pint of blood from my bleeding heart became colourless. It’s never easy to bury your own heart. Life remained in me, exhausted, even as my dreams, hopes, and memories washed away in the waves.

I took a deep breath. Crouching down, I took some of the bloody water in my hands and whispered to it, ‘Remember to come back to me.’

The sun sucked my blood, grew redder, then dropped dead

into the sea and eventually disappeared. I saw couples walking along the beach, hand in hand, cheek touching cheek, mouth on mouth. Love still exists on this planet. Romance would never be extinct.

Then why was I sitting alone? Why, through all these years, did I only feel the pain of love, and not the happiness of love that Mom talked about? Why did Adi find happiness with other girls and not me?

I lay on the sand and stared at the stars which had begun to appear rather reluctantly. There is nothing more amazing than a star-studded night sky to realise how mysterious this world and love is. I had had some wonderful moments under the stars with Adi.

Did he miss me the way I missed him?

Of course not. If that was the case, I wouldn't have been sitting here with a hole in my chest instead of a merry heart.

I put some sand on my body and lay down. It made me feel better. Maybe that's how the dead feel when others put the sand on them.

I sang my "Breakup Anthem".

It was the first poem I had written for Adi, for us, on our very first Valentine's night.

I lost you, I lost me,
I feel nothing, you are my life,
Bring back my heart, bring back my soul,
Bring back my dreams, bring back my smile,
You are my love, you are my life . . .

CHAPTER 12

The First Valentine's Day

2013

The Valentine's Day preparations in our class brought on a bit of extra romance in the air. This year, many of my classmates had a valentine's date for the first time. Speculations were rife about Adi's probable valentine. Riha—the beauty queen ever since her toddler days and every boy's crush in the school—remained the top contender. Dia stood at the sixth position purely because of her closeness to Adi. Girls prayed, made cards, and wrote love songs; so did the boys.

But someone hated all this drama—me.

The sleepless nights I spent in the run-up to Valentine's Day had turned me into a poet. One night, I wrote in my diary:

What do you want? Why do you stay in my head all the time? I can't sleep, I can't eat, I can't laugh, I can't study. I don't know what to do with you . . . Leave me alone.

Riha, Ann, Kaya, Megha, Arpita, Dia . . . I know Riha is going to be his valentine. Since the beginning of time, people have loved beautiful faces. Everyone wants a Cleopatra and every girl wants to be like one. But how many care that history is just another lie, that the present is just a dream, and that love is a blind man's game?

PS: There is one name missing from the list of girls who want to be his valentine.

Who cares? Me. Probably only me.

D-day arrived. Everyone in St. Michael's had been waiting for it more eagerly than an Indo-Pak World Cup final.

'How cute he is . . .'

'I can die for him . . .'

'He smiled at me today . . .'

'Is any of this voodoo stuff real?'

'I will leave this school if he dares to date someone else . . .'

Girls spent a considerable amount of time talking and dreaming of Adi.

Valentine's Day morning went without any chaos at home. At school, however, a lot was happening. Couple were sneaking off to hidden corners of the school to make out. Gifts, cards, flowers, bands, and chocolates filled every classroom, especially ours, thanks to Adi and Riha. Dia blushed most of the time.

Girls like Dia are always noticed by the good-looking guys. Her boobs had grown bigger while mine still refused to develop into a decent shape. Mom had taken me out bra shopping, but whenever I wore a bra, it suffocated me. Looking at Dia, I decided to wear one from the next day. Boys and boobs seemed to get along well.

Krish had proposed to a girl from a senior class, a girl who was Rahul's friend. Rumour had it that Rahul had helped Krish woo this girl. Whatever, she said yes!

Adi beat everyone else in receiving the most number of anonymous gifts, cards, and roses. And everyone waited for the greatest moment in the history of Valentine's Day. That's when I stepped on a card lying right next to my table. Maybe someone's card had fallen out, just to remind me, Tina, look what a big loser you are.

I opened the card and read it. Bad habit!

Tina, even when nobody is around you,

I will be there, watching over you.

The card fell from my hand, this time out of sheer surprise. It didn't have a sender's name, and it wasn't a fancy card. A simple card with some colours, clouds, stars, a rainbow, and a fluttering butterfly in the centre.

I hid the card in my bag and looked around. Nobody saw me, except Urmi, the girl sitting in the corner of the classroom, lonely and sad like me, and possibly, sulking like me. Why had I never noticed her before even when I had been going through this shit? I smiled at her, she smiled back. I devised a plan to check her handwriting by borrowing a notebook from her. She wasn't the sender.

Just then, I saw Adi in the centre of the classroom with a beautifully wrapped gift in his hands.

'Would you be mine?' He pointed at each girl, making a zigzag motion in the air. My heart pounded fast and loud, my hands became sweaty, and I saw the same colours of love. Adi pointed at me, looking straight into my eyes. He never looked at me in class. Everything became blurry, I felt dizzy, and then his hands moved on towards Kaya, the girl sitting next to me. Then he stopped right at me, again. My heart stopped. I wanted to get up, I almost did. I tried and had almost succeeded, but then I saw Riha, who sat right in front of me, running to Adi and jumping on him. She was hugging him, kissing him, and laughing, tears running down her face. She looked like a princess next to him.

I sat back, pretending that I had gotten up to pick up something. Kaya looked at me weirdly.

'You thought it was you, right?' she asked. How could I agree with her?

'I wanted to take out my inhaler.' She just uttered a long hmmmm. It meant, don't think I am an idiot.

I picked up my inhaler. Asthma poked in my throat.

Riha displayed her gift—a beautiful candid photograph of her in a golden photo frame. There were two extras in the background—Kaya and I. In fact, we made Riha look more beautiful. I could have easily beaten the saddest person to have ever lived on this earth with my gloom. Adi had included us in the picture on purpose. He wanted to make me realise just how beautiful Riha was and how pathetic I was. For the world, it was a candid photograph, but for me it was a warning from Adi—our war was not over yet.

'I fell in love with her the very first time I saw her. She was looking at me, and something hit me. I have never felt it before. I sense the same feeling now whenever I see her.' Adi stopped dramatically and kissed Riha on her cheek. I thought they would have sex right there in front of us. My muscles twitched. Why should I even bother? I dropped my head into my diary, which I had started carrying to school fearing my mom would search for it in my room.

I wrote:

"Tina, even when nobody is around you, I will be there, watching over you . . ."

I don't know who you are. I don't know if you are ever going to tell me your name. But I want to tell you that every day, I will say thanks to God for making me realise there is someone thinking about me, even if it was for a day. God, please keep her or him happy and loved.

PS:

Hope that we meet one day.

For the rest of the day, I felt like I was in a dream. Adi and Riha celebrated their first day together. Many of the girls cried out their hearts in the bathroom. When I looked at Riha, I got incredibly jealous. And whenever I saw Adi, the dancing colours of love moved from him to me. I observed Dia from time to time as well. I knew her heart was broken too. If she had come to me, I would have let her cry on my shoulder. I missed being her friend. I smiled at her, but she looked away.

After school got over, I headed to my tennis coaching. But I was feeling so low, I couldn't concentrate in the practice match. I tried but the ball kept hitting the net. All I wanted to do was go home and lie down on my bed.

My coach shouted at me and kicked me out. As I was walking out of the stadium, I saw a tall boy with toned up muscles—probably two or three years older than me—approaching me. He smiled at me and said, 'Hey, happy Valentine's Day.' I showed him my middle finger and walked out. Time to go home.

On my way home, I started crying for no reason. Mom didn't ask me the reason for my early return. My coach must have called her up and told her.

'We are going to RockS for dinner,' she said.

'Why RockS?' It was a restaurant in which Adi's father was a business partner.

'You used to say it's in—'

'Mom, it's too expensive,' I cut her short. 'It's for those Adi types.' I hurried towards my room.

'We can also go occasionally . . .' I heard her. I knew she wanted to cheer me up.

I came out of the room with a painting of white lilies which I had made for my mom for Valentine's Day. When she read what I had written at the back—I am so proud to be your daughter and I will always love you—she hugged me and said,

'I am proud to be your mom, Angel.' She gave me a lovely golden chain along with a butterfly locket. I thanked her. It looked amazing on me when I put it on, and yet, I wasn't happy.

'Is there anyone special in your life?' She pulled my nose. I showed her the card from my secret admirer.

'This is so cool!' She borrowed my favourite phrase, which I didn't use anymore, as nothing seemed cool anymore.

When Mom left to get her purse, I logged in to my Facebook account. I had stopped updating my profile and posting anything ever since my "ass-show", though I still checked Adi's and the others' accounts religiously. He had the same photo of Riha, rather us, as his cover photo with a caption which read "My valentine, she has the most beautiful eyes which have taken away my sleep . . ." I had never heard anyone admiring Riha's eyes before this. I used to get compliments for my big eyes. Not anymore though. What'd happened to the world? All good things had stopped coming to me.

'They look cute.' But Mom's eyes were on the corner, on me.

'He didn't even crop us out. In class, he was giving a speech about Riha, like they were getting married there.'

'Someone is getting jealous, huh?!'

'No. Dia is the one who is jealous. She wanted to be his girlfriend.'

'But you said every girl in school wanted to be his girlfriend . . .'

'That is just because he gets them autographed photos of film stars. So, they think he is great!'

'Now I know why you don't like him.'

'Mom, I am hungry.' I wanted to change the topic.

'Get ready, you can even put on some lipstick today.'

'I don't want to put on any lipstick today. When I want to, you don't let me.'

I wore a peach frock and left my hair open. Mom helped me put on a little lipstick. The butterfly lay silent on my neck. My hair flew under the fan. Mom looked at me, and smiled.

'My little girl is turning into a beautiful young woman.'

I clicked a selfie with Mom and uploaded it on Facebook with the caption, "Love you, Mom!".

'I will like it after we come back home.' My mom liked my updates and posts on FB. It would, probably, be the only like I would get now. I didn't care. I wanted to tell anyone looking at my page that I had my mom, if not a valentine.

Mom drove to Juhu. I remained sullen throughout the drive.

'Angel, do you want to say something?'

'Something like what?'

'I mean anything.'

'No.' I lied.

We saw the oh-so famous RockS for the first time.

It looked majestic, done up in heart-shaped balloons, roses, and colourful lights. Romantic songs were playing and candles danced on every table. The fragrance of the roses lingered everywhere. Everything looked perfect.

'It's the quintessential restaurant,' Mom said. A girl dressed in a red gown ushered us to our table. Mom ordered some red wine. The girl waited for a second and then asked,

'Ma'am, one glass?'

'Yes.' The girl gave me a smile and left.

'You are going to taste wine for the first time.'

'Dad told me I couldn't drink before I turned sixteen.'

'That still stands. But today is an exception.'

The wine, when it arrived, looked like my own blood had been collected into a glass. We toasted.

'To Angel's happiness,' Mom said.

'To God's happiness,' saying that, I took the first sip of my very first drink. And coughed. Not because of the wine. But because I saw Adi and Riha walk in, hand-in-hand. The manager ushered Adi in as if he owned RockS. Mom saw them too, with surprise visible on her face.

'They look wonderful together.'

Can you believe this? That was my mom. I gave her a stern look. Across the room, Adi pulled out a chair and helped Riha sit, much like the chivalrous hero one only sees in the movies. Riha kept smiling like an idiot.

'I didn't know Adi was a gentleman even at this young age.' Mom was impressed.

'Mom, don't be fooled by his etiquettes. I'm sure they must have had sex by now. You should have seen their kiss.' I didn't say the kiss had been on Riya's cheek. What difference did that make? A kiss was a kiss.

'Angel, sex is a wonderful thing. In the earlier generation, it used to happen only after marriage. We can't expect that nowadays. But you have to wait till you turn eighteen. There is a difference between making love and having sex.'

'At the end of the day, it's all the same.'

'When two people are in love, that's love making. When there is only lust, that's sex.' My mom always had a definition for everything. Shit! Adi saw us. He looked as surprised as we had been. Riha only gave us a forced smile. Adi got up and approached us, alone. I became nervous.

'Mom, what should I do with this wine? He will go and tell everyone. Mom . . . Do something fast, he is almost here.'

'Don't worry. You are with me.'

'Hey, Aunty, what a surprise! When I met you earlier today, you didn't tell me you were coming here.' Then he looked at me with a smile, as if he was my best friend. I hated that fake smile he always flashed when Mom was around.

'Is it your first one?' He looked at my wine glass.

'Yes, I just gave it to her to taste,' Mom helped me out.

'That's cool. What's the occasion?'

'We are also celebrating Valentine's Day, just like you,' Mom said.

'Oh yes, it's Valentine's Day. Happy Valentine's Day, Tina.' Adi took the glass from me and took a sip. I sat there, numbed. Then he returned to Riha. On the way back, I saw some people exchange pleasantries with him.

He was bloody popular even in a restaurant.

Riha grinned proudly. I hated her more.

'Did you meet Adi today? You didn't tell me about it.'

'Yeah, Adi came to me after his cricket practice. He asked me about our Valentine's plan. I told him I was waiting for you to come, so we could decide. It was Adi who suggested RockS could be a good option. But he didn't tell me about his plans.' Mom sipped her wine.

I was speechless. Adi planned this. Poor Mom. She didn't know.

'There wasn't any Valentine's Day hype when I was young,' Mom said. 'But I love this. Every day, life is not colourful, romantic, and musical. It's good to have one day to just remind us all that we love each other no matter what.'

After that, I didn't enjoy the wine or the dinner or the conversation. My thoughts wandered, my stomach burnt, and I wanted to only look at Adi.

'Angel, is something bothering you?'

'I don't know . . .'

'I have been noticing you for some days now . . . Don't lie to me . . . You can tell me whatever it is . . .'

'What have you noticed?'

'I think you are in love. Tell me, who is the one?'

'How do I know if I am in love?'

'What do you think of when you go to sleep? What do you think of first when you wake up? Does thinking about someone give you butterflies in your stomach? Is there someone you want to see all the time?' She waited for my reaction.

'Nobody.' That was my answer.

Later, when we were leaving RockS, Mom said bye to Adi and Riha. She even complimented Riha.

Grrr . . . That's not funny.

'Aunty, let's take a selfie.' Adi got up. Riha, however, wasn't excited.

'Mom, let's go.' But she pulled me in. I looked like an alien forced to take a group photo with humans. What a tragic Valentine's Day! Everything turned out imperfect, except the fact that I had the most perfect mother with me.

I reached home, sad and lost.

Adi had already uploaded our group photo on FB with the caption: #FirstValentine'sNight #ManyMoreToCome

Adi and Riha looked perfect together. He made me look like a clown again, without cropping me out from their romantic photo.

I wrote in my diary:

When Adi proposed to Riha in class, I wanted to cry. My heart burnt. I was angry. I realised I loved him from the moment I had first seen him in our building lift. All those colours I was seeing around us were the colours of love. I lied to Mom today . . . It's Adi I think of before I sleep and when I get up. It's him I search for all the time. I am in love. I love Adi. Did he choose Riha because of her beauty? Does he know Cleopatra wasn't a mirror-cracking beauty? I wish I could take him to Egypt and show him the coins that have Cleopatra's face impressed upon them . . . She wasn't beautiful, but she must have been intelligent and smart to have Julius Caesar and Mark Antony fall for her.

I wrote under my wish list:

8-I want to celebrate all my Valentine's Days with Adi until I die.

9-I want to have my first kiss with Adi.

10-I want to have sex for the first time with Adi when I am seventeen. Mom, sorry, eighteen would be too late.

11-I want to hear from Adi that he loves me and that he will love me forever. Only me.

I read my wishes again and again. But I could see Riha getting all these things, not me.

I wrote again:

My dreams got shattered today. Before I could tell him how much I love him, he left me empty. This is my Breakup Anthem:

I lost you, I lost me,
I feel nothing, you are my life,
Bring back my heart, bring back my soul,
Bring back my dreams, bring back my smile,
You are my love, you are my life . . .
Do come back to me, kiss me in love,
Don't turn away, love me in love,
Tell me once again, you love me always,
Until the stars dance, the moons smile,
Until the sun shines, the rain cries,
Tell me once again, you love me more . . .
I am here, my love, under the sky,
To look up, to see the stars again,
When you aren't here, I see nothing,
Nothing but black, teary black,
You are my love, you are my life . . .
Come back to me, kiss away my tears,
Cross my heart, love me again,
Hold my hand, show me the smile,
Show me the colours, the colours of love,
I am still here, waiting for you,
Remember to come, come back to me my love . . .

I closed my eyes. And in my imagination, I went back to RockS, and saw Adi waiting there, for me. He hugged me, then looked into my eyes, and said, 'You are my first love, Tina. You will always be mine . . .'

CHAPTER 13

The Purple Rain

May 16, 2016

The sea turned dark and continued to grow darker until it was all black. I had been sitting there at the beach, staring at the stars and trying hard to forget Adi.

'This is crazy.' I heard it clearly—the familiar Adi drawl.

Was I also losing my sanity?

'Let's go, Tina.' It was him. Adi was standing right behind me.

Just then his phone rang. He walked ahead and spoke to someone in a hushed tone.

Who else could it be but Shruti? Why was she around wherever I went?

'What the hell are you doing alone at the beach? Man, someone could just—' He held my hand.

'What? Rape me?'

'No, hurt you.'

'Nobody can hurt me more than you. So don't worry.'

I got up and began walking ahead.

'Why did you leave your phone at home?'

'How do you know about that?'

'Tina, do I need to be Einstein to guess that?'

'Are you fucking PMSing, Adi? Did I ask you to come after me leaving your girlfriend behind? I want to be alone.'

I walked towards the main road.

'Do you want to have coffee at Chai-Coffee?'

'Oh, that's beneath your class.'

Why was I PMSing now? I should've been happy to see him back.

'I have to go. Mom would be worried,' I said.

'At least you thought of her now, at nine in the night.'

'Why do you do this? Huh?' I screamed at him.

'Do what, Tina?'

'You screw my happiness. Then you show this bloody concern for me while you are dating half the planet.'

'What has that got to do with you?'

'What do you mean by that?'

'Come on, Tina. Don't fight now. I've had a long day.'

'Did you fuck her for the whole day?'

'Tina, you are becoming bitter and vicious. I told you if you can't respect the girls I date then don't talk about them. Do I say nasty things about your boyfriends?'

'Oh, really? Tell me when have I had a boyfriend? I wish I had one who would love me back the way Mom describes.' Adi didn't answer that. He possessed this great talent of going mute whenever I got angry. 'Adi, I am not made of latex. I can't go through this shit every time.'

'Do you want to know what's wrong with you?'

'No, I don't want to know.'

'That's the problem.'

'Okay then, tell me what the problem is. Also tell me what I don't have that the rest of the girls do.'

'Forget it. If you don't want to be civilised, then there is no point of having a discussion.' He walked towards his car and opened the door for me. Hardly any boy showed such chivalry nowadays.

I didn't want to act pricey. I wanted to sit next to him more than anything else in the world. He drove. There wasn't any music. The best part of our drives used to be that we both loved noise. Music broke our eardrums even if our fights didn't break our larynx.

'Can I borrow your phone?'

'I spoke to your mom already,' he said, looking straight ahead.

Only this very morning, Mom had asked us not to see each other until I learnt the reality of life. And then she actually sent Adi to fetch me. I couldn't have been happier.

'What did she say?'

'You ask her when you see her.' *Ohho.* This conversation wasn't going anywhere.

His phone rang again.

'I can take the call.' I sensed it was Shruti calling him. But Adi ignored my generosity. He knew I would have screwed up somehow.

Adi took a turn towards Juhu. That wasn't the way to my house, but his. In fact, Minu had called me in the morning saying she wanted to meet up to know what had happened between Adi and me.

'Adi came home and went straight to sleep, asking us to not bother him. He looked constipated. Did you guys fight again? I mean, I know that's nothing new. But why he is angry at me? I can't understand that!' Minu had sounded confused.

'Oh, he must have fought with Shruti. I will meet you tomorrow. I've got tennis practice in the evening.' Saying that, I had kept the phone down, though I always loved meeting her.

'Where are we going?' I asked.

'To have coffee and hear some music . . .' That meant we were going to RockS. The same RockS. His phone rang again.

'I am not in the mood to listen to any music.' I sulked. Adi picked up the call.

'Shruti, I will call you when I am free.' Adi disconnected the call and turned to me. The same chill ran down my spine that I had experienced in the lift.

'W-What?' I stammered.

And then, just like that, Adi began tickling me until I laughed.

'You look better when you smile.'

'What do you mean by "better"?'

'Do you want to fight again? I can get upset too. Why didn't you tell me about Florida? Am I a nobody?'

'I wasn't planning to go. Then why should I tell everyone?'

'I am not asking about everyone.' He looked at me.

'Do you want to know the answer? I thought you will be sad that I won't be here. Once I got the admission, I realised I didn't want to go, leaving you . . . I mean . . . Mom . . . but I was stupid. I was an idiot. I should have known . . . My bloody heart refused to think then . . . But now I am okay.'

'Tina, your mom has so much hope in you. I have never seen someone love her kid the way she does . . .'

'Then you can take her home . . .'

'My mom would be happy to have her at home. So don't tempt me.' He smiled. How did this boy always know how not to fight? The more time I spent with Adi, the more I hated all the other boys. They didn't have what Adi had, I mean as a human being. His way of seeing life, of making others smile, of forgetting fights and caring for someone, the way he loved the whole world. Do you know how scary it is? Why does a person have to be so good, perfect, adorable, and lovable? Why was he not mean and crooked? If he wasn't what he was, my bones would have been intact and my heart in the pink of health.

The security guard at RockS gave us a wide smile. Everyone knew Adi, some knew me too. I got my share of little popularity in RockS . . . hmmm . . .

'You come here regularly?' I wanted to know how often he brought Shruti here.

'I remember my promises, Tina.' My heart skipped a beat. He had promised me once that he would come to RockS only with me. He had promised me another time that he would never leave me and that we would be best friends forever. I wanted to hug Adi and tell him that I loved him. Rather, I wanted to tell him that I knew he loved me. But I didn't. And my heart blushed.

Adi held my hand and walked into the pub section of RockS. We made heads turn. We were probably the youngest couple there. Or rather, the youngest people, as we weren't a couple and that was the whole issue.

'Do you want to drink?' Adi asked.

'I stopped drinking for real, unlike you.'

'Yeah, that's good. I stopped too, this time for real.'

'Good. So, tell me what's the problem with me?' I couldn't kill my curiosity.

'Hmm . . . The problem with you is that you are too cute, I mean you think you are cute, not exactly, you think every girl is cuter and not you. You don't value yourself.'

'Same old one.'

'Shut up, Tina. The problem with you is that you think your life is me. How can you stop living—'

'What's wrong with that? I know you love spending time

with me. Even after dating all these bitches, I mean stupid girls, you come back to me every single time, even though you claim that many of the girls broke it off with you because of me.'

'I come back to you because we are friends.'

'Is there a rule that says friends can't be lovers?'

'Do you mix scotch with beer?'

'What happens if we mix scotch with beer?'

'People don't do such stupid things.'

Well, I had quit drinking after our infamous sexual encounter. But I asked the waiter for some scotch mixed with beer, or beer mixed with scotch, to prove my point. The waiter stared at me as if I was already drunk. Minutes later, I was gulping down scotch mixed with beer, or vice versa.

'Holy shit. This is bloody awesome. Do you want to try?' Adi looked at me, amused. 'Don't be shy,' I tried to coax him. 'Anyway, you are going to pay the tab. So feel at home.' But Adi didn't drink. The scotch and the beer started to kick in. Alcohol always made me fearless and more loving. That was the only good part of it.

'Yesterday, you insulted me, you killed me. It wasn't fair, Adi. I will never forgive you for that. You made me feel like a whore . . . That was so mean . . . You think people who don't have any legacy are gold-diggers?

'I am sorry, Tina. I didn't mean it . . . I was angry, I suppose . . .'

'Even when we are angry, we don't hurt someone so deeply, Adi. We don't hurt someone who cares for us. I did that once, and now I know how much it hurts.' He just hugged me.

'Tina, don't go back to yesterday. We should let go . . .'

'How can I? It was like you get pregnant, wait for nine months, and after the delivery, the doctor tells you that your kid's been stolen. What the hell has money got to do with love? Which bloody asshole said something like that?'

'I don't know who said it . . . All I am saying is that we are good friends.'

I gave him a look. He corrected himself, 'I mean . . . We are best friends. I want it to be that way for ever, until one of us dies.'

'Best friends should be lovers.' Adi's phone rang. It was Shruti again. I drank more. Adi stopped me.

'Let me drink . . . I want to forget . . . You called me a whining pig . . . You called me pathetic and a gold-digger . . .' I got louder. 'Sh-Sh-Sh-Shruti . . . I hate her . . . She just dropped into your lap . . . Sh-Sh-Shuuti . . . It's not fair . . . It's bloody not fair, Aaadii . . .'

'This is what happens when you mix scotch with beer.'

'Shhh . . . Have you ever fallen in love at first sight?' Adi just looked at me. 'I mean, did you have butterflies in your tummy when you saw either Riha or Shruti? Did your heart beat like this?' I drummed on the table, faster and faster. 'Did you see the colours of love? Huh . . . Did you see them?'

'What are these bloody colours of love that you always talk about? You never want to say what the hell these colours are . . .'

'You are a loser, Adi. One day, if you are blessed, you will see them. I saw them when you looked at me for the first time. And I have seen them a million times since then. It's the most beautiful sight to behold . . . It's like becoming a part of the cosmos . . . Swirling around . . . But what's the point?! Why did we meet when there are a billion other people in this world? Why did you come to my building and into my class? I would have never known you, I would have never broken my bones, I would have never hurt my mom, and I would have still had my heart here . . .'

'You would have never seen the colours of love or rainbows in the sunshine, if it were not for me,' Adi shot back. 'You wouldn't have seen stars during the day, or the wind dancing, or the sun crying. You would have missed the music from hell and life would have been less exciting without me. So, you should thank me for coming into your life and tolerating you for all these years.'

'You are right . . . Thank you for tolerating me. But no thank you for making me sad and breaking my heart . . . I want to dance . . . No . . . I am going to dance . . .'

'Okay. Let's dance then.'

'I stopped dancing with my best friend.'

'When did that happen?'

'Right now . . . You think I can't dance without you? Get a life . . . okay?'

'I hope you remember what happened the last time.' I showed him my middle finger and walked towards the dance floor. I saved myself from taking a fall. By the way, I was the only one in sportswear at that fancy restaurant.

I danced. Alone. A man in his mid-thirties, who seemingly wanted to save lonely hearts, approached me. He danced about five feet away from me at first, but then he came closer and put his arms around my waist. He didn't ask for my permission. I didn't move away either. I danced like there was no tomorrow. The man tilted my face towards his, his face was inches away from mine, and then, someone suddenly pushed him away. The next instant, Adi twisted my hand and began pulling me towards the exit.

'What's wrong with you, Tina? He was all over you!'

'Why are you bothered? You are not even eighteen, but you have had more sex than anyone in this room. You even fucked your so-called best friend!' I slurred. 'You raped me. Adi, you raped me . . . You raped my heart . . .' I didn't care about embarrassing him or me. That's the best part of getting drunk. The world doesn't exist for you anymore.

'Tina, you are drunk. Just keep your mouth shut.' My drama was beginning to attract some audience.

The manager of the restaurant came to Adi to help him.

I wasn't ready to go just yet.

'I want to drink more because I don't have a heart now. It is floating in the sea somewhere. Alone. Bleeding purple . . . red . . . not purple . . . bloody orange . . . no . . . it's black . . .' I started crying.

'Purple sounds better. But I will go if you don't stop this now.' I heard Adi say.

'That night, you told me I was the most beautiful girl you had ever seen and you said you loved me. I thought we made love. Then you told me, you were just tolerating me. All fuckers are rapists. They should be in jail, rotting their asses and dicks off.' Adi covered my mouth and walked me towards his car. His phone rang just then. This time, it was my mom.

'Aunty, we are coming home.'

'Nobody loves me, not even my mom . . . I hate my dad . . . I hate me . . . I hate you . . .'

'Tina, let's go.'

'I want to be with you now, yesterday, and tomorrow . . . after your death . . . after my birth . . . after your wedding . . . after our kids . . . after my death. Don't leave me, please . . .' I kept abusing Adi, and kept on talking about how much I hated him and then how much I loved him. I meant everything. That was weird.

'I am not leaving you, Tina. See, I am right here.' We stood on the road. But I couldn't stand.

'I think I forgot one of my legs on the dance floor. I can't walk.' I looked around for my leg.

'You've got my legs now.' Adi carried me to the car.

'You can take it back tomorrow.'

'Okay, I will . . .'

'Why we are in the space shuttle?'

'We are going to Kirumurchi.'

'What's that?'

'A new planet made just for you.'

'I named a star . . . No, two stars . . .' I tried to continue, but my tongue refused to move and my head fell on Adi's shoulder. His phone rang again. I got back my senses when I heard Shruti.

'Shruti, please go to sleep. Yes, I am with Tina. So? So what?' He disconnected the phone.

'You kissed me in the morning and married me in the night . . . Thank you . . . When we will have kids?' I giggled.

'Tina, are you just faking that you are drunk? Don't play games with me.'

'I am drunk . . . not dead. I want to sing a song . . .'

When all the undefined feelings, the sleepless nights, and the endless days made me miserable, I poured my heart out into words.

Hence, Adi had made me a poet.

He made me crazy.

He made me happy.

He made me cry.

He broke me. He made ME.

I sang,

When I saw you for the first time,
I saw the colours of love
Whenever I see you,
My heart leaves me to be with you
Wherever I go,
My eyes search for you
When you ignore me,
My hopes give up on me
When you are around and not around,

My body aches, I don't know why
Sleep leaves me, so does hunger,
All I do is think about you.
When I am awake, when I am asleep
I hold your hand, I look into your eyes
I hear your breath, I see your smile
I feel your kiss, I stop the time
I smile in tears, I cry silently
If this pain is love, let the pain be me . . .

I slurred. And I heard Adi completing the rest of the song:

Embrace me and engulf me . . .
I love you yesterday, today, tomorrow
I love you until I take my last breath
And I would love you again
As we never go away.

'Did I send this to you too?'

I couldn't remember, nor did I hear Adi's reply.

A long-awaited calmness washed me ashore.

And I saw my heart beating, dancing, and smiling.

CHAPTER 14

The Love Blues

2013

Love bloomed in my heart. But I couldn't swallow it or spit it out. I couldn't sleep or stay awake.

Instead of praying for Adi to change his school and his home, I was now praying twice as hard to keep him next to me. Yes, I changed my requests like politicians. They say everything is fair in love, so I guessed it was okay. The Gods would understand me. Instead of hating school, I now eagerly looked forward to being there. I smelt Adi's perfume; I heard his chuckles; I saw how his moustache had sprouted and how his hair grew, and I could even guess the colour of his underwear. I didn't know any magic tricks like him, but I could see through him. I saw his heart beating, as if I was looking at a 3D colour X-ray. I saw his breaths making their way inside his lungs, writing my name there, then coming out, and entering me. I saw all of this, but he didn't see anything. That was the saddest part of my love story. And the end too.

I had heard that visiting the Mahim Church for nine consecutive weeks could make any wish come true. I made new additions to my wish list:

12-Break-up of Adi and Riha.

13-Go to the Mahim Church for nine consecutive weeks with Adi.

My horrifying days continued even after we graduated to the ninth grade. Everyone got extra busy with their studies, while I was busy creating my ultimate "love world" with Adi.

Around the same time, St. Michael High School's social media website was created. It was a mini version of Facebook, where students could create profiles, update and upload photographs, comment on each other's profiles, and chat. The best part was that one could do all this while choosing to be anonymous. Adi was the brains behind it. Some students made their profiles usinng their real names and display pictures, while others chose fake names and random pictures of the sun, moon, water, lips, people kissing, legs, or whatever else caught their fancy.

I made an account as well with a fake username "I LOV ADI", and used a photograph of Adi's dimpled face as my display picture. Soon, my profile became the most discussed and viewed profile in the school. The students speculated about the person behind it. Some said it was a boy, some said it was a heartbroken girl, while others guessed it was someone close to Adi. My nights became busier. I made sure I uploaded a candid photograph of Adi every day, titled "Adi of the Day". My updates never got a response from Adi himself, although many commented on them and challenged me to come clean.

Finally, one day I got a private message from Adi. I jumped

off the bed and then jumped back on. Then, I ran all around the house. Luckily, my mom was in the garden with her friends. I waited for five minutes so that I could regain my composure before reading Adi's message and replying to it.

Aditya: Why are you scared?
I LOV ADI: What do you mean?
Aditya: You are just a coward. But I know who you are.
I LOV ADI: Tell me who I am.
Aditya: Show some guts to face people rather than hiding behind a fake profile. I hate cowards like you.
I LOV ADI: ☺Love you, Adi. Get some sleep. Don't think about me.

Then I went offline.

Though I had sent him a smiley, Adi had left me spooked. What if he really knew it was me? He could be bluffing. I had never downloaded the mobile app on my phone. So unless someone checked my laptop at home, which I had protected with a password, I would be safe. I calmed myself.

When I went to school the next day, I heard everyone in class talk about Adi's mystery fan. Even Riha seemed worried. However, she and Adi looked happy together and continued to break many hearts. I guess my ex-friend Krish had no time to waste on finding out who "I LOV ADI" was. He had his hands full with his demanding and suspicious girlfriend. Thanks to her, he spent less time with Adi and Rahul. Dia too had her mind on other things. She had broken up with Jeevs. So she looked lost and unhappy.

A week later, another private message from Adi appeared in my inbox.

Aditya: Call me, this is my phone number. Who knows, we may hit it off.

I LOV ADI: Good night, Adi. Miss me.

I went offline. I decided not to use his number. I had to act pricey, only then would I get enough attention from him. I had no clue if any of this made sense. I thought it was working. I could almost imagine Adi frowning and saying what the fuck. He was probably getting frustrated because he couldn't unmask me. I danced. Again.

My online rendezvous progressed and it added some spice to my world. My mom started noticing that I was spending a lot of time on my laptop. She warned me, 'Angel, I hope you are not forgetting that your exams are approaching.'

I hadn't forgotten, but I was just too busy. I had to plan how to click Adi's pictures without being noticed. Then, I had my tennis coaching, the inter-school match was also coming up, and above all, I was in love. Some busy school days these were!

Adi was now the captain of our school cricket team. It had been some years since St. Michael's had brought home the winner's trophy in an inter-school match. I sent a private message to Adi a day before his match.

I LOV ADI: All the best for tomorrow.

Aditya: Will you be watching me?

I LOV ADI: No.

I went offline. The next day, Adi's team faced St. Xavier's team, the defending champions. The whole school was there to cheer for Adi and his team. Krish and Rahul shined as opening batsmen. Adi became the man of the match, but I wasn't there to watch his team lose. That night, I couldn't sleep. I knew Adi would be upset over having lost the match. I posted on my page: *When you lose, your wins are sweeter.*

I waited for a comment from Adi on my post. But he didn't. Mom asked me to get some sleep. The next day, I had my final tennis match.

The next morning, Dad called to wish me luck. He had never seen me play in a competition. I asked my mom not to come for the match since I knew no one from my class would be there to cheer for me. It would only make her sad.

Before the match, Mr. Khan gave me all the motivational speeches possible. My opponent, a tenth standard girl and a two times inter-school champion, stood tall in the court. Her schoolmates rooted for her, their school flag fluttering around. I felt like a loser even before the game had started.

I took deep breaths to calm myself down. That's when I heard the St. Michael's anthem in the air, accompanied by the beating of drums. I turned around and saw Adi, Riha, Rahul, Krish, Dia, and most of my classmates and many other schoolmates there, cheering me on. Urmi smiled at me.

Were they really there for me?

I couldn't believe it. Riha leaned on Adi, speaking non-stop. He looked uninterested and irritated about being there. Behind Adi, Miss Rose—wearing a white T-shirt and a pair of tracks—waved at me. I gave her a big smile. She looked almost like a student from our school in her casual attire.

I assumed my classmates were there because of Miss Rose. She could always influence students easily. That had nothing to do with the fact that she was the most beautiful teacher in our school, and that the boys and even the girls always sought a glimpse of her when she walked through the corridors. She always wore a sari, her long, thick hair was braided, and she wore a thin gold chain with a small cross on it around her neck. Miss

Rose was known as a strict teacher and she made sure not to miss any student in the class. Some joked that she had an extra pair of eyes at the back of her head. Absolutely true! She could see us even when she wrote on the blackboard. While most of the girls admired her collection of saris, which she hardly ever repeated, I looked at her neatly kept feet and at her pink nails. She inspired me to take care of my feet.

This unexpected turn of events made me happy and nervous, especially Adi's presence. He could be right, I was being a coward. I could smile at him, kiss him, and sleep with him in my dreams. Instead of going to the court, I wanted to run away as fast as I could. It was too late though. My opponent, the reigning champion, served first. I didn't see either the ball coming towards me or the hundred students wearing white T-shirts with St. Michael's logo. All I could see was Adi and his white cap with a red heart and two words on it: I WIN.

My hands shivered, no, they froze. He wanted to remind me it was he who always won.

If you win this, you will win over Adi. You've got a chance.

Make it or break it.

Then, I hit. I hit, and I hit the ball as if I was hitting at Adi's hatred for me. I won the first two sets. St. Michael's had won the tennis championship trophy for the very first time. I heard my schoolmates, I heard their roar, their slogans, whistles, and cheers.

My eyes searched for Adi and found him missing from the group. I missed him and wished for his hug, or at least a smile. I had earned it.

'You made us proud,' Miss Rose congratulated me.

I thanked her and walked to the changing room. I turned around and she was still there, smiling at me. In the changing room, instead of Adi, Miss Rose's presence bothered me. Her eyes and her smile cut through me and frightened me. It was like she knew my secrets. That made me sick.

My mom took me out for dinner to celebrate my win. Our win. She was happy, but I wasn't.

'I am definitely coming to watch you play next time.' If I had had any idea about my cheering classmates and schoolmates, I would have asked her to come too.

All through dinner, however, I wanted to rush home to check my I LOV ADI page. I had updated the "Adi of the Day" photo with his I WIN cap.

When we reached home, I ran to check my page.

What a wonderful night! Adi had sent me an instant message.

Aditya: You think I don't know you, huh?

I LOV ADI: I saw you sulking there at Tina's match. I know you don't like her. Then why were you there?

Aditya: You know all about me! I wouldn't have given a shit, but it was for St. Michael's sportsman spirit.

I LOV ADI: I always see her alone nowadays. It was good to see her win.

Aditya: Oh! So you must be aware why she is seen alone nowadays!

I LOV ADI: No, I am not her friend.

Aditya: Then, who is her friend?

I LOV ADI: You should know. You are in her class!

Aditya: I don't have time for others.

I LOV ADI: Because of Riha? She is beautiful. But I love you more than anyone.

Aditya: Prove it to me.

I LOV ADI: I see you in me. You are in me. You are me.

I didn't need to think. He was in me always.

Aditya: You are a poet, huh? Why can't you write one more poem now?

I LOV ADI: Okay, here it is. ☺

You are from the clouds, you are from the heaven
You fell into my heart
My heart bled, so you could grow
Because I love you more than my life
Because you are my life, you are mine
I will live in you and I will die in you
Today, tomorrow and today, tomorrow.

Aditya: If you love me, meet me tomorrow at nine at RockS. I will wait for you.

Adi didn't wait for my answer and went offline.

How would I go and meet him at RockS?

I went to my mother. When she heard my weird request, she asked me to go and sleep.

'Mom, I want to talk to you. Please!'

I pulled her out of the bed and told her how much Adi meant to me. For the next three hours I poured out the story of my life, with and without Adi. She didn't laugh. She didn't smile. She didn't blink. Instead, she stared at my "I LOV ADI" page on my laptop. I saw shades of fear in her eyes.

'Mom, he is the only one I always think about. I see him everywhere, even when he isn't there. I see the colours of love around us . . . I am in love, Mom. Adi is the one you asked about . . .' She stared at me.

'What're these colours of love, Angel?' Now, I stared at her. I had thought everyone who had ever been in love had seen them.

'Mom, don't change the topic. Help me out.'

'Angel, he just wants to find out who is troubling him. How can you stalk him or anyone? I want you to stop this nonsense immediately.'

'Mom, this is my first love. You won't understand.' Why was she telling me to stop? Maybe she thinks my love for Adi will hurt me and break my bones.

'You said every girl in your class likes him. That's called infatuation. When I was a young schoolgirl, I thought I was in love with the carpenter who worked for us. That was my first love. Then in high school, I fell in love with my Hindi teacher. For two years, I daydreamed about him. Then I met Sharan, when I was in the twelfth standard, and he said he loved me. We didn't have this kissing and all back then, but we exchanged letters and promised to be together forever. Then I shifted to Delhi for my MBBS. I don't know where Sharan is today or where that carpenter or my Hindi teacher are, and neither did I ever try to find out. This is what happens mostly with first love, second love, and many more loves. It's all a part of growing up and learning.'

I was happy to know that my mom had also felt the same things that I was going through. That's how she could figure out that I was in love much earlier. I hugged my mom. She let me sleep with her that night. I loved these rare opportunities to sleep next to her, especially when I had asthma attacks.

'The first love cuts the deepest, baby. Be prepared for it.'

I was ready to take any cut, no matter how deep, anytime. Seeing Adi with Riha gave me more pain than any cut could ever give me.

And, I went to school the next morning without knowing if my mom would become my partner-in-crime.

In the school bus, Krish, Dia, Rahul, and some of the other students congratulated me for my win the previous day. I was happy. Finally they were speaking to me again, my mean old friends. Adi was on his phone and ignored me. Nothing new! My classmates seemed happy for me as well. My only friend, Urmi, gave me a wide smile. She even gave me two laddus in a small box. I thanked her.

Not much later, I stood in the staff room with a wide smile smeared on my face as my teachers and the principal praised me, until Miss Rose asked me, 'Do you want to come with me for coffee? Maybe tomorrow evening?' My smile vanished.

'I've got my tennis practice.'

'Friday looks better then,' she said.

'Okay.' This wasn't okay. I was scared.

'Please tell your mom that you will be with me.' I nodded. What else could I do?

I wasn't sure about Mom's reaction. Why would a teacher take a student out for coffee? What if the eyes at the back of Miss Rose's head had spotted me stalking Adi?

Miss Rose made the rest of my day miserable. And Adi took over the baton from her during our lunch break.

'I see you in me. You are in me. You are me.' Adi shamelessly stole my lines and recited them to Riha in front of the students remaining in the class, including me. 'I always wanted to confess this while looking into your eyes.'

What the hell and what more? I waited.

'How touching Adieee . . .' Tears rolled down Riha's cheeks as she hugged Adi. She could have easily given any Bollywood actress a run for her money with this melodrama. Dammit! I tried to hold back my tears. I felt a little better because Adi's attention was on his phone and he had missed Riha's drama. Riha realised that and glanced at Adi who was looking at his phone. She faked a smile and got a sneak peek of what was on Adi's phone. Now she had that million-dollar smile, laced with pride.

'How cute, Adi!' Riha exclaimed.

She snatched his phone and showed it to the class. Adi was looking at his display photo with Riha, the same one where I was in the corner like an unwanted alien.

This time, I swallowed my anger, dashed to the bathroom, clutching my diary.

Fuck . . . I hate everything that is happening in front of me. Adi, you stole my love for you and gave it away to Riha. This is not cool. You are re-confessing your love for her on the same day you challenged me to prove my love for you. This is not fair. It hurts me all over. This must be what Mom was talking about—the first love cuts deepest. It's horrible.

PS: I wish Riha cuts you deep.

In the evening, my coach gave me a racket signed by Sania Mirza. Then he introduced me to a boy, Rohit, the same one I had shown my middle finger to on Valentine's Day.

'Rohit will be your match partner from today onwards.' Mr. Khan spoke less and worked more. The handsome Rohit smiled back and shook my hand. But Adi was the "handsomest".

I started believing in miracles when, after I got home, Mom agreed to help me stalk Adi. I promised her this would be the last stupid thing I would ever do in my life. Soon, she would come to know that all promises were made to be broken.

'Why can't you just tell him that you like him?'

'I can't. Maybe I will . . . I mean, one day . . .' I didn't know what exactly love was. Was it the colours I saw, or the feelings which I couldn't name? Nothing was absolute. What if love was just an illusion? When you opened your eyes it was gone. Like it had never been there. I wanted to wait and see.

Mom had the perfect plan. She wore a pair of jeans, one

of Dad's shirts, a cap, and spectacles. We would go to RockS before nine, I would stay in the car, and she would wait inside for Adi. A drink and some starters would make her look like a genuine costumer. When Adi would come in, she would use her cell phone camera to click his pictures. This way, I could keep my identity hidden, and still be able to post a candid photograph of him.

As we were nearing RockS, Mom started to worry.

'If I can't recognise you, then how would Adi? But if anything goes wrong, just WhatsApp me. Okay? You are the best mom.'

'Stop buttering me now. Are you sure Adi will come?'

'Yes, Mom, he doesn't know it's me, I mean . . . I think so.' She didn't look convinced.

It was silent in the car after that. I sensed that Mom was dreading going to RockS. Well, too late to turn back now. We had arrived.

Mom headed towards the restaurant. I waited in the car and prayed to Mother Mary. An image of Riha and Adi having sex rocketed into my mind instead. I wanted to shut them away. Then an image of me being with Adi flashed in my mind. And then I couldn't stop the tinkle between my thighs. It spread all over me.

My phone rang. It was Mom.

'I can't see Adi.' It was already ten past nine.

'Mom, look properly, okay?'

'Shhh. Adi is here with Riha.'

'Riha? What is she doing there?'

'He is holding her hand and looking around.'

'See, he is looking for me.'

'No, they are looking for a place to sit.'

'Mom! Don't be so heartless.'

'Let me take some photos and get out before he sees me.' Mom disconnected the call.

I got out of the car, suffocated, worried, and sad.

Five minutes later, I saw Mom rushing toward me.

'I think he saw me.'

'How?'

'I don't know, I just feel like he did.'

'You are just scared.' She gave me her phone.

'Mom, you should be a paparazzo. What a superb pic!'

'I am a paparazzo daughter's mother.' I ignored that.

Adi looked devilishly handsome, and I didn't want to admit it, but Riha looked stunning as well.

'He was holding her hand . . .'

'Does it make any difference, Angel?'

'I think it makes a difference.' Why does Riha have to be so pretty? Frustrated, I cropped her out of the picture and gave Mom her phone back.

'Mom, I have been wondering how you fell in love with a carpenter.'

'Jesus was a carpenter.'

'But this guy wasn't Jesus. Was he as handsome as Adi?'

'He was just an average-looking guy. He never spoke to me. But the way his eyes spoke to me whenever he looked at me, I knew he loved me too.'

'Why didn't you tell him that you liked him?'

'I was scared and confused. Most first loves remain unknown to the other person and they fade away as time passes. Then, once in a while we look back in time and remember it all. That's the fate of first loves.'

'I will change the sad fate of first loves.' From where did I get such confidence?

'Time will tell,' Mom said.

Half an hour later, we reached home. I raced inside, and immediately uploaded Adi's photograph on my page.

Almost immediately, I got a message from Adi. I wanted Mom to go to her room. But she didn't.

Aditya: Why did you hide again?
I LOV ADI: Why did you come with Riha?
Aditya: Did it break your heart?
I LOV ADI: Yes. And you stole my lines. I saw them on your page.

I lied.

Aditya: You stalk me, you check my page more than I do. A coward can never be a lover.

That was rude, nasty, and unacceptable. Adi went offline before I could tell him so. I stared at his words. So did Mom.

'He is right. Don't sulk. The sooner you understand, the lesser pain you'll be in.'

My mom added another pinch of wisdom and left the room.

The night passed and I just sat in front of my laptop, angry and upset.

In love and in hate.

In tears and in smiles.

CHAPTER 15

The Broken Tears

May 17, 2016

The sun hit me hard and shook me.

I felt as if my head was still on the pillow and I was walking around headless. My mom became fretful when she saw how miserable I looked. She gave me warm lemon water to make me feel better. I smiled.

'Good morning, Mom.'

'Even after you promised . . .'

'I am going to pack my bags now . . . What happened yesterday?' I couldn't remember anything.

'You babbled about burying your heart in the sea, leaving your leg in RockS, and leaving your life with Adi. I am tired of this nonsense.'

'Mom, don't rub salt on my wounds.' I remembered Adi carrying me out of the lift and saying I should lose some weight.

'Where is Adi?'

'I kicked him out.'

'That was mean, Mom . . .'

'Tina, you decide if you want to stay here, in the sea, in the pub, or on the road. Don't come home after drinking.'

'Mom . . . I have only two weeks . . .'

'You are just seventeen, for God's sake. Every damn kid on this planet falls in love. Nobody becomes a mess like you. Why do you want to play the victim? Whom are you punishing and for what? Me or Adi? You think all these tricks will get him back? Any boy would run away after seeing your theatrics. How can I help you if you want to dig your own grave?' She pursed her lips. Was she debating whether she should say something more or not? Was she about to cry?

'Tina, maybe you shouldn't go to Florida. You are so used to being protected by me and Adi. You will not be able to survive there for even a day. Oh God, I don't know what to do anymore." Mom stormed out and locked herself in her room. This time, it was my turn to plead with her to open the door.

'Tina, leave me alone. I need some space too . . . I am tired.' I lingered outside her room. Then I went and cooked lunch for us. Rice, dal, and fish fry. Even after my pleading with her again and making another set of promises, Mom didn't respond or open the door.

My head ached. I needed a shower.

The cold water made me feel better.

The doorbell rang once, twice, and then thrice. I got out of the shower and opened the door. It was a delivery boy at the wrong door!

I called out for Mom again, but there was no answer. I repeatedly banged on her door, but still there was no response. Terror seized me. What if something had happened to her?

I ran down to Sarojini Aunty's home, forgetting that I just

had a towel wrapped around me. I couldn't bring myself to say anything. I just burst into tears and kept saying "Mom . . ."

Sarojini Aunty and Shyam Uncle quickly ran up the stairs to my house. I didn't even realise the towel had dropped off until Aunty pulled out a dress for me once we were back home. I was naked, but I didn't have the time to be ashamed. All I had in the mind was my mother. As Mom didn't respond to Shyam Uncle's calls, he began hitting the door to break it open. That happens only in the movies. It took us another ten minutes to open the door, but it seemed like an eternity.

Mom lay on the bed, facing the wall, as if she was fast asleep.

I tried to wake her up. But she didn't open her eyes or speak to me. Shyam Uncle checked her pulse, then he picked her up and rushed to the lift while shouting at Sarojini Aunty to get the car. Sarojini Aunty ran to her house to get the car keys while I followed Uncle into the lift.

Moments later, I sat next to Mom in tears, praying for her safety. Aunty kept on telling me, 'Tina, don't cry. Don't cry. Rachel is fine.'

And then she started crying too.

Once we reached the hospital, the stretcher with Mom disappeared into a long corridor, and time stood still. The wait, the prayers, the tears, and the guilt increased.

A little while later, Adi came running towards us. I hadn't called him nor had I taken my phone back from Mom. But how could I forget that though Adi and his family weren't staying in Daffodils anymore, they had made friends for life. In fact, he had more friends than I had.

He hugged me hard, as if I had been lost and found.

I stayed in Adi's arms.

'Shhh . . . I am here . . . Everything will be fine.'

Adi kissed me on my forehead.

'How can I tell her that I will not hurt her, ever . . . This happened because of me . . . We had a fight . . .' I cried.

Adi wrapped his arms around me and sat down next to me.

'I swear to God, if I have to choose between Mom and you, I will choose Mom. I am done with my one-sided romance . . . I am done . . .' He tightened his grip on me and rested his chin on my head. Did a drop of water just fall on my forehead?

Yes. Adi was in tears and I heard his silence.

The next few hours stretched on. Finally, when the doctors spoke to us, I cried like a kid. Mom had had a heart attack. They let me look at my mom through the glass door of the ICU. I kept my hands on the glass and whispered, 'Mom, can you hear me? You know how much I love you, right? I am sorry . . .' I stood there, hoping she would open her eyes. I now realised what my mom had gone through in the past. The same pain, guilt, uncertainty, hope, tears, prayers . . . God, don't give this pain to anyone.

I sat outside the door with Adi beside me. He was still holding me close to him.

'Adi, I am sorry for everything I ever did . . . I know have I always troubled you all. Mom must have hated me . . . I wish I could go back in time and correct my past. I really wish—'

'Tina, I wouldn't want anything to be erased from our life. Nothing, not a thing. I am sure she also feels the same way. She loves you the way you are.'

Did Mom really love me just as much after everything I had done? Would I love a daughter like me? What if we don't get a second chance in life?

I had no answers, just more questions.

The doctors had said that the next twenty-four hours were going to be crucial. I didn't leave the hospital even after Adi's parents came to take me home. Neelam Aunty and Sarojini

Aunty stayed with me most of the time. The more I saw them, the more I realised how blessed we were to be loved and cared for by people who did not expect anything in return.

May 18, 2016

The next day, late in the evening, I held my mom's hand. She looked pale, but her smile gave me another life. Only I knew how precious that moment was.

'I don't know how to live without you even for an hour.'

'I am sorry, Angel. If it were up to me, I would have never done anything to hurt you.' I wanted to hug her. But her stitches might hurt. I cried. Again.

'I am sorry for what I did, Mom. Now I know what you must have gone through at that time. Did you hate me then?' A few years ago, I had my mom worried to death when I had been admitted to in the hospital.

'No, Angel, I loved you more, I prayed more for you . . . And I wanted to be a better mother for you.'

'Mom, no more Adi drama. He is just a friend now. You can trust me. I promise.' She smiled. Of course, she didn't believe me. Soon, Adi joined us.

'Thank you for taking care of my girl like always. I can't say how much—' Adi stopped her and sat next to her on the bed. They must have been mother and son in some previous birth. They adored and loved each other.

'You both need to get out of this hospital. You two should go to RockS. Tina just told me you are only a friend now.' Adi turned to look at me. I showed him my thumb, not my middle finger.

'Did Angel tell you it was me who had gone to RockS that night to get your picture?' I covered Mom's mouth.

'Mom, nooo. We should have some secrets also.'

Adi didn't look amused. It was as if he was aware of it already. 'It's okay, Aunty, everybody should have some secrets . . .'

I looked at him. What more was he going to say?

'So, let it be Tina's secret.' Adi gave me a knowing smile.

I wonder about Adi's secrets. Were his secrets about his girlfriends? About their kisses? About sex? He never discussed his personal life with anyone, even with us, his four a.m. friends. I should ask about his secrets later.

Neelam Aunty and Sarojini Aunty waited impatiently to meet their friend. Shyam Uncle came to visit Mom in the evening. Everyone was happy.

I must say, bringing back a loved one from the very doors of death is the best moment one can have. That feeling of snatching our dear one back from the hands of God is the purest form of victory. Everything looked unimportant in front of that. For the first time I wasn't thinking about Adi.

Then I realised I had some unfinished work to take care of.

I looked at Adi.

He saw the unexpected and the unavoidable coming between us. He frowned. I smiled.

CHAPTER 16

Rainbow in the Sun

2013

I had no constipation, yet I had spent an hour in the toilet on this particular Friday morning. I was anxious, wanting to delay reaching school as much as possible.

Mom knocked, knocked again, and then banged on the door.

'Mom, let me sit in peace for five minutes.'

'Don't say you don't have peace in this house, Angel. That's not a fair thing to say to your mother. And you have been sitting there for an hour. If you don't come out now, you'll be late for school.' She sounded upset.

I came out of the washroom and told her about the dreaded coffee date with Miss Rose.

'That's nice. It is rare to find such a wonderful teacher in life. It is clearly no reason for you to skip school.' Mom wanted to cheer me up, but she was definitely wondering why Miss Rose would go out for coffee with me. Exasperated, I left for school.

Riha's birthday fell on the same day.

Adi, the proud boyfriend, made sure his so-called pal Shah Rukh Khan wished her through a WhatsApp video call. Every girl in our class wished for a boyfriend like Adi.

My jealousy evaporated as the time for my coffee outing neared. I sat in the staff room, bit my nails, and probably ate some of the skin below them too. As Miss Rose was wrapping up her work, some of the teachers smiled at me and some enquired about my tennis practice. Did they know Miss Rose was taking me out for coffee? Our maths teacher, Mr. Anwar, looked at me. It was the kind of look I threw at Riha. He showed all the signs and symptoms of being a Devdas. I was sure he kept a secret diary about Miss Rose.

Minutes later, I was sitting next to Miss Rose, in her car. She drove well and faster than my mom.

'Did you tell your mother?'

'Yes.'

'She loves you very much.'

All mothers love their kids, I wanted to tell her. I didn't understand how everyone figured out how much my mom loved me the moment they met her. She had always stood out at the parent-teacher meetings.

My mom had what Adi had. Everyone loved them.

'Do you have any favourite hang-outs?' I didn't have a favourite hang-out anymore, as I didn't have any friends except Urmi. But why should I tell Miss Rose about that?

'No.' I spoke in monosyllables.

Ten minutes later, we sat at the same coffee shop where my friends and I used to go, once upon a time. Starbucks looked the same. My caramel frappé tasted the same.

'Tina, I know you are wondering why we are here. I wanted to let you know that when I am out of your class, you can see me as a friend.' Miss Rose sounded genuine.

Did I need a teacher to be my friend now? No, I needed my own friends.

But I nodded my head.

'What would you like to eat?'

'I am not hungry.'

'I thought you loved smoked chicken sandwich?'

How the hell did she know that? Was she a stalker like me?

We had two sandwiches on the table in no time.

'Tina, do you want to tell me something?'

Whenever a woman throws that question at you, she wants to know your secrets and the onus is on you to figure out what exactly she wants to know. My mom did the same with me too.

'Tina, I want to help you,' Miss Rose said.

Well, I didn't ask for your help, did I? No, wait. Did she know that I had stalked Adi for some time? Is that what she was hinting at?

'Do you want me to talk to your classmates and sort out the issues between you guys? Your exams are just around the corner, and after that there will be a class picnic and many cultural programmes. It would be fun to have a good time with friends.'

Hell, now she knew this too.

She could have been the most talented and beautiful CIA agent ever.

'I do have a good time with my friends.'

Only cowards show their weakness to others. Though Adi believed I was a coward, I was not going to be one at the moment.

'When I was a teenager, I lost my mother,' Miss Rose continued. 'My sisters were studying in different colleges. We were all drifting apart. I was reckless, stubborn, and rebellious.

Then I met my principal in my college. She threatened to throw me out of college. I became more difficult. Some of the teachers hated me and I hated them more. Then one day, my principal asked me to meet her every day during the lunch break and share with her whatever problems I had faced during the day. I took it as a joke and didn't go. The next day, after the lunch break, she stormed into our class and threw me out. I had no choice after that but to end up in her office and give her a list of troubles I had created and faced that day. Now, she wanted to know the good parts as well. That list was short, close to nothing. I hoped this charade would end in a day or two, but it continued until I finished college as a state topper. "You proved that I wasn't wrong." The principal said that and hugged me after seeing the result. Everything she had done for me made sense in that moment. My family thought I would become an IAS or a doctor or an engineer, but I wanted to be a teacher. Like my principal, I too wanted to help someone as troubled as me . . . Tina, we all have a life. It has to have a purpose, and it's never easy to find one. We have to evolve every day through our ups and down. Every storm we face helps us learn something about ourselves.' Miss Rose stopped.

What her principal had done and what she was doing was great. But why me? What had I learnt from my life experiences? That first love is just a concept that looks good in books and movies? That friendship is an overrated word? That love means pain? My thoughts hurt.

'Anything to share?' Miss Rose asked, again.

'Thank you for the coffee and sandwich. It was nice,' I said. She smiled. I got up.

'I want you to do some homework.'

All the beating around the bush ended and now we were getting to the main point. I didn't feel good.

'Write down all your fears on a page and show it to me in school. It will help you.'

'I don't have any.'

You are my fear now.

'Everybody has some fear or the other. You think about this over the weekend and give the list to me on Monday.'

She wanted to spoil my weekend also. That's cruel.

We left the coffee shop. Miss Rose drove in silence till the car reached my building.

'Don't worry. All will be well,' she spoke like a saint.

I understood the meaning of her words, but not the context.

'Thank you. Good night, Miss.'

Miss Rose said goodnight and took a U-turn. I had a bad feeling that she wouldn't take a U-turn away from me easily. The coffee date was just the tip of the iceberg.

I made my way to the lift and saw Adi sitting on the garden bench, fiddling with his cricket ball. Why was he sitting alone? Oh God, he must have seen me in Miss Rose's car at school. I hung my head and walked as fast as I could. He could also throw the ball at my head. Again.

As I walked past Adi, a movie-like scene played in my mind. My hair fluttered in the air in slow motion, my cheeks blushed, and my skirt had a Marilyn Monroe moment. The colours of love danced before me. I held the school bag tight against my chest and stopped my heart from jumping out of my body. Adi didn't throw the ball at me, neither did he look at me. I walked towards the lift with a feeling that his eyes were on me.

I told Mom about Miss Rose and her principal, but not about Adi or the homework I had been assigned by Miss Rose. My mom became Miss Rose's fan in the fraction of a second.

'I wish we had more teachers like her.' That alarmed me.

No, I didn't wish that.

That night, I went to the terrace to watch the stars to take Miss Rose out of my mind. She and the story of her principal had instilled more fear in me than Hitler himself possibly could have. The stars looked like a thousand diamonds in the sky. I spotted Jupiter, thanks to the clear sky.

That's when I heard Adi, Krish, and Rahul. They had come to the terrace to have a smoke. I quickly hid behind a few boxes. Nobody knew they smoked, not even me. I held my breath and watched the smoke spiralling up in the air.

Rahul was talking about how one of his classmates used to email love letters to Miss Rose. That day, she had confronted the sender of the letters, and said, 'If you wrote these letters to someone in your class, the probability of you being in a relationship would have been much higher.'

'How did she figure out who the sender was?' asked Adi.

Rahul had no answer. That's the answer everyone wanted to know in his class.

'She must have used some hacker,' Adi guessed.

'Adi, you should take her help to find out who your stalker is. What the fuck are you staring at the stars for?' Krish asked.

'I am trying to see if I can spot my girl in them . . .'

'Asshole, Riha is in your pocket already. Now you want her in the stars too? Man, you know Tina used to be crazy about these stars. She knows about them more than the NASA guys. Krish used to hang around with her hoping that one day he could get into her panties.' That was Rahul.

'Rahul, I didn't want to sleep with her,' Krish said.

Adi turned towards him. 'Krish, you told me the very first day, after our cricket match, that you will fuck Tina before the year ends.'

'I thought I would. We used to be together all the time. I've still got a chance though. I bet she will run behind me if I talk to her.'

'At least you saw her bum.' Rahul laughed.

'That's all you'll get. She hates us for what we did. Any self-respecting girl would do the same. So forget about having another chance with her.' Adi surprised me with his response. I thought he'd agree with Rahul.

I had no idea Krish wanted to fuck me. How gross! They even discussed these things with each other. Assholes.

'Adi, have you fucked Riha yet?' It was Krish again.

Was this all that boys talked about—fuck, fuck, and more fuck?

'Guys, you don't fuck the girl you are in love with. You make love to her and I—' I wanted to go and hug Adi, but my phone cried out like a bloodthirsty ghost before Adi could complete his sentence. Who could be the spoiler? My mom!

'Holy fuck, I'm shitting my pants,' Rahul screamed as they all whirled around. They turned on their cell phone light and spotted me. I got up calmly, picked my telescope, and walked to the stairs. I stopped midway, and showed my middle finger to Krish. He deserved a slap and a kick and all the bad names I could think of. But I was scared to follow through with that urge. Three against one? No chance! And I wasn't wearing panties that night too!

'Fuck man! She heard it. Shit man!' I heard Krish.

'She watches the stars even now.' That was Rahul.

How memories become cursed because of the present!

How friends turn into enemies and strangers!

I didn't bother much. I could still see the stars from the window in my room.

I remembered a movie where a boyfriend had named a star after his girlfriend. How romantic that would be!

I wrote under my wish list:

14-Name the stars—Adi loves Tina.

I even spotted "Adi loves Tina" up in the sky.

This was crazy. The more I heard Adi, the more I adored him. How could a boy be so sensible? I slept well that night after having spent many sleepless days because of Adi.

And the stars "Adi loves Tina" smiled upon us.

'I waited for this day to tell you how much I love you,' Adi whispered in my dream. Why do dreams only show us our fantasies and not the reality? I sometimes wish they helped me with the reality too.

If I had any idea about what was waiting for me in the future, I wouldn't have dared to get up from my sleep.

I wouldn't have gone to school anymore.

I wouldn't have loved Adi.

I wouldn't have done anything I did in the past.

CHAPTER 17

The Love Games

May 18, 2016

Adi drove me home from the hospital.

We both needed a bath and I needed my phone.

I showered while Adi waited. As always, I walked out in a towel, with my hair wet.

'Do you want to fall sick again?'

Adi threw his towel at me. He ruffled my hair before going in for his shower. I loved these little things that only he could do. I closed my eyes and remembered my promise.

No more of this one-way romance, instead, it was time to set things right for my mom. When Adi heard about my plan, he wasn't so sure any more about driving me to Ajit Uncle's bungalow.

'Are you sure about this? It's not funny . . . You should have asked Aunty first.'

'If I go by the book, I won't reach anywhere . . . I don't see any other better options.' He knew I was right.

And we were on our way to meet Ajit Uncle. Adi didn't forget to cheer me up.

'Don't worry about Ajit Uncle. I know he would be delighted.'

'How do you know?'

'It's a guy thing, yaar . . . You won't understand.'

He could be right. I didn't argue.

When we reached, the same security guard peeped out from behind the gate. He reluctantly opened it. We found Ajit Uncle watering the plants in his garden. I hugged him.

'Is everything okay? Don't tell me you both are planning to elope!' Was it the same guy thing Adi had been talking about?

'How is Dr. Rachel George?' She wasn't "George" anymore, but I didn't correct him. Her name sounded better as it used to be. After Adi and I had had breakfast, I broke the news about Mom's heart surgery. How could someone have a heart attack at just thirty-nine? Ajit Uncle expressed his shock and wished to visit her.

Life brings up surprises when they are least expected. Who knew it better than Ajit Uncle? His son, Jai, became my friend when life bombarded us both with its twisted surprises. The first time our paths crossed, we were both at the end of a dark tunnel from which there was no hope of a return. But Jai had his amazing father and I had my amazing mother to hang on to. Jai, who lost his mother to cancer when he was ten years old and was struggling to cope with it, found a mother in my mom. She loved him, and his little garden and his birds. He loved her and the sea. Ajit Uncle reminded me of a father who was always there for his daughter. He invited us for weekend lunches followed by visits to the beach in the evening. As Jai and I swam, a proud mother and father would watch over us and chat.

Sometimes Jai used to ask me, 'Can I take your mom home?' And I would say, 'Please take her, but I will take your dad home.' We laughed. But I remember thinking, this could be a perfect family. But again, life throws up surprises and our wishes become meaningless.

'Tina . . .' Adi nudged me. We hadn't come to give Ajit Uncle a visiting pass or to have breakfast with him or to water his plants.

'Uncle, you can say whatever your heart feels like. If you don't like what you are going to hear, I promise you it won't go out of this room.' Ajit Uncle had never seen me getting so melodramatic. That made him visibly anxious.

'Spit it out, Tina. You know we have come a long way. You can tell me anything.' He was right, but I was a little nervous.

'Do you like my mom?'

'Of course. She is one of the finest ladies I have ever met.'

'Great. Would you like to marry her and be my father?' Ajit Uncle's face turned red. Was he blushing or was he angry? I couldn't tell.

'Sorry, Uncle, you can give me your answer by tonight. I didn't want to hurry you this way. But you know I have very few days left before I go to Florida and I can't leave her alone in this situation. She wants me to have every happiness in this world and wants nothing for herself. But she has so much of love to give, and she deserves the best in her life. Uncle, I thought you like her and I trust you completely that you won't break her heart like my father did.'

Ajit Uncle held my hands.

'It's not that I need time to think, Tina, but your Mom wouldn't agree to it.'

'How do you know?'

'You know that I am fond of you and your mom. Some months ago, I had discussed this with her . . . I didn't tell you anything because your mom never encouraged that conversation. I understood her completely.'

Ajit Uncle didn't need to tell me further. Knowing my mom, I knew she wouldn't have thought about marriage or a man because I had become her only purpose in life. I was the one to be blamed for putting her through all this.

I smiled and planted a kiss on his cheek.

'Thank you, Uncle. I will call you soon.' I was thrilled like a little girl.

'Uncle, get ready for a date with Rachel Aunty.' Adi hugged him as we were about to leave. Uncle came to the garden to see us off. My favourite roses were in full bloom.

'Do you want to take some flowers for your mom?'

'No, she would love to see them here. And more than that, these are for Jai . . .'

'I would never let your mom or you down. If I get the chance, I would love to have a daughter like you.' He hugged me. This time, he held on to me longer. I smiled a content smile. Adi was as happy as I was. This is what friends do.

We heard some music as we drove back to the hospital.

'For a moment, I thought Uncle had gotten angry.'

'Come on, I told you he loves your mom.'

'Hmm . . . It is funny how everyone seems to be in this secret admiration group. I am the only one who shamelessly wears my heart on my sleeve and says how much I loved you.'

'That's why you are different.' Adi gave me a look of disbelief. Fuck! I had said how much I "loved" him. Was my mind starting to give up on my dreams and on Adi? I didn't know. I wasn't happy, but I wasn't sad either. It had to happen one day. The sooner the better.

'You have matured ten years in just two days.' Adi pulled my hair. I loved it when he did that.

'I wish I could have matured without my mom's ribs and heart being cut open.'

'Are you going to tell your dad?'

'My ex-dad, Adi.'

'A dad is a dad.'

'You sound like my mom now.'

'I always sound like her. Sensible.' The smile I always wanted to see in my dreams melted me. I controlled myself.

That evening, Mom was shifted from the ICU to the ward. She had lost weight in just one day. Adi and I went in and sat with her.

'Did you two fight again?'

'No, Mom, we have stopped fighting. Friends don't fight, I suppose.' Adi remained tight-lipped. Maybe he didn't want to get into a private family matter. Or he thought I had gone insane. Or he wanted to let me handle it.

'Mom, I think you need to date.'

'Don't you think your dating stories are terrifying enough for me?' She smiled.

'Well, that's the point. No dating, just get married. You need a life too. For years and years, all you have been doing is taking care of me. How many times have you had sex? I was trying to calculate that today.'

'How can you talk to your mother like this?'

'Well, you are not just my mother, okay? You're also my friend. Why do you always have to be so nice, Mom? Why can't you be upset and angry and hate me and others? Your heart wouldn't have been broken then. Anyway, I know someone who loves you and he wants to marry you.'

'Angel, I will get another heart attack if you continue to talk such nonsense. You need some sleep. Adi, will you please drop her home?'

'All I am asking is for you to start a new life, Mom. Let's do it together, as you always say.'

'Who is this secret groom that you have picked out for me?'

'You will meet him today evening. Don't scare him away. And I know you like him too.'

'Huh. That's good. How do you know that by the way?'

'Mom, it's a girl thing. Do you remember when you asked me if I was in love?'

'You are becoming impossible.' She smiled, and joined with the physiotherapist who came to take her for a walk.

Mom hadn't agreed to the marriage yet, but I knew I could convince her. In a single day, I had begun fixing my mother's life and my fucked-up relationship. How cool was that?!

My phone rang just then. It was Rohit, my tennis partner. Now, I had to fix my own life. Better late than never!

I took the call and Rohit and I chatted for a few minutes. Adi stood next to me, uninterested in my conversation. So, I told Adi, 'Oh, I forgot to tell you, yesterday, Rohit asked me out again. He just called me to confirm our dinner date.'

I looked at Adi to see if he was hurt. Unlike him, I hadn't had many occasions to make him jealous.

Bloody hell, he wasn't!

'Again? I have been hearing this for some years now,' Adi shot back, looking at his phone.

'This time I am taking it seriously.'

'Did you tell Aunty?'

'She knows.'

'What did she say?'

'What would she say?'

'I don't know. That's what I am asking.'

'My happiness is her happiness.'

'That's good. You need to take some rest before your dinner date. Let me drop you home.'

'Hmmm . . . But that's tomorrow.'

I wanted him to know, I was free "today" if at all he wanted to spend time with me. Who cares! Get a little jealous, you idiot. I'm about to date another guy.

On reaching Daffodils, I was just about to get out of the car when Adi said, 'Let's sit in the garden for a while. I miss this place.'

I hid my excitement. It was the same garden where he used to play cricket when we were young. 'It was good to see you play the matchmaker today, so far you have only been a match-breaker.'

Adi was right. I had done some pretty adventurous things to shoo away his girlfriends.

'I want my mom to be happy.'

'She will be happy if you are happy.' I looked at Adi. He just stared back at me, as if he was seeing my heart.

'I want to be happy, Adi . . . I am trying. I hope I will be.'

'Let me help you.'

'You are not a psychiatrist.'

'Nobody knows you the way I do, Tina. So, let me help you. Go and sleep now.'

'Any words of wisdom about Rohit?'

'Of course. He is a great guy. Now you can stop blaming me for everything: if you smile it's because of me, if you cry it's because of me, if you sleep it's because of me, if you don't sleep it's because of me, if you fart it's because of me—'

'Adi, if I fart, it's definitely because of you. You give me indigestion! Period.'

'Okay. Now run. Good night.' He gave me a good night kiss, got up, and started the car while I stood there. Adi reversed his car, then stopped next to me, and rolled down the window.

'Go home, Tina. It's cold.'

'I was just checking whether you know how to reverse or not.'

'Yes, Miss Tina. I was born reversing this car. Now run before I spank you.' I waved at him. I thought he would come back again. My heart was stupid and not too pleased about my brain's interference between me and Adi. Whenever possible, it showed me the colours of love. But I decided to ignore my heart, or at least I was trying to.

Good night, my best friend. I texted Adi.

My phone beeped. I jumped to get it.

I can't sleep. I think I am in love.

I had been waiting to read this message for years. Only, it had come from the wrong number and the wrong person. I remembered my promise. I typed:

Looking forward to our date, Rohit. Good night.

How weird is life.

How unpredictable its moments are.

How strongly can the heart and the brain contradict each other!

How funny are these love games.

How mysterious is our future.

CHAPTER 18

My Missing Dreams

2013

Monday blues are never a good feeling.

Miss Rose stared at the blank paper. I bit my nail.

'Miss, I don't have any fears.'

'Then why are you scared to face Aditya? Don't you think one day he will find out about what you have been up to?'

My lungs nearly burst out. How did she know everyone's secrets?

'I don't have anything to tell anyone.'

'Okay. Your assignment still stands.' The discussion ended, for the day.

That night, I saw Aditya's message.

Aditya: You don't like me anymore? You don't stalk me. You don't message me.

I LOV ADI: I am not going to trouble you anymore.

Aditya: I will miss you then. My life would be less colourful without your stalking.

Was this really Adi? He had never said something like that before.

I didn't reply.

Aditya: Hey stalker, you seem worried. Why? You don't like that I miss you? I thought you would be happy to know that I know you and I will miss you if you stop loving me.

What game was this? Was he bluffing or did he know it was me? Fuck! It was not Adi.

Aditya: But I want you to come before me and tell me that you love me. Lovers have to be like warriors; they should not waste time playing hide-and-seek. Love has to face the storm, not flow with the wind.

I LOV ADI: What would you do if I came before you and said I love you?'

Aditya: I will marry you. ☺

It hurts when he makes fun of me.

I logged off.

While the world adored and wondered and wrote stories about this enchanting word "love", I proudly lived in love. No, I died in love. No, I have no idea how to explain this. It was insane, insane enough for me to lose my every sense and sensibility over him, over my life. That was the best part of it. I knew it would hurt every cell in my body, still I longed for it. I would have bartered my life for these crazy feelings. I cried, I laughed, I jumped, I rolled. I was happy and I was sad. I loved him and I hated him at the same time. I would have given up this world for him. I would have defended him and never given up on him even if the world turned against us. The cold war between Adi and me continued, but my love for him multiplied. I was breathing him every day. It was like his soul was embracing mine every moment. My love for him was weightless, shapeless, speechless, and invisible, but it was in me everywhere I went. When I was with him, I was happy and complete but sleepless. When he was not with me, I was sleepless again. Weird! But that's the way it was. It was all tears, all sleepless nights, all excitement and daydreams. The truth is that my perfect Adi existed only in my imagination. I daydreamed about Adi all day, every day. In reality, however, we didn't throw cricket balls at each other. Because I didn't play cricket anymore. I didn't keep my foot on his open shoelace. Because he learned to tie them up. He didn't grin at me anymore. Because he never looked at me.

He hated me, but I loved him.

It sucked. Big time.

I wrote in my diary:

Nothing is worse than falling in love with the one who will never love you back.

Nothing is worse than hoping that one day your love will be reciprocated.

Nothing is worse than ignoring others just because you see only one person everywhere.

Nothing is worse than seeing that your love is dating everyone except you.

Nothing is worse than hearing from him how much he loves her.

It tears my heart, it breaks my hope, it burns my soul.

But my love for Adi is beyond this pain.

My passion for him is beyond my tears, my loyalty is beyond my ego.

My hopes are beyond the rejections, my prayers go beyond this reality.

I love him truly, madly, wholeheartedly.

And my pain becomes my strength.

The more he breaks my heart, the more I am in love with him.

I am not ashamed, loving someone is not a crime.

I know this is my love story, not his.

These are my dreams, not his.

This is my redemption, not his.

And I pray that one day we won't be him and me,

We will be one. Just one.

These would be the last lines I would ever write in my diary. For the next day, my dear diary disappeared from my school bag. Time stood still. I wished for the earth to split open and hide me in its folds. What if Adi had taken it? My heart was beating out of my chest. But he didn't seem bothered in the least about my missing notebook even after I ran around the class in panic.

I had just one person to turn to. I ran to the staff room.

Miss Rose asked me to sit and take some deep breaths.

She couldn't figure out why I was being so hyper about a missing notebook.

'Would you please come and ask . . . But please don't say it's my diary . . .'

'It's okay, Tina, almost everybody writes a diary.'

But nobody writes about a crazy make-believe world with Adi.

Miss Rose came to our classroom ten minutes later. It wasn't her period. But the students weren't bothered about her coming to the classroom as far as Miss Rose did not ask them any questions. When they heard her, there were whispers in the classroom—who wants to read Tina's notebook? In a minute, they forgot all about my missing notebook and started whispering about Miss Rose's special attention on me.

That evening, I decided to go to Adi's house. I had to make sure that he didn't have my diary. If he had it, I had to get it back anyhow, even if it meant falling at Adi's feet.

I rang the doorbell at Adi's flat and Neelam Aunty opened the door. She gave me a smile and welcomed me inside. Neelam Aunty asked me why I never joined the others for group studies or sleepovers at their house. I didn't have any answer. I just gave her a smile and asked her if Adi was in his room. He was, so I walked towards it with trepidation. I saw the cautionary notice on his door—*Enter after taking permission.* And I entered without permission.

The first thing I saw when I opened the door were the life-sized naked blondes on the huge TV screen on his wall. Their breasts appeared extremely close to Adi's face. Krish jumped off the seat.

Was he jerking off? Oh God. Yes, he was!

I turned to run. Adi saw me.

He neither paused the video nor turned it off.

'Why the hell didn't you knock? Can't you read the board?' Krish screamed and rushed to the bathroom. Adi muted the video and looked at me.

'I think I knocked,' I lied. 'I . . . I mean . . . Have you seen my notebook?'

'Do you really think I would waste my time stealing your notebook?' Adi had a point.

I stood there like an idiot.

'Hey . . . Do you want to watch these blondes with us?' Adi snapped.

What a jerk! I hadn't expected this from Adi.

I ran out of his room. Neelam Aunty looked at me with a quizzical expression.

'Is everything okay?' she asked.

No! Your son and his friend are watching porn!

'Yes. Sorry for bothering you, Aunty. I will go home now.'

When I reached home, I had a message waiting for me in my inbox.

Aditya: Stalker, I miss your poems. Sleep tight.

I didn't reply. Maybe he had started loving me.

I shook my head. It was just my wish. And I couldn't write about all this since I didn't have a diary anymore. Putting my feelings on paper made me feel better.

Just then, Mom came in and in her hand was another diary! 'You can keep it at home. I won't snoop around,' she said.

I never found my first diary again. It gave me asthma attacks, sleepless nights, constipation, everything. Then the memories started to fade away. Whoever had it, never spoke about it. I was happy. I LOV ADI's identity remained a secret. At least that's what I hoped.

But, one day, someone would dig out my secrets. That would take me down the cliff. It was like my first love. When I look back, I miss my first diary and my silly world. Perhaps, the firsts in life are supposed to be lessons and memories, which get buried deep down as years pass by.

CHAPTER 19

The Second Love

May 19, 2016

The white lilies that Ajit Uncle had brought looked pale in the white room.

Mom seemed better though. Was she blushing? Yes!

'You are such a bad liar, Angel. Ajit didn't know what to say!'

'Who knows, Mom, you might be his first love. The same way I couldn't tell Adi and you couldn't tell your carpenter . . . Don't waste time. Trust me, if you don't get him, someone else will.'

I was the happiest. My mom was hopefully going to date a great guy and I had decided to move on in life. Rohit might not have been my first love, but he would give me the love I deserved.

'Mom, now we can bore each other with our love stories. How lucky are we?!' Someone knocked on the door just then. It must be Rohit. I opened the door and Adi walked in.

'Am I bothering you guys?'

Why was he being so formal?

'You are not bothering us. Why didn't you take my call?'

'I was busy.'

'Why did you come here then? Did Shruti kick you out?'

'I came to meet Aunty.'

'Good, be with Mom. Rohit is waiting for me downstairs.'

'That means I can't sleep today as well.'

'Will you come to see me off?'

Adi gave me a "what the f" look. Then he kissed my mom and followed me out.

'I have to take Shruti out for dinner.'

'Really? I thought you broke up.'

'I have already had fifteen breakups, all thanks to you.'

'You tell me this almost every second day. Sixteen sounds better, so break up with Shruti before I go to Florida. She is not your type. You know that.'

'Oh, I don't know. Enlighten me. What's my type?'

'Someone like me. Mind you, I didn't say me, okay? I am just a friend now. But I think your type is someone cute, like me.'

'Give me a break, Tina.'

'Okay, given.'

We got out of the building and walked towards the exit gate. Rohit was waiting there.

I wanted to flaunt Rohit. He was tall, muscular, caring, and already a national-level tennis player. Not a bad choice after all.

'If you want, you can take Rohit's autograph. He will be playing the US open soon.'

Adi gave me the finger. But he wasn't jealous. He seemed happy instead, happy that I was finally going away!

'I am a little busy. You guys have a good time. Rohit, don't make her drink. You won't able to handle her.' Adi was behaving as if he was my guardian.

'What's wrong with you? Nobody is perfect after a few drinks.' I stopped him.

'Yes, but you are too imperfect after just two pegs. Oh! I forgot, she stopped drinking. So don't force her.'

'Yes, she shouldn't drink anyway. She is still underage.' Rohit took Adi's side with a smile.

'See, you understand. Good. Also, she can't have mushrooms or garlic. She will forget about this and you will have a heart attack seeing her rashes.'

'Are you helping me or spoiling my date?' I asked.

'I am helping Rohit, and I am being selfish and helping myself so I don't get panic calls and run to get you. Go, have a super time.' Adi patted Rohit on his shoulder as if they were chuddy buddies and left. Man, only Adi could handle situations like these. The way he had spoken and behaved had made Rohit sweat. He had seemed breezy but it felt like he was also being possessive of me.

I turned and looked back. Adi wasn't there.

'Right, shall we go?' I heard Rohit ask.

Rohit turned out to be a great date.

We didn't go to RockS. We both had some bad memories of the place. And above all, RockS was a dedicated place to Adi and me. Rohit made sure I didn't drink or eat mushrooms and garlic. For the first time, I genuinely and truly wanted to know this guy for who he was. We had known each other for years. But I had had no time for anyone except Adi.

'What other things give you allergies?'

'Shellfish and cats. I don't catch colds as often as I used to earlier. And I don't get asthma attacks anymore.'

My phone beeped. A WhatsApp message from Adi.

He had sent a picture of Mom and Ajit Uncle. They looked cute together.

'My mom's date.' I showed Rohit the picture.

'They look cute. You know, I was kind of jealous. Aditya knows everything about you.'

'Yes. I know everything about him too.'

'Give me a chance to know you . . .'

I kissed Rohit on his cheek. He deserved it for being understanding, especially after the failed date we had had in the past.

'I don't know if you'll believe it, but I fell in love with you the moment I saw you. My heart said you are my girl, I swear.'

I believed him.

The same thing had happened with me too. Irony was that it wasn't him, but Adi.

'On that Valentine's Day, when I wished you and you gave me the finger, you must have been in a bad mood with one of your Adi bouts.'

'Maybe. No more talking about Adi now. We are just friends.' But I felt a lump in my throat.

'Yes, indeed. Do you want to dance?'

'Adi says I dance like a monkey.'

Rohit just smiled.

Yes, Adi . . . again!

'I am worse than a donkey. It will be a nice combo.'

We started dancing. I wasn't expecting it to be fun. I always believed Adi was my only happiness. A few minutes later, my phone rang. It was Adi. Of course, I was thrilled but I ignored his call. I hoped this would make him a little jealous. Adi called thrice more in the next half an hour. When the phone rang for the fifth time, I moved away from the dance floor to talk to Adi. Rohit accompanied me.

'Are you okay?' This was Adi's first question.

'What makes you think I am not?'

'My phone wasn't reachable, I thought you must have called.'

'No, I didn't.'

'What are you guys are up to?'

'We are dancing.'

'Where?' I didn't answer.

'I mean . . . if my phone becomes unreachable again, at least someone should know where you are. Aunty would be worried . . .'

'Don't worry about my mom. Rohit is here.'

'I know, but still . . .'

'How come you phoned?'

'Just wanted to remind you that don't call me to come and pick you up.'

What's wrong with Adi? He just wanted to irritate me.

'I do remember,' I said and disconnected the call. This wasn't the normal Adi. I could very well imagine his "what the fuck" expression.

Rohit looked uncomfortable.

'Adi had called to check if everything was okay.'

'Of course.' He took me to the dance floor again.

We continued dancing. I saw Adi's face in Rohit.

'Let's go out. It's noisy,' I said.

Rohit held my hand and led me out.

The garden outside looked beautiful under the shining moon. Two days later, it would be a full moon night. I didn't recite or write any poems for Rohit. Yet, it was nice to be loved, and to love.

'Thank you, I had a good time,' I told him and my phone beeped at the same time.

Don't you think you should come home now? It's cold outside. It was a WhatsApp message from Adi.

Rohit has got a jacket. Sleep now. I put my phone on silent.

Rohit's hand had the warmth of a new friendship, the promise of a future. He looked at the scars on my wrist. They remained there to remind me of my past, of the mistakes I had made, of the hate and the love I had received.

'Do they pain?'

'Not now.'

'Then?'

'Not as much as my heart did.'

'Do you want to tell me about it?'

'You will hate me.'

'Nothing from your past is going to make me hate you, Tina. We all have a past, even I do. Even I had my first crush, my first love, and I've had bad times too. Someday, you can tell me about your past, whenever you are comfortable, and listen to my story too.'

'Hmm, one day. I want to know if everyone acts as stupid as I did.' He laughed.

'More or less. That's the best part of it.'

'My mom used to tell me that the first love is the best feeling, but it cuts the deepest.'

'All wounds can be healed with the right medicine.'

I leaned against Rohit. He smelled great.

I didn't see any butterflies around me.

I didn't see any colours of love.

I didn't float in the clouds.

My heart didn't stop.

My hands didn't sweat.

Maybe love is beyond all the overrated dramas that we associate with it. Maybe love is just unnoticeable, like the air we breathe, the plants in the garden that we never notice, an ant trying to cross our feet, a touch that doesn't have any sparks, and the water running in the fountain day and night. It could be black.

It could be just anything. It could be just nothing.

'I love you, Tina.' Rohit's face touched mine.

His lips brushed against mine.

His breath warmed me.

He brought back memories of my first kiss, its excitement and its aftermath.

CHAPTER 20

The First Kiss

2013

The stargazing trip to Panchgani didn't cheer me up.

After a heavy lunch, all the students rested in the afternoon prior to a busy night. The girls in my class were divided into groups of three and were required to share a room in the hotel that had been booked for us. I was clubbed with Riha and Dia and that made me feel like an unwanted entity in the room. Adi visited them to make sure all was well for his girls, but he avoided me.

The evening activities started with the students setting up tents at Table Top, a place that gave a bird's eye view of the entire valley. It couldn't be just an accident—Riha shared a tent with me. I spoke to Miss Rose to figure out if there was a chance I could change my "tent-mate".

'We don't always get choices in life,' Miss Rose said and went back to her work.

Exactly at seven p.m., the team from the planetarium guided us to watch the eastern and the northern sky. There were so many constellations—Cassiopeia, Polaris, Perseus, Double Cluster, Auriga, Taurus, Orion "The Hunter", Canis Major, Canis Minor—but I had seen them all earlier. However, the Celestron 400x80 refractor telescope tempted me to spend my whole night behind it. Still, I got distracted seeing Adi and Riha watching the stars together and sharing jokes.

Two hours later, we broke for dinner and students were asked to go to the hotel's restaurant. It had gotten colder outside. I went back to the tent allotted to Riha and me to get my sweater and my inhaler. By then, everyone had gone to the hotel but I decided to lie inside the tent in the silence of the night, alone, away from the fear of dark for the first time.

'Riha, I told you I'm sorry. Come on. Don't behave like a kid.' It was Adi, speaking from the other side of the tent. It was dark, so I couldn't see him properly.

What should I say? Why do I become speechless around him?

'If you are not coming out, then I am coming in.' I put the blanket over my head. I was nervous. Adi got into the tent in no time. He sat next me, holding my hand over the blanket.

'I said I am sorry. You know that I love you.' Adi bent over me. My breath stopped in its tracks. I wanted to tell him it was me, Tina. But I didn't.

Then something happened.

I lost my senses, still I remembered.

Adi removed the blanket in one swift motion and then, his lips were on my lips! Oh my God! Adi kissed me! I had never heard how a lip talks to the other. When I heard it for the first time, I didn't know how to answer. Adi didn't stop at the kiss, he separated my lips with his tongue. My mouth burned like hot iron. I wanted to pull away before I started to float, but I just couldn't. I couldn't think straight, or else why would I have arched up towards his chest, hugged him hard, as if I was a part of his body. He didn't push me away. He held me tight and our breaths became one. I felt his heart beat inside my heart. The kiss sent warmth through our bodies, quickened our breathing, and we hugged as if we would never separate. His tongue danced inside my mouth, waited for mine to join. I felt something in my abdomen, then all over my body. The cold disappeared, the tent vanished, the world dropped into nothingness, a million stars illuminated the darkness around us, I drifted up in the air as if by magic. I arched towards him, and he held me tight.

'I love you . . .' Adi said.

I had never heard such divine words in my life. I saw the colours of love around me. My brain was on fire, my whole body trembled. Something oozed out of me without my permission. My thighs got wet with it. We were still kissing and I was floating in the clouds, the way I had always dreamt of. Until then, I never knew how beautiful these moments could be.

It was my first kiss from my first love.

It would be the most special moment until I died, and even after my death.

Adi stayed in my arms, both of us short of breath. I had tears in my eyes, tears of joy and love.

'I love—' Before I could complete my sentence, Adi opened his eyes. He looked at my face as if he had seen a ghost. Then, he jumped right out of the tent.

'Would you please come out?' I heard him say. 'Please, I want to talk to you.' Adi saying "please" sounded sweet.

I walked out towards him.

Adi sat on the ground outside the tent, staring up at the stars. I stood behind him. He moved a little to give me some space.

'You can sit.' I sat, obeying him like a kid, but keeping my distance from him. I saw the stars, they looked brighter than usual, much like the ones in my dreams. My heart fluttered.

'Which star is that?' He pointed at the one that twinkled the most. I looked at him like I was in a dream.

'Pole Star,' I said.

'I want to say I am sorry. I thought—'

'You don't need to be.' I wanted to thank him for fulfilling my wish. They say if you truly wish for something, your wish comes true. I believed it now. I have more wishes. Let's see how the universe was going to help me with them.

'I have to go. I came for Riha.' He underlined it again. I just shook my head. 'Again, I didn't mean . . . I am sorry. I hope it remains between us . . . Please . . .' Adi got up and waited for me.

'Ye-yes,' I stammered.

'Why didn't you go for dinner?' I didn't answer.

Was he really concerned about me or was he just wondering how to leave me alone there? That was the moment we saw some flashlights moving towards the tents.

'Maybe they are here for you.' Adi disappeared into the night. Would he have stayed back if no one had come looking for me?

I would never know, not unless he told me.

I got up and went inside the tent.

Miss Rose, along with some of the hotel staff, came to fetch me.

'Are you okay? You scared us. How could you just stay back here alone?'

'I wasn't hungry.'

'I have heard you know quite a bit about stars.'

'My dad taught me.'

'Do you want to teach me about them after dinner?'

Miss Rose gave me company for dinner, raising some

students' eyebrows high enough to touch the ceiling of the restaurant. Riha, Krish, and Dia shared a table and Riha kept on dialling someone's number on her cell phone—Adi, of course. And he too turned up not much later.

The dinner got over pleasantly. Adi's magic still stayed with me. I saw Miss Rose looking at me with curiosity.

'You look happy today,' she said.

'I love the stars.'

I couldn't tell her that I had just had my first kiss from my first love.

After dinner, we went to Table Top again to watch the stars. This time, I helped Miss Rose spot Leo.

'Can you see the sickle? The bottom star of the backward question mark is called Regulus. You can see the triangle as the tail in the eastern side. The brightest star is called Danebola.' She was as excited as us kids.

'It's interesting. I have never seen stars so closely.' That was Adi.

'Aditya, what are you doing alone there? Come here. Tina knows them pretty well.' Miss Rose made way for him.

I looked at him nervously. Shit. Miss Rose knows that I love him. What if she told him right now?

'Where should I look?' an unenthusiastic Adi asked.

I started to sweat. I became mute and deaf this time. I could still feel his warmth on my lips. I wanted more of it, but somehow, I controlled myself and managed to explain to Adi about the sickle and the tail, about the legends behind Leo and how the Egyptians were influenced by Leo's structure.

For a change, Adi listened intently. And so did Miss Rose too. I must say, it was the best night I had had ever since Adi had walked into my building and into my life. It was nice to be with people who care for you, like Miss Rose. It was enchanting to be with the person whom you love so much. If the person loved you back, that would be the best thing.

I wished Adi and I were alone there. I wanted to tell Adi how much I had waited for this day, just to be next to him, to look into his eyes, to hold his hand, to hear his breath, to feel his presence . . .

The students watched the stars for another hour. Then, it was time for a game of truth and dare. Everyone gathered around the bonfire. I started walking towards my tent, but Miss Rose stopped me and made sure I sat for the game.

'I don't want to know anyone's secrets.' She went back to the stars. I thought she was generous, like my mom.

I looked at Adi and Riha. It looked like they had patched up. I sat there in a corner, worrying about the rotating Pepsi bottle. It stopped, pointing at Adi.

'Adi, do you really love your girlfriend?' Riha asked.

'Yes.' Adi didn't take even a moment to answer. Riha blushed.

Then, it pointed at Mihir.

'Have you had your first kiss?' one of my classmates asked.

Mihir shook his head.

The bottle pointed at Adi again. 'Adi, did you kiss your girlfriend, I mean French kiss?'

'Yes,' Adi said calmly. Riha's face fell, but she looked at him curiously.

It was Dia's turn next.

'Stand near Miss Rose's tent and shout "I'm in love!"' Mihir said.

Dia scoffed. 'This is so easy that it doesn't even qualify as a dare.'

And without any hesitation, she did it. Nothing happened and Dia came back and sat down, her head held high.

It was Adi's turn to spill the beans next.

'Adi, is your future wife amongst us?'

Adi smiled. 'Yes.' Riha blushed and gave a flying kiss to Adi.

Then, the bottle pointed at Riha. 'Riha, when did you kiss Adi for the first time, I mean French kiss?' It was Krish.

But Riha didn't answer and chose, instead, to take a dare.

'Kiss the person you hate the most, on the lips.' Riha got up and walked towards me. I had just had a bath in rainbows and in the colours of love. But I hadn't seen this kiss coming even in my wildest of dreams. Riha bent over me, the students clapped, her lips touched mine, and then she opened her mouth.

'You bitch,' she whispered, and then she bit my lower lip. I thought she had seen Adi kissing me and wanted to chop off my lips in revenge. I wanted to scream, but I didn't. As she walked back to her seat, my lower lip bled. I wiped it on my sweater. Everybody saw the blood, but nobody said anything, not even Adi.

'Did you like the kiss you got today?' It was Adi's chance and he asked me that question!

Was he talking about his or his girlfriend's kiss? What an irony, I got kissed by both on the same day! I had no time to complain.

'Yes,' I said. Blood still sprouted from my swollen lip. Then, as I walked back towards my tent, I heard Riha saying, 'I didn't know she was a lesbian. I should change my tent.'

I took my inhaler once inside the tent. I wondered if Adi would ever think about me after that kiss. Had he been replaying our kiss in his head the way I had been doing? Was he getting goosebumps thinking about it like I was? Was he flying with the clouds? Was he seeing the colours of love? Would I ever get any answer from him?

I closed my eyes and saw Adi bending over me, his lips touching my lips. I felt the same tingling sensation I felt whenever he was around. I smiled and kissed him again. Wow. The touch was surreal. The kiss was immaculate. The feeling was divine. The moment was sacred. The night was magical.

I was grateful.

I got kissed, again and again and again.

CHAPTER 21

It Gets Better

May 21, 2016

What a feeling it was to come back home, to give death a miss, to get a second chance with your loved ones, to smile and to live once again. Who would know this better than me?

My friends and I had decorated my home with balloons and lilies. Ajit Uncle, who stood next to my mom at the door, doubled up the twinkle in her eye. Still, she had tears in her eyes. Now, it was her turn to cry. She was in love too. Well, she was getting there.

'They look cute, like us,' Krish commented, looking at Minu. Another one-way romance! He was madly in love with Minu, but she had started dating her first crush—her tuition teacher.

While the ladies rested and chatted, the men seized the kitchen under Ajit Uncle's supervision. Adi and

Krish became his assistant chefs while I uploaded their pictures on Facebook with the caption, "Love in the kitchen".

Before we started lunch, something happened.

Shruti called Adi and threatened to leave him. Again. She had seen my post on Facebook and didn't appreciate the love that was happening in our kitchen.

'Why the hell did you do this, Tina?' Adi barked at me.

'This is about Ajit Uncle. I have no interest in you anymore.'

'Oh really, Tina?' Adi asked, looking at Ajit Uncle's left hand, the only part of him that was visible in the pictures.

Adi spent the rest of his time on the phone with Shruti.

'You started it, you fix it now.' He gave me the phone. But Shruti disconnected the call as soon as she heard my British accented 'Hi, Shruutiiii!'

The doorbell rang a little later. Adi opened it.

Rohit walked in with a bouquet of beautiful roses and a great smile.

'Oh, I thought someone had come to deliver flowers.' Adi tapped on Rohit's shoulder, as if he was giving him permission to come in. 'Let me give this to Aunty.' Adi offered his help.

'Thank you, Adi, but these are for Tina,' Rohit said.

'Oh yeah? But she loves lilies. Maybe next time . . .' Adi's smile was a silent killer.

'I have started liking roses from now onwards.' I took the flowers from Rohit.

Krish and Rahul stared at this new, irritated Adi. They shot him a weird look, and then looked at me.

'Is something cooking between you two?' I ignored Dia's question and instead, introduced Rohit to the aunties and uncles at home.

Rohit mingled with everyone, while Adi sulked.

'Don't lie, Tina. Why is Adi PMSing? It's not like him.'

'Dia, the probability of the Taj Mahal moving into this kitchen is much higher than Adi ever loving me back. I am trying to get out of this mess. Don't give me stupid ideas now. Go give him a head massage or kick his ass. He is upset about Shruti.'

Dia pinched my bum, and gave a long "hmmmm".

After lunch, Adi, Krish, Rahul, Minu, and Dia left for their cricket match. Adi was courteous enough to invite Rohit. Then, he pulled me towards the kitchen. Rohit noticed us with a pinch of jealousy. 'The match starts at four,' Adi said.

'Rohit is taking me out.' I said with a sweet smile.

'I can't believe this shit. You just started dating him and you are not bothered about our match. Whenever you aren't there, I lose.'

'Really? I didn't know this . . .'

'Eighth standard, our intra-school final, you weren't there.'

'We were enemies back then.'

'Ninth. You weren't there. We lost again.'

'I was in the hospital, visiting stars . . .'

'Tenth, you were there. We won, and I was man of the match. Eleventh, you were there. We won. Man of the match again. Twelfth, you weren't there, we lost again. Do you want me to lose this time as well?' His eyes held my gaze. It had the same lightning effect. Then, Adi just left.

Tina, it's all an illusion . . . No, an infatuation. Don't change your mind . . . Think about your life. I reminded myself that I had to stay with my plans.

'What are you doing here?' Rohit came into the kitchen.

'I saw a butterfly . . .'

'A butterfly in your kitchen . . . Where is it?'

'It just flew out.' I pointed towards the window.

Rohit saw the closed window and smiled.

'Let's go. My time starts now. Aunty has asked me to drop you home by eleven.'

What should I do? Adi or Rohit? Tina, don't make a mess again. The voices fought inside my head. Rohit held my hand. His warmth made me warm too. I walked along with him, making my mom smile. After a long time, she was at peace.

Rohit drove like a racer.

'I have a surprise for you.'

'What?'

I loved surprises. Why was I not excited?

'If I tell you, how would it be a surprise?'

'Rohit, I have to go for Adi's match.'

I didn't want Adi to lose his match while I waited for some surprise. I loved the idea of being Adi's lucky mascot. How cool was it that he had his girlfriend Shruti and hundreds of other girls praying and cheering for him, but he thought I was the one who mattered most? Some more days . . . Then I would be gone. It was confusing, but thrilling.

'It's just a club match, right?' Rohit looked baffled. 'Tina, can I ever get ten minutes of you without Adi? Don't you think I deserve that much?'

'I am trying, Rohit. He is just a friend. And I want to spend some time with my friends before I go. I am really sorry.' I had started using the phrase "just a friend" which Adi used frequently while referring to me. 'I will see you at the court. I hope that's okay.'

'You have no option but to see me at the court, Tina. Do you want me to come with you?'

'Not this time.' Adi didn't like Rohit, neither did Rohit like Adi. Why? Maybe it was a guy thing.

'I don't see Adi getting possessive about his own girlfriend the way he does about you,' Rohit said.

'Really?' I had never thought about it or felt it before. I would be the happiest if that was remotely true. I hugged Rohit and ran to get a taxi.

The taxi driver threatened to drop me off right then and there if I nagged him to drive any faster again.

'If I don't reach soon enough, I will end up missing something very important.'

'Let me guess. It has got to do with your boyfriend.' He gave me a look.

'No. Just a friend.'

How much my tongue wanted to say, yes, boyfriend.

'I have never told my wife that I love her. Today, friends also say I love you.'

'You tell your wife once and see what happens.'

'What would happen?'

'You have to find that out.' He wasn't convinced, but he broke all the red lights for me.

'How old are you?'

'Seventeen.'

'I have a daughter. She is sixteen.' He looked worried.

I knew the reason!

I reached Azad Maidan, where the match was happening, ten minutes after four p.m.

Adi had made just three runs in two overs.

His team members, including Rahul and Krish, sat as if they were at a funeral. I saw Shruti, Minu, and Dia cheering for them. I joined them.

'Hey, Shruti . . . Friends?'

'I have more friends than I can handle.'

I offered her an olive branch and she slapped me on the face with it.

'You don't need to handle me. I don't want to be your enemy. I am going to the US next week.'

'I don't hate you, Tina. Just that I could never understand how you are always in their heads.' She had said "their", but I knew she meant just Adi's. She looked at me like a cat—an angry, fussy cat.

'We are just friends. You know that. Ask Dia.' Dia nodded without much interest.

I don't know if I was indeed Adi's lucky charm, but just then sixers flew up to the eagles, runs rained, and Adi's team won the match. Shruti's jaw dropped and mine too.

Adi raised his bat up in the air and then gestured towards us, towards me, with his charming, dimpled smile. He ran to us. I stood there in anticipation that he would come and hug me. He did indeed, but he hugged Shruti first, then Minu, and then Dia.

'Thanks for coming,' Adi said to me. I wanted to say that I would be there for him always. But before I could, Shruti dragged him away for her surprise celebration plans. Adi wanted to take us all along.

'I am sure they don't want to interrupt us. I hardly get to see you as it is.' She gave us, me in particular, a nasty smile.

My phone rang just then. It was Ajit Uncle.

'Would you join us for dinner? I am cooking for your mom.'

'Three's a crowd, Uncle. I have plans with my friends. I can also stay over at Adi's.'

'Angel, behave . . .' Mom! Oh, he was on the speaker phone.

My mom was in love. That's super cool.

'Okay, I will behave.' I disconnected the call. I was happy; my mom deserved the best. Dia and the gang offered me a lift, but I wanted to be alone. I lied about having a dinner date with Rohit and left them.

I walked towards Marine Drive, and sat on the cement

blocks there. I saw the setting sun. I saw the silent sea. I heard my beating heart. I started to realise that loving someone is about being happy for that person. It was a cliché, but it calmed me.

I thought of Rohit. And WhatsApp'ed him.

I think . . . I love you. I felt happy, blessed, and loved.

Are you already drunk? You want to really screw it up by sending me a message when you know I am with Shruti.

Fuck, I had sent the message to Adi!

Don't feel so important. It was meant for Rohit.

Adi didn't believe me though.

Finally, I was going to move on from Adi by going to Florida. I had to share this happy news with one more person who had been a part of my journey.

I dialled Miss Rose's number and she said she would be thrilled to meet me for dinner. When I met her at her building gate, she looked as beautiful as ever with the same warm smile.

'Tina, you look vibrant. Is your impending trip to Florida keeping you so happy?' She smiled.

'Well, that and my decision to move on from Adi. But I guess I needed Mom's heart attack to jolt me back to reality.'

'We never know what the future has in store for us.' Miss Ross smiled.

They say teachers are the future of the future. They are the ones who make history. Only the most blessed students meet teachers who guide them towards the future they desire for themselves. Only chosen teachers walk with the students, holding their hands. Miss Rose was indeed a chosen teacher and I was a blessed student. She not only showed me the future, but she was also there to hold me whenever I fell.

CHAPTER 22

A Birthday Missed but Celebrated

2013

My life and my routine didn't change much in the ninth grade.

I continued making up my perfect make-believe world with Adi while he still dated Riha. After all the hard work, all I had gotten in the bargain was that mistaken kiss which had fallen on my mouth and the tingling sensation I had felt all over my body for the first time. I had also started to live without my ex-friends. The saying that time heals everything could turned out to be true. They couldn't hurt me anymore. They didn't expect that I would be okay without them. Urmi had replaced every friend I had had. Quality over quantity was the priority when it came to friends.

Before I knew it, it was September. The month I looked forward to, the month I was born in, and the month my dad visited me with birthday presents. Our plans were dashed this time around when Dad called us to say that he wouldn't be able to make it for my birthday, blaming some emergency at work. Mom rushed to her room and locked the door. I heard fireworks erupt between them for the first time. They were divorced. But my mom didn't want him to desert his daughter.

And on 21st September, my birthday came without my dad around. Since it was a Saturday, there was no need to worry about birthday wishes from my classmates and ex-friends. But I had my mom.

'We are going to RockS tonight. We should celebrate,' Mom told me while fetching me from tennis practice. She had given me a beautiful blue dress and a DVD compilation of all the precious moments of my life, right from my birth.

It's good to grow up and it's bad to get hit by its side effects.

At RockS, everything looked just as majestic as before.

Mom ordered champagne.

'Is everything okay?' This time, it was my turn to quiz her. We weren't rich enough to splurge on expensive drinks except for the ones Dad got from the army canteen.

'We can also celebrate occasionally. To my Angel,' she raised a toast. I took a sip. Well, it tasted better than wine.

'Is everything okay with Dad?'

'Of course. You know what a doctor's life is like.'

We laughed and drank.

'Mom, Adi is here.'

'Where? Angel, that's Shah Rukh Khan!'

'Nooo! I just saw Adi.' Both of us were right.

Mom saw Shah Rukh, and then Adi, who was with him.

My eyes, as always, spotted only Adi.

'Shah Rukh looks smart in real life too,' Mom said.

'Mom, don't drool. Let them go.'

'Adi saw us,' she said. I didn't raise my head.

'Hey, Aunty. What a surprise! Are you guys regulars here?'

Sarcasm! I hate you man.

'No, Adi, we are celebrating Angel's birthday.'

I gave my mom a look. She gave me a big smile.

By then, Shah Rukh Khan had reached our table. He was just following Adi.

'My classmate, Tina. It's her birthday today,' Adi said, introducing us.

I hadn't expected that.

I wanted to look at Shah Rukh Khan. But my head refused my wish.

'Wow, what a fantastic day, Tina! Happy birthday, sweetheart. Well, what should I gift you? Huh . . . Okay, here you go . . . It's a little small for you, but still . . .' He removed his watch and put it on my wrist. Then he smiled, showing me his dimples.

I sat there looking at him like I was in a dream.

Mom nudged me. I got up and smiled, but I forgot to thank him.

I remembered what I had written in my lost diary. *What would I tell Shah Rukh if he wishes me on my birthday?*

Nothing. I didn't say anything.

'As Miss Tina is not asking for a selfie, and I am not used to people ignoring me, birthday girl, can I have a picture with you?' Shah Rukh held out his hands toward me, exactly the way he had done for Kajol.

I wanted to pee.

I wanted to go and hug him.

I wanted to kiss Adi again.

But I didn't do anything.

Dumbstruck, I stood next to the superstar like I had just woken up from sleep.

'Come on, Adi. You should be a boyfriend like me.'

Shah Rukh, perhaps reading my mind, pulled Adi to join us. What if he could read Adi's mind too? I wondered.

Adi stood next to me and Shah Rukh Khan took the picture.

'I will make sure you get this pic. Post it on Facebook. I will feel good knowing you didn't delete it.' He smiled and wished me again before leaving. My mom thanked him.

The rest of the night was a blur. I don't even know how we reached home. I was in a trance, and embarrassed about having behaved like a mute person in front Shah Rukh Khan. Then I saw a tag from Adi on my FB page. It was a picture of me with Shah Rukh and him, with the caption: #HappyBirthdayTinafromShahRukh

I called out to Mom and showed her my birthday photo on Adi's page.

Wow! This was super cool.

'Now you are speaking.' She tickled me and then left, saying, 'Shut the laptop and sleep. I know what's in your head.'

I didn't doubt her, and closed the door.

I looked at Adi and me. My smile vanished when I realised that Riha definitely looked better next to him than I did. However, I went to sleep staring at us. It looked like the Gods had stopped fighting with me. Some of my impossible wishes were getting fulfilled in the most magical of ways. What I didn't know was that this was the calm before a storm, the feast before the slaughter, the kiss before the murder, the bath before the burial.

When I went back to school on Monday, a surprise awaited me. I found a card in my desk drawer.

Happy Birthday, Tina. I still watch over you.

Automatically, my head turned toward Urmi. She smiled at me. I asked her about the Valentine's Day card and then this one. She said the cards weren't from her. I trusted her. We wondered about the mysterious guardian angel.

My mind wandered. I didn't hear my teachers. I didn't think about my missing Dad, or about my birthday gift from Shah Rukh. Instead, I tried to put a face on the words which stared at me. How could anyone remember my birthday? Why did someone want to be nice to me? Why was that person hiding behind these cards? Now, I realised what Adi must have gone through.

I showed the card sent by the invisible ghost to my mom.

'This is called karma,' she said.

'I don't stalk Adi anymore. You know that.'

'But you used to.'

'I will apologise.'

My mom smiled, proudly.

Her daughter was finally showing some sense.

I logged in.

I LOV ADI: I am sorry. I should never have stalked you. I was scared to tell you how much I loved you. Someone told me, loving someone without any reason is the purest love and it makes us perfect. And someone taught me today that loving and caring do not have to be confessed or named, they do not need to have a face. It's a prayer we keep for the other, the soul we save forever. I have yours now and ever . . .

My mom watched me in silence.

My heart pounded. It wasn't easy.

Being sensible could never be easy.

Now onwards, Adi will exist only in my world.

We will be happy there.

Just before deleting the profile, I saw Adi's message.

Aditya: I am looking forward to seeing you honouring your words. You better do that.

Nothing more. My happiness drained off in a second.

Was he really happy that it had all ended? I thought he loved this game too.

Mom looked at me.

I had tears in my eyes.

I pressed that delete button, and then I hugged her.

My mom didn't say anything.

I didn't say anything.

CHAPTER 23

Finally, A Marriage!

May 23, 2016

A marriage never guarantees happiness. But this time, I truly believed that my mom's marriage would be a happy one. It wasn't easy for me to convince my mother to marry again even after my father had moved on with his new family. As always, she had a thousand reasons to say no, but everything started and ended with me.

'Angel, I am happy. I have you.'

I didn't counter that. I hadn't ever been sure about anyone but Ajit Uncle. We had seen how much he'd loved Jai. We had also seen how shattered he had been when Jai had drowned in the sea in the cold December of 2013 when he had gone out with his friends for a swim. The only thing which had given Ajit Uncle a little peace of mind was the fact that Jai had loved the sea. He had lost his son. Mom had lost a boy she considered her son and I lost the brother I never had.

'Mom, if you want me to be happy, please . . . I am scared to leave you alone here.'

I hugged her and cried. This was the first time I was thinking about someone else other than me. I was scared to death thinking that while I would be out exploring the world, full of happiness and love, my mom would be all alone. I was afraid we would never find a wonderful person like Ajit Uncle again. I was scared that one day, my dad would stop communicating with us altogether. He would never actually do that, but when you are scared, you think the worst.

Mom was in tears too. She kissed me and complained, 'I hate seeing you so grown up, and that too in just a week.' I smiled. Yes, she was only used to seeing my selfishness and my heartbreaks. Not anymore though. That was a promise I made to myself.

'I need to talk to your dad too.' I knew she would. That was how unique and forgiving she was. I nodded.

I had more to do. I called Adi, my partner-in-crime.

'Are you sure, Tina? You should probably give them some time,' Adi advised.

'Shut up, Adi. Only I know how hard it was to get her permission. Now please don't spoil it. Anyway, you are the least qualified person to offer any advice on this. You can't even keep a girl for six months.'

'Once you learn to live without me, my girlfriend will remain with me forever.'

Funny . . .

'You will miss me and come running to me and fall at my feet.'

'Tina, don't live in your bubble of illusions.' Adi laughed.

'Truce. Are you with me on this?'

'Of course, Tina, you should honour your words. Also, Ajit Uncle and Aunty are made for each other.' Adi's favourite line. If he was on my side, nothing was impossible.

In an hour, Adi reached my home with a registrar. Meanwhile, I had gone to get the groom while Dia and the rest of the gang collected Mom's friends. And my mom was newly married with the blessings of her friends and her daughter. Not many children are lucky enough to see their own mother's wedding. I hoped Jai was happy at this turn of events, wherever he was.

Ajit Uncle would stay at his house till I was in India. Mom must have found it difficult to have him around. We were both not used to having a man in the house. It had been just the two of us ever since Dad left us.

My mom had another plan instead of her honeymoon trip. She wanted to take me to see my dad before I left the country. I wasn't much convinced about visiting my ex-father.

The divorce hadn't made my mom bitter. Later, she had something to tell me about how we are not all perfect. She told me how we all drift apart but how we could still care for each other and how Dad would always be a part of my life.

I didn't cry. I didn't question her. All I said was, 'I guess.'

My dad had kept his word. He was there even when he wasn't there. We learned to live without him. But when I had wanted him the most, when my mom had wanted him the most, he hadn't been there. When Mom was in a hospital, I had wondered about the meaning of family. And I stopped talking to him even after my mother tried hard to bring my father back into my life.

'I don't want a father who stays only at end of the phone, Mom.' It hurt her. It hurt him. She tried to make me understand what the life of an army doctor was. But as my mom had said, sometimes we drift apart. And I had drifted apart from my dad.

Memories are like broken pieces of glass. The harder you grip them, the more you bleed. I wanted to put mine in a box and lock them away forever. Still, I thought about my dad on our way to Srinagar to meet him. Deep in my heart I knew it was me who had made us drift apart. Staying away from their family for long months and working in such a demanding condition could change people. However, guilt appears in different ways. That's what happened with Dad and me.

He wasn't there when we arrived at his doorstep even after Mom had informed him about our visit. I felt relieved at his absence.

My dad's current wife, Pooja, looking drained and lost, opened the door and wiped off the sweat from her face when she saw us. The two-year-old baby in her arms cried like an alien who wanted to revolt against the entire planet even after his mother's pleading and her kisses. My mom took the baby and had some funny conversation with him, which nobody understood except the little one. He smiled and pulled her cheeks, her nose, and her hair. It was like magic! Pooja watched them in awe. She didn't mention Akash—whose hand I had fractured—until Mom asked about him.

'He has gone out with some friends. Can I get you both something to drink?' Mom didn't discourage the host.

I looked around the house like a spy. After about half an hour later, Pooja brought us coffee and some biscuits. There was more silence than words, except for Mom's baby talk with the kid.

'He's got congenital cardiomyopathy,' Pooja informed us.

'So sorry to hear that.' My mom and she then continued their conversation on the treatments. At least they had found something to talk about.

An hour later, we heard my dad park his bike outside the house. He didn't look surprised or excited when he came in and saw us. I couldn't ignore his love for me as I saw it clearly in his eyes. But I guess he was guilt-ridden because of what he had done to us, so he didn't say anything. He noticed the diamond ring sparkling on Mom's finger. The awkward silence made everyone uncomfortable. How relationships change! The same dad who used to carry me on his shoulders now sat a few feet away like a stranger. And I told him,

'I just want to let you know, I didn't die in the hospital that time. And Mom is now married to a great person. Oh, and I will be going to the US for further tennis coaching.' Even though I knew my mom would get his blessings for her new life, I wanted to tell my dad that Ajit Uncle was a rich guy with a nice bungalow, a factory, and luxury cars.

'Congratulations . . .' That was for me for sure. But he didn't call me Angel any more, not even Tina. Everyone was silent again.

'Would you like to stay for lunch?' Dad asked.

'No. We have some work to finish,' I said. Mom gave me a look. Why was she looking at me like that? Oh my God! Did she still love him? What a tragedy that would be!

My mom whispered, 'Tina, he is your dad. You can't behave this way. Say sorry.' Mom addressing me as "Tina" reminded me that she was angry. I was rude. I was angry. Because I was upset and I still couldn't forgive my dad for what he had done to us.

'Sorry,' I said.

'It's okay, I understand.' I wanted to tell him how much I hated him. But all the years of anger I had hidden in my heart had numbed me.

It was time for us to go. We had been there for just about two hours. Dad walked with us till the front gate and he seemed more comfortable away from his wife's scrutiny and his kid's howling.

'I am taking an early retirement.'

'Are you okay?' Mom sounded concerned.

Who cared if he wasn't?

'The kid's treatment is taking a toll on us,' he said. He must have been regretting what he had done to us. Looking at his beefed-up wife and my mom who shone like a star must have brought him back to his senses.

Oh, love has got no rules.

The kid came outside, smiling at Mom. I looked at him. Maybe he wouldn't be living long. I carried him and took his hand in mine. He looked at me, and then he smiled at me as if he knew me. It surprised me. I smiled too, for the first time after reaching that house. Kids are cute. And he was my stepbrother after all.

'Shall I drop you?' Dad asked.

'No, we want to take a walk,' I said. That's the answer he must have been hoping for. Otherwise, he would have said let me drop you, let's have lunch, etc. His questions had a hint that we were not supposed to overstay our welcome. Or was it that he wanted to hide his miseries? Dad took the baby from me. The kid frowned and started to cry.

'If there is anything we can do . . . I mean, anything, please let us know . . .' Mom told him before we started to walk away. He just nodded. Then he called out to me.

'Angel . . .' I stopped. I hadn't heard him call me Angel since I was in the hospital. He took my hand in his and just held it. The scars were still visible.

'I am sorry for not being there for you. I regret it every single day.' I saw his eyes well up.

'It's okay. It's okay, Dad.' I hugged him for the sake of the few good moments he had gifted to me. Then Mom and I continued our walk. I wanted to turn back. But I didn't. My mom did and she waved at him again. All I had left there were some chocolates for the kids. All I took were my own doubts about the magic called love and family.

'You made him feel better. Thank you.' I didn't say anything. I didn't forgive him. I will not forgive him. Adi used to say, 'Don't forgive, but forget what he did. You will never be happy hating him all your life. Let it go.' He was right, as always. I wanted to let my dad go.

'I think he is broke and needs help,' said Mom.

'You should ask him.' We weren't rich enough to look after one more family. Still, one need not be rich to help others. That's what Dad had taught me, once upon a time.

'Where do you want to go? We still have some more days here,' Mom asked.

'We've met our co-family, now let's go back to our family.'

CHAPTER 24

Love Casualties

2013

This happened two days after my birthday.

I reached the class relatively happy, proud, and determined to let go of Adi. As soon as I entered, I heard "I love Adi, I love Adi" in a chorus. All the students were huddled around the blackboard. And this was what I saw on the board:

I LOV ADI is Tina.

Right below those words was a cartoon of a cat jumping out of a basket. The next lines were even more heart-wrenching.

#TinaLovesAdi #AdiLovesRiha

Adi read it aloud, while Riha looked at me angrily.

My mouth went dry, my body started shaking, and I wished to disappear. Every girl in school loved Adi. At that moment, I was the only one who didn't want to love Adi.

Who wrote this? Someone who had my diary? Then why had he or she waited for so many months? How could this happen the day after I had deleted the account? What should I do?

'I can't believe this!' Dia gave me a nasty look.

'She is mad. You should tell the principal.' That was Krish.

They had been my best friends, once upon a time.

Finding true friends was more difficult than finding water on Pluto. Trust me, two great friends are better than twenty friends who bark behind your back, who are not happy for you at any point in time, who discourage you in everything that you do, who dance with joy when you are in trouble, who light candles at Mahim Church when your boyfriend cheats on you or ditches you like an asshole, and to take one more step ahead, who are not ashamed and will try hard to snatch your boyfriend from you. I never wanted to steal Adi. I had fallen in love with him before anyone else. Like most people, I kept my first love close to my heart, and locked him down right there. This will save you from more miseries. Looking at Krish and Dia, this was what flashed into my mind though I should have been thinking of ways to protect myself from the mess I had created.

'We can't believe it is you! Is this true?' Rahul who studied in the tenth standard had come running upon hearing the breaking news. Students from other classes had also queued up in the corridor outside our classroom to get a glimpse of what was going on between me, Adi, and his girlfriend.

'You still want to be a coward?' Adi twisted my hand and turned me around to face the class.

'It's not me.' I was scared, but I decided to face him.

'Here is the one who claims she loves me more than anybody else in this world. She says she goes to sleep thinking of me, she wakes up thinking of me . . . and she says more . . . wait a sec.' Adi scrolled down on his cell phone and started to read:

'When you are around, the sun becomes shallow
When you are around, roses become colourless
When you are around, you become my breath
When you are around, you are my reason to be alive.'

'Wait guys, there is more.' Adi got carried away.

'When I look into mirror, I see you
When I breathe, I feel you
When I sleep, I miss you
When I cry, I love you.'

Riha tried to stop Adi, but he continued.

'My love for you makes me miserable
My passion for you makes me complete
My prayers for you make me happy
Your one smile makes my life.'

I stood next to Adi, looking down and hoping the interrogation and the insults would end. The way Adi held my hand hurt me, but not as much as his words did.

'Guys, you should hear this. Where do you copy these lines from? Huh?'

'Tell me once you love me,
Tell me once you miss me,
Tell me once I am yours,
Tell me once you will never leave me,
Tell me once we will be together forever,
Because I will die without you.'

Riha and Dia started to fake tears, while the others laughed. Adi went on:

'What is love? I asked the Gods,
What is love? I asked my mother,
What is love? I asked the wind,
What is love? I asked the moon,
What is love? I asked my dreams,
What is love? I asked my heart,
They said close your eyes, what you see is your love,
I closed my eyes, I saw you, so you are my love.
I opened my eyes, I saw you, so you are my life.
I love you Adi, then, now, and forever . . .'

Adi wasn't ready to stop.

'I dream of you holding me, I dream of you kissing me,
I feel your lips on me, I taste your tongue in me,
I forget the tears of darker times,
I am blessed, because I've felt you,
I freeze the moment in me, in you, in us.'

Adi took a dramatic pause. I thought his grip loosened.

And he smiled at me.

'Thank you for taking away my sleep. I must say these poems sound so romantic. When you have taken so much pain to write all this and stalk me for months, why can't you say it in front of everyone that you love me as you claim to?'

'Adi, stop it. She is a psycho, like the ones we see in the movies.' Riha fumed. 'You should say sorry to me. Adi is my boyfriend.'

I ignored them and walked towards my seat. On my desk,

written in red paint, were the words "I LOV ADI". The same words were written on Adi's desk as well. Whoever wrote this had done me a favour. I wouldn't have been able to write something like that even if I had wished to do so a million times. But what was the point now? I wanted to be out of this Adi maze. Adi came up behind me.

'I am giving you a chance to come clean. Accept it in front of everyone that it was you. Let me see how much you love me.' I didn't look at him. I didn't want to fall for his trick.

'Stop bothering me,' I managed to say.

'Do you love me, huh? Do you? Look into my eyes and say you love me.' I raised my head and looked into his eyes. I saw the colours of love coming out from him and into me. I opened my mouth, but at that same moment, Riha pulled Adi away.

'Adi, let's go to the principal,' she said. Adi brushed off Riha's hand from his. His face turned red; he looked like he was trying really hard to control his anger. After a few seconds, he just flew off the handle. When he banged his fist on my table, I was jolted out of my thoughts.

'I asked you a question.' Adi pulled my chin up.

I wanted to scream and tell everyone that yes, I loved Adi. I had no days or nights or moments without him. I wanted to tell Riha that she didn't deserve him. I wanted to ask Adi why he had taken so long to find out it was me. But I didn't say anything. My stomach ached, my heart fluttered, and I felt dizzy. I wanted to run, I wanted to die.

'It's not over. You are such a coward that you will make your father, who is serving in the army, ashamed of you. Didn't your mom teach you to tell the truth? Or did she help you write these poems? Was it her idea to stalk me?'

'Please leave my mother out of this,' I said rather loudly.

'What will you do if I don't? You want to beat me? A liar can never love someone! A coward is never to be loved. You are a coward, a liar, and a cheat.'

I pushed Adi. No, I jumped on him. I had no clue how I got this idea to bash him up. Adi hadn't been expecting it either. He fell. I didn't stop. I saw everyone's eyes flick from him to me. They shouted, 'Adi, get up! Get up, Adi!'

It was like we were in a WWE ring, where everyone was cheering for Adi. Adi grabbed my tie and pulled me down. Now my face was only inches away from his. His eyes swam into mine. I looked at him like in a dream, then hit him on his face with my hands and moved away. He could have grabbed me and smashed my head with his hand. He didn't. He just lay there on the ground, blood oozing from his mouth as he continued looking at me. Then he touched his mouth, and saw that his fingers were smeared with his own blood. The noisy classroom turned silent; they couldn't believe that Adi had lost in a fight against me even before it had started.

I sat on the floor, next to him, and extended my hand towards him. I was scared. I was sorry. I was hurt.

'I am sorry, I didn't mean to . . . There is blood . . .'

'Honour it if you have the guts to start it.' What's this bloody honour he was always talking about? Adi got up and returned to his seat.

'Be careful. He will not leave you, that's what it meant,' Urmi told me. She could be right.

Not much later, Miss Rose came in.

'Who wrote this?' she asked, pointing at the blackboard. The class remained silent. 'Class monitor?'

The class monitor, Ashwin, explained the turn of events in brief, making sure he didn't leave out any point, including the fight between Adi and me. Miss Rose didn't say anything and went back to her class, leaving me surprised.

In this weirdest of situations, if something had brought me happiness, it had been Adi. He had spoken to me and had held my hand even though he had twisted it hard enough to almost break it. When he had pulled my tie, his breath had fallen on my face, tickling me. I thought he would kiss me. I had the same divine feeling that I had had with him in the tent. When his hands touched my neck, I had goosebumps, I forgot the fight and it was like . . . like he was in my bed and we were rolling and pulling each other's leg. It was like he was trying to kiss me and I was teasing him before kissing him back. I must have blushed and I felt the wetness below. It was weird.

Before the lunch break, Adi and I were called to the principal's office. That was unexpected. I walked behind Adi. I thought Sita must have walked a step behind Ram just like this. Neither of us expected the surprise that awaited us inside the principal's office. Our mothers were sitting there when we walked in. My mom's angelic smile was missing. Miss Rose was seated next to her.

'Here they are.' The principal proudly presented us, as if we were some prestigious trophies. Adi stood there without any apparent excitement or tension. I bit my nails in anxiety.

Nobody spoke until my mom broke the silence.

'I can't believe you picked a fight. That too with Adi?'

'From being the top student, Tina has gone down to the bottom now. Dr. Rachel, if she doesn't improve, you may have to find another school for her. This is not a sports school, though we are glad for all the trophies she wins.' The principal stopped and turned to Adi. 'You are causing enough ruckus for the girls. Is this the time to have girlfriends and exchange kisses in class? And how can the two of you fight like animals?'

'Sir, we are all supposed to fall in love,' Adi said. Neelam Aunty looked at Adi with a pleading look to keep his mouth shut. 'I just wanted to know who my stalker was. Someone wrote it was Tina. I wanted to confirm it, but she answered with a punch. I didn't start the fight.'

'Sir, I told him it wasn't me. Then he brought my parents into it.' I had to win this, I didn't want my mom to be embarrassed of me for stalking her friend's son.

'Aunty, you tell me, would you advise someone to lie? Why can't you ask if it's her? If it's not her, at least the others won't call her a liar.' Adi trapped my mom too.

'Adi, Tina told you it's not her. This is high school. Kids do have crushes on others. We should just leave it at that.' Neelam Aunty came to my help. Mom turned to me.

'Tina, why can't you tell the truth?'

'It's not me, Mom,' I choked. I thought my mom would help me rather than siding with my enemy.

'Tina, it's okay. Nobody is going to scold you,' Miss Rose said reassuringly.

'Sir, Adi told everyone not to speak to me. They were my friends. And now they make fun of me.'

'Sir, she doesn't wear underwear and that's why everyone laughs at her. I have nothing to do with this.'

'It's okay, Tina, you have a skin allergy which your friends do not understand about. I told you if you stop reacting, they will leave you alone,' my mother said. I had started crying by then, so she gave me a tissue from the principal's table. Adi had a winning smile on his face.

The principal saw that the situation was getting worse.

'You both can go to your class,' he said.

'It's okay, Sir. She needs to deal with this.' My mom didn't want to end it. I tried to stop her. Even Adi's mother felt so moved by my tears that she asked my mom to let go of whatever it was.

'Tina, if you want to keep your head up, you should know how to honour whatever you do and learn to face the consequences of your actions. That's the right thing to do. So why can't you tell Adi what you wanted to tell him? You will feel better. I told you earlier also. Try it once, it will be fine,' Mom tried to put some sense into my head again.

'I have nothing to say, Mom.'

'Tina, tell the truth and just put an end to this.'

'Mom, you know that I don't do anything anymore. Then why you are forcing me like this?'

'I know that. Still, Adi needs to know . . .'

'Tina, whatever it is, it won't go beyond this room.' The principal encouraged me.

'It was me. I even apologised to him and deleted the account,' I said without looking at anyone.

'See, now nobody can blame the one who wrote it on the board,' Adi smirked.

'Concentrate on your studies and your practice. You both can go now. No more fights or discussions about this topic.' The principal gave us permission to leave.

'You broke my trust, Mom,' I told her before I walked out of the room. Instead of protecting me, she had thrown me to the wolves. I had shared every secret with her. I shouldn't have done that. I'm not saying that one must lie. But this small a lie wouldn't have caused any harm. It wasn't like I would have become a con artist or a criminal just because I hid my love for Adi. I hated my mom for the first time.

'Tina, your mom didn't break your trust. She helped you face the truth.' Miss Rose stopped me in the corridor. I didn't say anything. If they all were so proud of my mother, then they could appoint her as a teacher here. She could teach everyone to tell the truth and become a laughing stock.

I walked back towards my class. Adi walked behind me.

Would he tell me let's forget what happened and be friends?

'I thought love is just another story,
I thought love happens only in books and movies,
I thought love is just an illusion,
I thought love lives only in our minds,
I thought love is just some broken dream,
I thought love disappears when we are awake,
The day I met you, I realised love is real,
Love is as real as you and me
Love is you and me.'

Adi recited one of the poems I had sent to him.

I stopped, Adi smiled.

'Where did you get that from? It's funny, but I like it.'

'I am sorry for everything and I won't do it ever again. Please don't tell anyone.' I was ready to fall at his feet if he asked me to.

'I make a promise only if I can keep my word.' Adi walked ahead like a warrior who had won the battle.

Should I go to the classroom or go home or go somewhere else?

Would Adi tell the others that it was me?

I had no clue. I hated my mom, I hated Adi, I hated my school, I hated my principal, and I hated Miss Rose. I hated everything I had done to get Adi's attention. I had combed my hair again and again, worn the best dresses, stood at the balcony watching Adi play cricket. I had stalked, prayed, cried, and dreamed. Adi shouldn't have been so mean to me. With that thought, I decided to go back to the classroom.

I was about to enter the classroom when I felt my phone vibrate. No one was around so I took my phone out to check it. There was a notification on my I LOV ADI account. Adi had uploaded an audio clip, captioning it #ConfessionsofILOVADI.

My heart started pounding. I heard the audio clip for a few seconds and then closed the website.

Everyone in my class carried mobile phones to school, including me. Adi had, I realised, used his phone to record what had happened inside the principal's room. By now, everyone must have heard my confession. The students must have called me a liar, a bitch, a coward, a retard, a naked bum, even a psycho.

I grabbed my school bag and ran out of the classroom.

I didn't cry. I wanted to save the tears for myself, for when I would be farther away from them.

I didn't know where I was heading or where I could go.

Mom had once said, 'You can run from your problems, but how fast and for how long can you run?' She was right. I never looked for solutions because I was scared of the answers. And then I had started to believe that my make-believe world was real and that reality was fake. I knew I would be busted one day, but it had happened sooner and was much uglier than expected.

The bathrooms looked deserted during class hours. I entered one of the toilets. I sat there, but my bladder was as empty as my mind. I cried. I was scared and humiliated. Time travel existed only in the books. Still, I wanted to go back in time and put an end to what I had started.

But how could I?

I found a solution, the only solution that was going to take care of my problems. I wouldn't be laughed at, or tortured, or neglected. I wouldn't need to see Adi and his girlfriends. For once, I would win. The number Adi had left in the messenger flashed in front of me like his dimpled smile.

"I WIN" I typed and pressed the green button. Then, I pulled out my instrument box and took out the blade inside it. I looked at my hands, the same hands which had held the tennis rackets strongly, the same hands with which I hugged my mom with all the love, the same hands which had wrapped around Adi passionately while I had kissed him. When I made the first cut on my left wrist, Adi's lips were on mine and I was lying inside that tent under the moon and the stars. I didn't feel any pain when the blade cut through my skin again and again. The pain inside me was bigger than what a blade could give me. Blood splashed on my uniform and became one with Adi's blood, then it drenched my feet and the floor below me. It sped out of the bathroom faster than it should have. I sat down on the floor in the toilet cubicle, leaned against the door, and started to feel better.

The laughter around me began to fade away; a strange weightlessness engulfed me. I met my mom and asked for her forgiveness. I searched for my dad, but I couldn't find him. Slowly, everything disappeared. I couldn't see the blood on the floor or my own hands. I couldn't feel any pain or even my own breath. A streak of white surrounded me and the brightest fire swamped in. I saw Adi on the other side of the flames, his hands extended towards me to pull me out. I tried to raise my hand to hold him, but couldn't. However, I fell on the floor, into a pool of my own blood. Adi reached over, held my hand, and said, 'You are the one I love, I would never leave you. Come back!' I tried to smile. But my hand slipped on my blood, and I drifted away, far away to a place where I floated on the wonderful colours I used to see around Adi and me.

'Tina, look at me. I am so sorry. At least hear what I have to say . . . The moment I saw you in the lift, something happened to me. It was like a part of me had jumped out of me and run right towards you. I looked back to see if I was standing next to you. Because when I walked out of the lift, I floated, weightless, and I couldn't feel me in myself. I thought I had left myself with you. Then I tripped and fell on the floor and came back to the ground. As I walked ahead, I saw you floating away from me. I aimed that ball towards your head to make you fall and bring you back to me. Then, you fell, and I had you back . . . Please don't leave me and go away now. I wanted to wait and see if there's love between us. I fought with you to test you. I wanted to know if we could still love each other when we didn't talk, when we hated each other. I ignored you to understand how difficult it was for me to see you without me. I wanted to know if you feel the way I feel. I had to test if our love could survive our hatred. I let you win because I wanted you to be happy. I let others laugh at you so you would learn to be strong. I flirted with other girls because I wanted you to know that our love is special and that nothing could erase it. I wanted you to walk even when I was not around you. I wanted you to be strong when I was away. I will always be there with you even if you don't see me. My love for you doesn't need confessions and words. I know you are for me and I will not let anyone take you away from me. When we are succeeding in our lives, why do you want to leave me and go away? I know how much you love me, but I never told you how much I love you. Because true love never needs words, it never needs clarifications, and it never changes.'

I smiled. Did I? Yes. I heard Adi saying how much he loved me. We were ready to go, to start a life where we played, fought, laughed, cried, loved, missed, hugged, kissed, made love, and lived. Our love was something unsaid and unheard. It floats out from you and resides in me. It fills me in you and you in me.

How wonderful it was to hear the unsaid! I floated in the clouds and kept hearing Adi's voice, like he was right beside me, whispering into my ears. Then I heard my mom calling me Angel and asking for forgiveness. I heard Miss Rose saying she wanted to see the stars and that we should go soon to see them. I heard more voices, most of them unclear and unfamiliar. But I didn't hear my dad.

Mom's sobs cut deep into me. I felt the warmth of tears falling on me, sometimes they were Mom's, sometimes Adi's. Mom kept on whispering to me that she was sorry. I told her I didn't hate her and I was sorry too. I told Adi I was not upset with him anymore. I told Miss Rose I could touch the stars now. They didn't hear me. But I heard them. Again and again.

When I opened my eyes, I was on a hospital bed, one week after I had infamously cut off the pain and the fear that had bled out the life from me. Was I dreaming? I thought so. Until then, I had been happily engulfed in ecstasy, which I failed to recollect and feel again now. I had loved being up there in my dream world, wherever it was, with Adi. Now, I lay on a bed, drained, everything looking blurred and disconnected around me. I looked carefully at the room I was in, as if I was seeing the world around me for the first time. I searched for the unheard. I wanted to hear the unsaid.

'Tina, it's me.' I heard a familiar voice, a voice which was always followed by warmth on my forehead.

I must be dying, empty, and hopeless.

Hope must be in the words I heard and the colours I saw.

'Tina, can you see me?' I recognised the voice now. It was Adi's. 'Open your eyes, you just opened them. Come on, open them again.'

I didn't want to die. I wanted to fly, float, love, and be loved. I looked for Adi. 'Tina, look at me once.' I felt the same warmth on my forehead now. I tried to raise my hand, but I couldn't. There was a heaviness in me that paralysed me. Shadows moved around me now and terrified me. They must have come to take me along.

'Please let me go. I don't want to come with you . . .'

I screamed voicelessly. I hit the shadows in my thoughts. I cried in my heart.

I heard more voices. They were coming nearer. Another shadow ran towards me. I saw her as she reached closer; it was my mom. Had I died? Perhaps. Otherwise she wouldn't be crying. Everything and everyone confused me. My mom fell on my chest. She hugged me and kissed me all over. Her hot tears drenched me.

'Mom, don't cry. I am happy here. Adi loves me here. And I can see the stars so closely here. I sleep on the colours of love . . . Please don't cry . . .' But nobody heard me. Some people dressed in white clothes joined my mother. They all looked happy and hugged each other. I looked for Adi. But I didn't see him, or my dad. My eyes pained, my ears couldn't take the voices around me anymore.

I shut my eyes.

Everything turned dark, and once again I was wrapped up in nothingness.

It took me two more days to adjust to the earthly world all over again. The light hurt my eyes and my body. Mom stayed back with me, the doctors spoke to me and checked on me regularly, a girl in white uniform helped me sit up and walk. My teachers, my classmates, my principal, and Miss Rose, they all visited me. I would just nod and try to smile at them. My voice was still feeble. I spoke to myself in my thoughts though.

During one such visit, Miss Rose sat near my head and smiled. 'We all are so happy to have you back.'

I wasn't happy. I had loved being up there in my dream world. It had been perfect.

'Sta . . .' I tried to speak, but the words wouldn't come out properly.

'Tina, come on. Try again.' Miss Rose held my hand.

'We touched the stars . . . I . . . touched them . . .' Hearing me speak made Miss Rose smile.

When everyone was gone, Mom sat next to me and cried. 'Angel, I love you. I will never do anything to hurt you. I am sorry . . . I am so sorry . . .' She hugged me. Her embrace had the same warmth that I had felt when I was drifting away. I raised my hands to hug her back. That was when I noticed that my left wrist had a big bandage.

'But everything is well now. We can go home soon,' Mom said. When Mom sat down, I looked around the room. There were bouquets and the get well soon cards arranged beautifully on the table beside my bed. I looked at one particular card with stars, rainbows, and butterflies on it. Where had I seen it before? It looked so familiar. In my dream world, I had heard the story of a butterfly that fell in love with a rainbow and had to wait for the rainbow to appear again in the summer. My mom picked up the card and gave it to me.

'Unsaid prayers are never unheard.' I repeated the line. The card didn't have any sender's name on it.

'Adi gave it to you.' I nodded.

Why wasn't Adi's name or his card making me happy?

I wanted to go back to my dream world. Why was I not happy here? Mom placed a pillow behind my back.

'Where is Dad? Did you tell him what happened?'

'He couldn't come, Angel. He is on duty. You know how . . .'

I closed my eyes. I didn't want to hear anymore. I tried to remember what had happened and I saw myself in a pool of blood, lying in the bathroom, feeling weightless and in the dark.

'Don't you want to meet Adi?' I wanted to tell Mom that he had been there in the clouds with me, holding my hands, never leaving me, telling me stories of rainbows and butterflies, taking me to the stars, singing for me . . . He was with me, always . . .

How strange was that? Was it just a manifestation of my dreams that I had always carried with me? My heart started to hurt.

'Adi and Neelam Aunty went to a few temples to pray for you. And Adi was here when you opened your eyes.' What had happened so suddenly? How could things change so drastically between my falling in the bathroom and then getting up in the hospital bed?

That night, I saw Adi again. In reality, not in my imaginary world up there. He was with his mom, dad, and Minu. They brought me a huge bouquet, one as tall as me. They all looked happy. Nobody asked me what had happened to me. Nobody asked me why I had tried to kill myself.

A little while later, Adi and I were alone in the room. He stood near my bed. I lay looking at him, checking his face carefully to see if this Adi and the Adi I had seen in my dream world were the same. His moustache had grown a little. They were the same!

Adi smiled. I smiled.

'I am so sorry.' Adi held my hand. It felt so familiar. 'I was so scared that I would never see you again and that I would never get a chance to tell you what I wanted to.' I wanted to tell him about the other world, about how much he had loved me there, and how much I missed it here.

'I promise I will always be there for you.' He squeezed my hand.

That night, my mom took me for a walk in the corridor outside the room. I sat on a bench there and looked at the stars.

Would she believe me if I told her I had touched the stars?

'Angel, are you still angry with me?'

'I am not. I just want to go back there . . .'

'Where?'

'Where I was. I was happy there, Mom . . . Everything was perfect there . . .' She held my hand and sat there, hugging me.

'Angel, when you were learning to walk, you fell down many times. You got hurt, you cried, but soon you would try to walk again. You never quit and we were there to watch over you. No matter what happens, however disappointed we might be, it always gets better. When you play tennis, when you lose the first game, do you walk away? No. You know that you've got another set to play. You are determined to play better. That's what hope and faith do for us. You should know that when everything goes wrong, there is something right waiting for us just around the corner. That's the way life has been designed. You have to blindly believe that. We will fall, we will cry, but Angel, we will never quit. Never. Whatever happens, we will walk again, okay? Promise me . . .' I promised. I had just understood that we never quit.

'I am sorry, Mom. Were you angry with me?'

'No, Angel, I wasn't. But I was so heartbroken. I thought we were friends and you told me everything and we would be friends forever. When you felt sad, or scared, or alone, or angry, why didn't you think even once that you have your mom? Even when the whole world leaves you, you know that I won't. When I looked at you lying in that room every day, it felt like I had killed you. Do you know how that feels? All I had wanted to do was tell them the truth. I prayed to God every day to take my life and give back yours. I would have never been able to forgive myself if you hadn't woken up, Angel. All I have is you and you have to believe me when I say that I love you more than anything else in the world. I want you to know that we won't have any more secrets between us. I know you hated me when I forced you to tell the truth. But you know, Angel, that's what you have to do. We have to own up to our actions. You should be ready to accept people the way they are, not the way you want them to be. You love Adi, I know. Everyone falls in love for the first time and that's why it's called first love. But first love doesn't mean it's the last love or that it has to be the last love. We all have a second love, a third love, a fourth love . . . Many more loves await us. Don't you want to experience all that? Adi too had never thought you would do something like this. He was here every single day, waiting for you to open your eyes so that he could apologise.'

'Why can't he love me, Mom? That's what I keep thinking.'

'Why are you not in love with Krish or Rahul? You have known them for longer than you have known Adi.'

'I don't see the colours of love around them.'

'The same way, Adi doesn't see the colours of love around you. When both people see the colours, it's wonderful. Otherwise, love is just disappointment and tears. Someday, you will meet someone who will also like you the way you like him. But you can't hurt yourself or push others away just because you love someone. Until you learn this by yourself, you have to trust me and listen to me. Now, the first step towards a happy life is accepting Adi as your friend.'

'Could you forget the carpenter?'

'No, but I remember him only when I want to. Once he finished his work at our house, he a found job nearby. When I used to go to school, I would see him, sitting inside his shed, carving his wood like it was the only thing that mattered in his life. Then a year later, I came to know that one of the girls I knew from the school—she had failed almost twice in every class—had gotten married to him. I was like, how did that happen?'

'Was she beautiful?'

'Then I thought she wasn't. But as I grew up, I understood that it is not about being beautiful or rich. It's something else.'

'What's that?'

'I don't know . . . I still don't know. I think it's just something unknown. We might love someone, but we may get married to someone else. We hate someone, then we fall in love with the same person. We love someone, but he loves somebody else. How is it possible? It's possible only if it's beyond our control, just like we have no control over choosing our parents, our gender, or where we are born, or whether we'll be born at all . . .'

'How we can control it? There should be something, a way out . . .'

'Can we? No. All we can do is experience and live. But we can alter our experience by moving on. Life is so much more than just today. What happens today may have no meaning after ten years . . . So, we have to look forward.'

My mom looked at me in hope.

'Okay. I will try.'

'That's the first step, Angel. I want my daughter to be happy and chirpy, the way she used to be. We deserve to be happy, but being happy is in our own hands.'

'I'm trying, Mom. I really am,' I said. Mom held my hands but I don't think she trusted me.

I don't blame her. After all, I didn't deserve her trust anymore. I wasn't proud of what I had done. Nothing could erase my guilt.

This is how I betrayed my mom's trust, broke her heart, and reached the hospital.

Adi had gotten my "I WIN" message and wanting to know what it meant, had looked for me in the classroom, only to find me missing. Then he went out, along with our classmates, and searched for me. He had looked in the washroom and had spotted the blood on the bathroom floor. Since the door was locked, he kicked it open and found me inside. They took me to the hospital. Apparently, the doctors had had no hope that I would survive as I had lost a lot of blood. Since I am AB-negative—it is the rarest blood group in the world—finding blood wasn't easy. Adi's dad did everything in his power to have the blood flown to Mumbai. All this had happened while I was unconscious, unaware of what was happening around me. I was happy in my dream world, visiting the stars with Adi, almost killing everyone around me with worry. I had also heard Shah Rukh Khan singing a song for me. Apparently, he came to visit me one morning. Adi said I smiled once when Shah Rukh said he loved me. I didn't believe Adi though. As for my father, was he worried about me? I wanted to believe he was.

I owed my life to Adi. If he hadn't gone searching for me, I would have been lying cold and dead in the toilet. My school principal gave me some time off from school to recover. My classmates sent me flowers, chocolates, letters, and cards. Rahul wrote a long letter saying he was sorry and that they had never realised just how alone I had felt. Krish hugged me and cried and wanted to know if I had forgiven him. He said he had told Adi that he wanted to fuck me just to show off. I believed him. Minu cried and told me her brother had been so scared that I would die in my sleep and that Adi had kept on talking to me, reading stories out aloud to me, and writing some poems for me while I had been sleeping. Adi didn't show me the poems later though.

I missed the year's tennis championship match. My coach and Rohit came to visit me in the hospital. Adi's cricket team lost the finals. He didn't sound upset about it though.

After I was discharged, I had to attend counselling sessions designed especially for people like me, people who had gone through a tough time and who needed professional help to cope with life's ups and downs. This was where I met Jai and Ajit Uncle for the first time. Jai had been depressed and distressed after his mother lost her battle with cancer. As our counselling sessions progressed, our friendship grew stronger, even though it was ultimately short-lived. We missed him. I hope death isn't the ultimate end. I wanted Jai to meet his mother "there" and be happy. I believe he is.

I started going to school in November, two months after my suicide attempt. Nobody made fun of me anymore. Nobody asked me how it felt to be so close to death. I had my friends with me. I also had Adi with me. Everything and every day was so special because Adi had become my best friend too. We all studied and played together. And Adi kept his word. He helped me sail through the post-hospital days, he accompanied me to my counselling sessions, to tennis practice, for coffees, music concerts, and dinners.

Time flew by. And before I knew it, it was Christmas. Mom and I were sitting in the living room, next to the Christmas tree with the stars on it. I had opened every present except the one sent by Dad.

'Love for someone never changes. It's just that the people we love, they change. That has nothing to do with the fact that they stop loving you,' is what my mom said to me.

'What do you mean love never changes? Everything changes. Look at Dad. He is your ex-husband and my ex-dad. Don't you see how everything has changed, Mom? He wasn't even there to see whether I was dead or alive.'

It was worth dying to know how much others really love you. I died once because I loved Adi more than I loved myself. I started to live again because Adi and Mom watched over me, as they had promised. However, I still loved Adi as deeply as I had earlier, while he was still in love with Riha. I was ready to wait for the day when he would tell me, looking into my eyes, that he loved me the way I loved him.

Until then, I was satisfied with transitioning to being Adi's best friend from being his bitterest enemy.

My mom could be right.

When we lose a person, we find someone else.

I might no longer have my dad, but I had found Ajit Uncle.

When I lost Jai, I found Adi.

When I lost myself, I found everyone.

That wasn't fair, but it was a good compensation.

On the night of Christmas, as I looked at the stars, Adi held me tight. He kissed me on my forehead and said, 'Tina, hope means: Hold On, Pain Ends.'

What a lovely thought.

And I opened the Christmas gift from my dad. It was an Orion telescope.

You are my star. The attached handwritten note read.

My pain didn't end, but intensified.

CHAPTER 25

The Farewell Memories

May 27, 2016

I smelled the surprise party my friends had planned for me. It would be our last night out before I left for Florida. The five of us had found our callings in different directions even before the results had been announced two days earlier.

Dia was aiming for IIT. Her coaching classes had started before we had even finished our board exams. Krish's future had been decided by his father. 'What's the point of going to college when I know this restaurant is where you will make money?' He had a point and Krish agreed happily. Rahul decided to go to London to be with his brother. He dropped out of graduation first year. Travelling may open up the blocked part of his brain and help him figure out his true calling. Adi proved everyone's prediction wrong and broke his dad's dream of seeing him as a movie star and instead, chose to work as an assistant director to a foul-mouthed, moody, aggressive, and successful director, that too not under his dad's banner. He said he wanted to make a mark for himself without having to fall back on his father's clout in the industry. His father let him be. But we all knew that Adi would be a superstar sooner or later and that girls would die for him. I wondered if the world would ever know about the failed romantic story of a girl who had wanted to die for him. Would he ever think about me when he kissed those heroines? Would he talk about us, his five friends, and our friendship? Only time would tell.

We were lying on the terrace, watching the stars together for the last time. The inevitable farewell thickened the air. The boys smoked; we took a few puffs from them.

I started to cough. Adi took away the cigarette from me.

'Not for people with weak lungs.' I didn't argue. Asthma had left me alone for a long time now. I didn't want it to come back.

'Do you miss Riha?' I turned to Adi.

'No.' I hadn't expected that.

'Will you miss me when I am gone?'

'I don't know. I can only tell when you are gone.'

'You are such an asshole, Adi.'

'I wonder if you'll become like Serena Williams with all those bulky muscles.'

'No . . . I don't think so.' Adi played with my bracelet.

'Do you remember this bracelet?' I asked.

'Tina, why do you think I have amnesia?'

Krish and Rahul wanted to know about the bracelet.

'It's not fair to have secrets from us,' Dia chimed in.

'Tina is the one with a photographic memory.' Adi washed his hands of the matter.

The bracelet incident had happened after our Table Top star

gazing session and that first kiss with Adi and before the words "I LOV ADI is Tina" had appeared on the blackboard.

2013

It was a regular day, except Riha met me in the library and apologised for her brutal kiss.

'Tina, would you come with me to Mahim Church? I want to go for novenas on Wednesdays, but I don't know anything about churches.'

This twist made my heart flutter. Devotees believe that visiting the church on nine consecutive Wednesdays would grant them their wishes. What could be her wish? Adi! What else?

'You don't need to know anything about it. Nobody asks questions there, anyone can go.'

'I know, but I wanted to take Adi with me.' Huh, why was she asking me to come along then? Adi was her boyfriend, not mine. 'He said his parents would not let him go as they are not Christians . . .'

Adi's dad wasn't a conservative man. His family celebrated every festival, including Christmas and Eid. I was confused. 'I am not his parent.'

'Tina, I am asking for help. His parents will let him go if he says he is going with you as they know you go to church.' She sounded cute for a change.

'They know you as well.'

'Adi told me to ask you.' That was news. Adi hated to even look at me. Forget about going to church together!

Who knows?! Anything to fulfil his girlfriend's wish.

'Let Adi ask me.' I showed my attitude.

In the afternoon, I met Adi and Riha near the school gate.

'If it's not too much trouble, it would be helpful if you

could come with us to Mahim Church.' That short, straight, firm request, stated while looking straight into my eyes, made me falter. I couldn't say no now, could I?

I didn't tell my mom about the details except that some of us from school were going to the church.

On our way, Adi and Riha sat together in the back seat while I found myself next to the taxi driver. All the way to the church, the lovebirds chirped nonstop. I could see Adi through the rear-view mirror. Once or twice our eyes met, but he looked away. I was jealous, and sad.

Like a moron, I stood behind Adi and Riha when they prayed for a successful relationship. Riha even kept two wax figures in front of Mother Mary to seal their love. All the while, I stared at Mother Mary's statue protected by a glass frame and prayed.

How could you have let me say yes to coming here when you know they are here to ask you to bless them? I will believe in you only if they break up.

Nine Wednesdays passed. Riha and Adi might have prayed for their divine relationship while I had prayed for their break up. But, Mother Mary must have answered their prayers as their relationship grew strong and stronger. I had my doubts about the power of Mahim Church, but cherished what little time I got to spend with Adi. Every day for those nine weeks, Adi would drop Riha and then me at our building gates with a single word, "thanks". Later, we would walk into the lift like strangers. And I would just stand behind him, and watch him.

On the last day of the ninth week, he gave me a bracelet.

'I got it for Riha, but it's big for her.' My brain didn't need to remind me what exactly it meant. I took the bracelet without much thought; I didn't even say thanks. I walked out of the lift when it reached the seventh floor. When the lift door closed, I jumped around in joy. The bracelet fitted me perfectly, as if it had been made for me and a part of Adi now resided in me.

Present.

I never wore that bracelet but locked it away carefully, only to see it and touch it every once in a while. I was scared of losing it, until now. Now I was ready to let go of things, I was ready to let go of Adi. I was ready to let go of this bracelet.

I was ready to live again.

'We never knew about this church thing. Man, what other secrets do you two have?' Krish sounded upset. They had no clue about my first kiss or my first sexual experience with Adi either.

'Tina, tell me the truth. What did you pray for during those nine Wednesdays?'

'For Adi and Riha's break up.' I told them the truth. Adi gave me the weirdest look.

'Well, Adi and Riha broke up. Who knows, it might have been the result of Tina's prayers,' Rahul said and Krish agreed.

'You guys must be stupid to think all this romance remains forever. Man, we all will marry someone else! We won't even remember these buggers we kissed and had sex with while studying. It's all just a hormonal phase.' Dia sounded like a prophet. She could be right. She was the most experienced girl we had known so far.

'We may forget the first kiss and the first time we had sex. But Adi, I won't forget you promised me the moon but gave me a fart . . .' I reminded him. Adi pulled my hair. Everyone else burst into peals of laughter. How could I forget?

The moon was mine.

And the fart was Adi's.

CHAPTER 26

You Promised Me the Moon but Gave Me a Fart

2014

Time ran faster than Bolt. It runs faster still when you are in love. And I was in love. Weeks and months spent with Adi had nursed me back to the pink of my health after my failed suicide attempt. I could've happily danced on the tip of an iceberg.

And then it came—Valentine's Day. The second one after I had met Adi. I was desperately hoping that Adi and Riha would break up. And my prayers at Mahim Church had been answered! A week before Valentine's Day, Adi broke up with Riha. No, in fact, Riha broke up with Adi. The irony was that he had proposed to her on last Valentine's Day. And a year later, their relationship ended, which made me happy.

'Am I your girlfriend or Tina?' Riha had screamed. She had accused Adi of spending more time with me than her.

'Do I stop you from going out with your friends, including those idiots from St. Mary's?

'Adi, they are my brother's friends. I can't stop talking to them just because they won a cricket match against you.'

'Then why do you expect me to leave my friends? I am telling you, Tina is just a friend . . .'

I hated the way he always put an extra emphasis on the "just a friend" bit. Why couldn't he say, 'Okay, you fuck off. Yes, Tina is my girlfriend and I love her.' This is what I expected him to do, which he never did.

'I swear on my mom, Adi, this is over,' Riha had said in front of us. So I believed she would keep her word. Who wants something bad to happen to their own mother, right?

I ran to the girls toilet and jumped in happiness. I must say, I had a great rapport with the toilets in school. They were witness to my highs and lows. I went back to class after releasing my overflowing enthusiasm.

'Adi, I am sorry . . . Riha really thinks we are dating . . . and it's not only Riha, other students also think the same . . . We look cute together, that's why . . .' I made that up when I caught up with Adi that evening.

What I meant was, it was not a bad idea for us to date as the road ahead was now as clear as my heart. And I deserved Adi more than any other stupid girl out there.

'Riha is also stupid like you. She will come back. This is not the first time we've broken up.'

Hell, I wanted to hit him with my bag.

'Are you sad? I know how it feels.' I tried hard to bring some empathy into my voice.

'Tina, don't fake it. You must be happy today.'

'I am just happy for you. You guys fight every second week. True lovers don't do that.' Adi gave me a "what the hell" look.

'Yeah, you always ensure we fight. Don't make me angry now. Go for your tennis practice.'

'You want to come with me? You will feel good.'

'By watching you practise with that moron?' Adi had never liked Rohit. I wondered why. And the fact was, Rohit hated Adi too.

'No, watch me, and I'll watch you.' I giggled, topped up with extra love. He walked ahead.

He always ignored my love for him . . . Why?

'Just fuck off, Tina.' He didn't forget to say that to me. And now my mind would be in overdrive wondering if he was going to patch up with Riha. That would be the end of my dreams. Again! How could I let that happen?

I had to do something . . . Huh . . . What? Huh! Got an idea.

'Adi, if you patch things up all the time, Riha will take you for granted,' I told him.

'Tina, I don't need your free advice.'

'Don't take it for free then, give me a hand massage in exchange.' This time he had both his middle fingers sticking up.

'Yeah, show me all your bloody fingers. That wouldn't change the fact that I get these pains in my hand because of you.'

I walked away with a grin. I knew he would come to the practice now and give me a hand massage afterwards even if he didn't want to. I had blackmailed him. And he would hate me for that.

That day, I had this great feeling that this was going to be the year when I'd celebrate my first Valentine's Day with my would-be husband, Adi. Luckily, Riha had fainted a couple of days ago. She was anaemic and her parents had pushed the panic button. Much to my delight, she had been admitted to the hospital rightaway. All thanks to my prayers! And even if they patched things up, she wouldn't be out from the hospital before Valentine's Day.

Adi could easily have been a reincarnation of Jesus. Under all his arrogance, he was someone who couldn't see any pain around him. That evening, we landed up at the hospital to meet Adi's ex-girlfriend and my secret enemy. I hoped Riha would remain in bed for a while.

Get well soon. We miss you, Adi scribbled on a beautiful get well soon card.

Good, he didn't write "I love you" or "I miss you". Riha cried and drew a heart over her chest. That was cheeky and I witnessed a patch up right in front of my eyes.

Now that Adi and Riha had broken up, I was absolutely sure that he would ask me to be his date. Three or four days before Valentine's Day, I started preparing for my night out with Adi. I was so excited that my imagination was running wild. I saw him everywhere, even during my tennis practice. I couldn't sleep, I couldn't eat, I could only daydream.

'Tina, at this age, everything is a distraction. If you want to be the best, you must be prepared to make a lot of sacrifices. This includes boyfriends, hanging out with friends, kissing, and any other dreams that don't revolve around playing tennis. Take two days off and think about what you want to do. Do you want to be like any other girl walking down the road? Or do you want to tread on a path less travelled and make a mark for yourself? And yes, this is a tough path. If you don't have that determination, don't waste your time. Or mine.' My coach kicked me out of the court. Again.

I wanted to play tennis. I wanted to be the best. But I wanted to be Adi's girlfriend first. Why couldn't I have both? Why should we always have to choose?

This was not fair. Not fair at all.

But the best thing happened the same night.

Adi came home, two days before D-day.

'Aunty, can I take Tina out on the fourteenth? If you don't mind, that is . . .'

My mom looked at me. I sat there as if I couldn't have cared less, but I wanted to jump up and hug him.

'Where is Riha?' That's what my mom asked!

'We broke up.'

'If Angel wants to go . . .' saying that, my mom went into the kitchen to do the dishes. She expected me to be sensible and say no to Adi instead of being a filler in his life. But I didn't care. I deserved him more than Riha did, more than anyone else did.

Over the next two days, I invested every bit of my creativity into making my first Valentine's night with Adi memorable. I had a thousand versions of it in my head, and I believed the best would play out on the night of Valentine's Day. Sometimes, reality is more awe-inspiring than fantasies.

I went out with Mom to pick out a dress.

'Angel, I don't understand why you are so excited. They have broken up a hundred times before. I can see that you will be sitting and crying over this soon.'

'That's not funny, Mom. This time, they've broken up for good. Period.' I wasn't sure though.

'I am not going to be a part of this. I would have loved to get you ready and send you off for a Valentine's Day date if I was even ten percent sure that it was the right thing to do. But I don't think so this time.'

'Mom, trust me, Adi loves me. He just doesn't want to tell me.'

'Do you want to start another never-ending discussion over this? Angel, please, don't start again . . .'

'No.' I picked up a red satin frock. It had a wide neck and hung beautifully over my body, except that the neckline didn't do much to accentuate my small breasts. Riha had bigger breasts. I had even asked Adi once why he liked Riha.

'You don't need a reason to like someone,' he replied.

'Adi, you fell in love with Riha just like that? I don't believe this crap,' I said.

'So you tell me what makes you like someone.' He didn't ask me why I was madly in love with him.

'I like someone only when that person becomes a part of me and when I can see the colours of love around him . . . If I can live when he breaths, if my days are brighter when he is around, if I can think of him the whole day, if I can forgive him for everything he does, if I can love him even when I know he has never said that he loves me back . . .' I stopped. I was talking about him and he knew it. 'So tell me, why do you love her?'

Adi didn't say anything.

'I know . . . Because she has big boobs.'

'Yes, you are so right, Tina.' He smiled, that asshole.

'And you give me a headache, Tina. What are these colours of love you always talk about?'

I gave him the finger and closed the door on him. Then I checked my boobs.

Grrr . . . When would they grow bigger?

D-day

During class, I swam among the clouds with Adi while he listened to the physics teacher as if he would prove that the sun goes around the earth. I made a paper ball and threw it at him. Adi continued to ignore me. I went back to my fantasy world, this time wondering about ways to enhance the size of my breasts.

I had already tried out some boob enlargement ideas and failed. I had even bought two different bottles of some so-called "sexy boobs cream" and massaged my breasts with them before I went to bed every night. I had waited for weeks to see my boobs grow bigger. But nothing happened, except that Mom found the bottles in my closet.

'Mom, it's gross. You searched my cupboard?'

'No, you never tidy up your cupboard. So I just did it as a favour to you. So stop frowning.'

'Thank you.'

'Angel, do you want to tell me something . . .' She looked at the blonde's watermelon-sized boobs on the bottle's label. 'No creams can enlarge anyone's breasts. You should know this.'

'Mom, who told you that? See what they say on the label.'

'You forget that I am a doctor.' My face fell.

'But I read that mammary glands—'

'Angel, that's all just conjecture that they use to make money from stupid girls like you.'

'Don't call me stupid, Mom. All my classmates have bigger breasts than me. Boys like big boobs.'

'Who told you this?'

'Adi.'

'Adi told you this?'

'He didn't tell me exactly, but I know . . . Dia gets all her boyfriends because of her boobs. And Riha too.'

'Just like some people are tall, some are short, some are fair, and some are lean, there are some who have bigger breasts than others. It has nothing to do with love. A real man will love you for who you are.'

'How will I realise if he really loves me for who I am?'

'Well, he would never try to change you. He would appreciate you and love you for who you are. So you don't need these bottles.'

'Mom . . . Can I go for plastic surgery? I still feel I need bigger ones.' I wasn't ready to quit just yet.

'When you were born, your dad told me that we've got an

angel. That's why we call you Angel. You had the most beautiful smile, your eyes shone. Now you want to be like Riha, and Riha wants to be like you. This is the game of hormones. So don't stress over it.' She then proceeded to throw the bottles in the dustbin. She made sense. However, I still wanted bigger boobs, at least for Valentine's Day.

Mom didn't interfere or help me get ready for my big night. I shampooed my hair, blow-dried it, and applied Mom's lipstick. I saw her peeping into my room to get an idea of what I was up to.

'Look at yourself.' She made me stand in front of the mirror. 'You don't need make up.'

'Why do you want to decide everything for me?'

'Because I am your mom.'

'You know why Adi doesn't date me? Because I am not like Riha . . . I am not like his dad's friends' daughters. Mom, they all wear Victoria's Secret bras and inners. They wear Gucci and Prada. What do I wear? Whatever we get from the Lokhandwala market! Did you take me to Beverly Hills to buy my first bra? No. But they did. So at least let me look good once. Okay?'

'Don't you think we should be grateful that we can still buy things from Lokhandwala? I can't take you to Beverly Hills, I can't buy Prada or Gucci for you. But I want you to be a much better human being when you stand next to these Prada-clad girls. People wouldn't know if you are wearing Victoria's Secret bras. But they see what you let out when you speak and smile and behave. Clothes never define who you really are.' Mom could have easily become a preacher and she always had some big logic up her sleeve. I could never win an argument with her. However, she helped me dress up, put on a light lipstick, add a dash of blush on my cheeks, let my hair open, and put a silver band with a single small red rose on it. My eyes looked bigger because of the kohl she had applied around them.

She made me stand in front of the mirror again.

I smiled. Yes, I looked beautiful and I was ready to have the best night of my life.

Mom drove to me to RockS. She'd expected Adi to pick me up, especially when he stayed a floor above ours. But it had been my crooked idea that she drive me over, just to make sure he didn't ditch the RockS plan. He couldn't have left me alone at RockS!

'Mom, are you proud of me going out for my first official date?' I asked.

'Don't you think it's a tad early?'

'I am fourteen. Riha must have had sex with Adi by now.'

'It's okay to fall in love and date and all. At this age, you want to challenge the world. But having sex at such a young age is something . . .'

'I will have sex with a guy you approve of, and when you approve of me having sex with him. And I hope it's not on my first night.' She smiled.

'I hope you are sensible enough to choose a guy I wouldn't disapprove of.'

'Tell me, what kind of a guy would that be? So, I can keep my eyes open . . .' I was curious.

'The one you love, the one who loves you, the one who is considerate of others and who gives you a reason to be a better human. That's all you need to look for.' I wondered who that guy would be.

'Do you think Adi is that guy?'

'No.'

'Why?'

'You are miserable when you are with him. You hate every girl who talks to him, you want him around you all the time. Instead of becoming a better person, you are only getting worse and worse. You are not fit for Adi.' How could she be so cruel and blunt?! Then she said, 'You look beautiful. Have a lovely time. But Angel, you should know that you are just being a filler here and don't read anything more into it.' She dropped me at RockS with a concerned look and then a kiss. Mom's predictions never failed.

My phone rang. I jumped and answered it.

'Where are you? Tina, I am so sorry, Riha is coming with me. She asked to be discharged from the hospital as she didn't want to miss Valentine's Day.' I became speechless with anger and disappointment, hating Mom's intuitions. I disconnected the call. It was a sign that Adi would never leave Riha.

I walked into RockS, all my dreams broken.

The waiter took me to a table.

RockS looked like heaven for lovers on earth. The fragrance of roses filled the air. Red roses and candles on all the tables made the place look ethereal. There were couples lost in each other, completely in love, unaware of the world around them. To my right, some couples had already started to show their karaoke talents, while others were busy kissing. The waitresses carried wine and flowers and roamed about like red butterflies.

I watched them all. I wanted to be one of them, in love and loved in return. That's all I wanted.

Adi and Riha entered the pub a little while later. She looked beautiful in a red gown. Her make-up was heavy and she looked no less than a Bollywood heroine with her well visible cleavage. She must have been wearing a size thirty-four bra while I had only recently started wearing a size thirty-two. They walked in hand in hand. Why did she get to have my Adi's hand in hers?

Adi pulled a chair out for Riha. She sat, still holding his hand. She opened her bag and gave him two roses tied together with a red velvet ribbon and kissed him on his lips. What should a girl do if she sees her valentine with another girl, both of them looking like the couple of the millennium together? I wanted to go and punch them in the face, first her, then him, and then her again until my hand bled. But I didn't. Instead, I hid and watched them, seething with jealousy. Adi scanned the tables, and then typed something on his phone. A moment later, I got a message.

Where are you? Don't go back home alone. Let me send the driver with you.

Shameless, heartless, bloody asshole!

Riha looked irritated.

It was nothing compared to what I was going through. Enjoy.

Over the next five minutes, I got three calls and five more messages from Adi. I didn't answer either the calls or the messages.

Fuck off, Adi. I typed, then deleted.

Riha took Adi's hand in hers and placed a watch on his wrist. He smiled and said, 'How beautiful.' She looked proud, and then she of course asked for her gift. Adi looked taken aback and said he hadn't gotten her anything. He held her hand and kissed her. Riha's disappointment disappeared, and she said, 'I love you.'

I couldn't hear them, but that's what their lips said. If I were to continue standing there watching them any longer, I would have learned to read anyone's lips. But I wasn't that strong-hearted or generous.

I dashed to the washroom. A few months ago, when I had sat inside a toilet to overcome similar feelings, I had opened my bag, pulled out a blade, and cut myself until I had bled myself unconscious. Now also I opened my bag and looked inside. It had some things—a bracelet with a blue locket and a tiny grain of rice with Adi and my name inscribed on it. I wished Adi would wear the bracelet on his wrist forever, but my wish died prematurely in my bag inside the toilet. The sponge bra cups—

my secret weapons to plump up my breasts—dropped out of the bag. The same feeling of a blackout washed over me.

I am strong. I won't quit.

I promised myself, promised my mom, and promised any Gods who were watching me, if they were watching me. I sent a message to Adi:

Happy Valentine's Day, Adi. May God bless both of you with all the happiness.

Tears blurred the words.

Thank you, Tina. Every day is Valentine's Day.

Hmm, I got it—every day was special for them.

I know . . . I hate it. But I know.

I deserved a special day too. I placed the sponge pads inside my bra and pushed my breasts up. I saw the faint line of a cleavage form. Not bad! In my new-found sexy avatar and confidence, I left the bathroom, went up to the bar, and ordered a drink.

It burnt my mouth and my stomach, but my heart burnt more.

What a lovely night. And what a sad night!

'Happy Valentine's Day, sweets. If you are alone, would you care to join us?' A group of drunken boys in their early-twenties approached me. Were they gay couples? The drink started to work on my head.

'Where are your girlfriends?'

'Our girlfriends ditched us for some bloody pigs.'

'My boyfriend ditched me too. We are all in the same boat then. Alone, ditched, ignored, unloved . . .'

'What is the meaning of unloved? Never mind, let's unwind together. Drinks on us.' One of the guys took me by my hand. And all of us, rejected and dejected souls, became friends, rather drinking buddies, in no time. At least, I wasn't alone.

'I am going to change this day from Valentine's Day to

Devil's Day. This day reminds me of the bitches and bastards who broke our hearts,' I announced.

'Cheers to Devil's Day. This is for the bitch who made my heart bleed.' One of the boys began singing the popular Celine Dion song, "My Heart Will Go On". The song was not really well received by the group. How could he glorify romance? Clearly, alcohol spoke only the truth.

'Where is your boyfriend?' another boy asked.

'Here.'

'Here where?'

'In my stomach, just coming out.' I burped.

'Don't worry, Angel, we are here. You've got five boyfriends now!'

How did they know my nickname was Angel? Some telepathic connection maybe. One of them pulled me towards him and squeezed my breast. I thought he had somehow pulled out my boob; it moved! Oh, the pads had moved. I stopped him.

'You pick your boyfriend from amongst us,' another one slurred. I looked at them.

'Let me p-pi-pick . . .' I picked up the mike. 'Hello-h-h-hello . . .' I burped again. My boyfriends cheered.

'I dedicate this song to the devils who ditch people for others on this Devil's Day.'

'You promised me the moon . . . but you gave me a fart . . .
You promised me a kiss, you kissed that bitch
You promised me a smile, you made me cry
You are my valentine, I waited for your love
But you made me your ex-valentine in a day
I hate you, I hate you more than I love you . . .
Love is like a fart
When it's in the stomach, it's a part of you

When it goes out it stinks
I hate to fart, I hate to love . . .'

My Devil's Day gang sang the chorus:

'I hate you, I hate you more than I love you . . .
I hate to fart, I hate to love . . .'

I must have been sloshed. How could I have dared to sing something like that otherwise? I didn't even dare to be a bathroom singer, lest I hurt my own ears. But when you get ditched and drunk for the first time, when you hate the world and yourself, and when you hate the one you loved the most, you don't care a shit about rhythm or voice or sense or meaning. Some people recorded my performance on their phones, others laughed, while yet others danced and sang with me.

Then someone suddenly snatched away the mike from me. That was my fart, the Ditcher, the Devil, the Asshole, Adi. I fought for the mike and sang two, three more lines.

'I want the moon . . . I don't want . . .' I screamed into the mike.

'Tina, don't make a joke of yourself. Let's go.' Adi held my hand and began pulling me.

'Let me sing. You don't have a heart. You only have a dick.'

'Hey sweetheart, are you okay?' The Devil's Gang didn't like the intruder.

'Who the fuck are they?' Adi pushed them away.

'Don't call them fuck. They are my boyfriends.'

'Tina, let's go home.' I gave him the finger. Riha walked up to us and tried to pull Adi away from me. But Adi brushed her off. The devils interrupted Adi.

'You people stay away. She is my family.'

'Huh. Let her decide if she wants her family or her boyfriends.'

I went with my boyfriends, slurring, 'He promised me the moon and he gave her the sun. He even had sex with her.' I couldn't stand properly.

'Let's have sex then.' One of the boys held my hand.

'This is for you,' I took out the bracelet from my bag and put it on the guy who wanted to have sex with me. And I fell on his chest. He walked me out of the pub, pushing Adi away.

'Where are we going?'

'We are going for our honeymoon,' he said, pointing to a car.

'By the way, who are you?'

We both sat inside the car. 'See, do you remember this?' He showed me the bracelet and started to kiss me. I stopped him, it was different from the kiss I had shared with Adi.

'Let me go.' I tried to get up.

'You whore. You want to play games, huh? Now you want to go?' He pushed me back to the seat. I lay there. Then I heard a thud, then someone pulled this guy out of the car, and dragged me out.

'I can't walk . . . I can't walk. I want to sleep here.'

'Tina, would you please stop this drama?' Was that Adi I heard? I laughed.

'See, I even hear this asshole everywhere.'

'What asshole?'

'The devil who ditched me. He broke my heart. Why do I see him everywhere all the time?'

'Because you love him.'

'No, I don't love him. NO. I love him. I don't want to love him, but I love . . . I love . . .' I slurred.

It suddenly started to rain. Was nature also crying with me? No, Adi had splashed water on me.

I wanted to sleep . . .

No, I wanted to pee . . .

'I will pee here.' I raised my frock.

'Tina, let me help you.'

'I know you want to see me peeing . . .'

'Tina, you are drunk.'

Okay, you want to pee with me?'

'No.' Adi took me to the corner of the parking lot.

'Where are my bathroom slippers?' I looked down at my bare feet. Adi removed his shoes and helped me put them on.

'You are wearing them now.'

'Okay. Thank you.' I raised my frock, pulled down my panties, and started to pee.

'Tina, don't do this to me! Why are you standing and peeing?'

'Why can't I?'

Instead of answering, Adi made me sit. I peed, but then I couldn't get up.

'I want to sleep.' Wordlessly, Adi helped me stand and then pulled my panties up.

'Tina, you have to walk to the car. I am not Superman.'

'Where is Shah Rukh Khan? He carries girls in his arms all the time.' Sighing, Adi carried me to his car. Finally!

The last thing I remember hearing was Adi's driver asking him, 'Do you need a doctor?'

When I opened my eyes, I was lying on Adi's bed, dressed in his tee shirt and track pants. I felt like drums were beating inside my head. I met Adi and his family at the breakfast table.

'Tina! You are here? When did you come?' Adi's mom asked.

'I think I got here last night.' I was still confused.

I saw Neelam Aunty giving Adi a look.

'Your son has started to lie. I can't believe it,' Neelam Aunty told her husband. Adi sat there as if he was a ghost.

'Were you drinking, Tina?' his dad asked me. Adi just continued to look at me.

'No . . . I think . . . I mean . . . I was . . . But Adi didn't . . .' Neelam Aunty twisted Adi's ear and then got up to serve me breakfast.

I got a flash of Adi removing my dress and putting me in the bathtub.

'Did you remove my clothes?' I asked him in a low voice.

'You were dead drunk.'

'So? How could you do it without my permission?'

'Shut up and eat.'

'What else did you do?'

'I removed your panties too, but don't worry, I had seen your bum a long time back.' I hit his leg under the table.

'Where is my . . . bra . . . I mean . . .' He hogged his breakfast.

I got up and ran back to Adi's room. I found my bra, the sponge pads, and my panty in his room—all washed and dried. Adi finished his breakfast and came to my room, no, his room. I hid the pads before he could see them.

'Adi, who washed these?'

'Your mom didn't and my mom didn't. So it has to be me. I think two round moons are missing from the pile though. Take these and go home. Your mom called. By the way, you are wearing my undy, you can give it back to me later.' I pulled the tracks I was wearing and saw Adi's underwear beneath. Oh my G—

'Adi, you suck. You stripped me naked when I was drunk, didn't you?' I studied my hands and my neck in the mirror, acting a bit melodramatic.

'Oh yeah, I have nothing better to do. Stop hurling such outrageous accusations at me. Minu changed your clothes. So, now go and get a life. Good, your mom is here.' It looked like I was in trouble. Looking at Mom, I sensed the worst.

She and Adi's parents were watching something on the computer. I joined them.

Holy shit!

The girl looked so familiar. It was me, singing the fart song! God, I was completely out of tune.

'Tinaaaaa.' My mom sounded like thunder now.

'I am here.' And I sounded like a reincarnation of the Buddha.

'When will you stop being so stupid, Tina? I am telling you this in front of Adi, stop your one-way romance and give him and us some peace. I beg of you.' My mom folded her hands.

'Tina, you have become a YouTube star now. See how the number of hits is going up.' Adi's dad winked at me, trying to lighten the situation.

'And now, people will blame the parents for raising such brats. How you can drink? You are just fourteen, for God's sake. You want to drink? Drink at home . . . At least, I won't get to see such nonsense then.'

'Mom, I swear, I won't drink anymore. I just got carried away last night. It won't happen again.'

I had never seen my mom so angry, not even when I had tried to kill myself. She stormed out, ignoring Adi's dad who had tried play the mediator.

And that Valentine's Day ended with Riha breaking up with Adi again and me breaking up with Mom. And although I patched things up with Mom in three days, Riha started to see a boy from the tenth standard.

Adi never reacted about their split.

I became a YouTube star. It embarrassed me. Some people recognised me while others made different versions of my "moon and a fart" song on YouTube.

Many girls in school, including me, were happy that Adi had broken up with Riha. But Adi then began dating a series of girls—Leena, Ria, Pooja, Kia, Sara, and Katy—over the next two years. Imagine how much my heart burnt, how my head broke, and how my dreams shattered every time I saw him with one of these girls. But the rest of the girls started to believe that Adi was unlucky with his girlfriends. When everyone wanted to date him, his relationships ended as fast as they started.

One way or another, Adi and all his girls blamed me for his barren love life. All this while, I was busy polishing my dreams with Adi, while he dated one girl after the other.

This was crazy.

This was the fact.

I wasn't ready to quit.

CHAPTER 27

Truth or Dare

May 27, 2016

The moon and fart song brought us back to the present. We had an unexpected guest on the terrace—Rahul. He had brought beer. He loved it, said it was divine water.

'Let's play truth or dare one more time.' Rahul spun the beer can. I wasn't excited about the idea.

'No, yaar, let some truths remain unknown,' Adi said. Minu supported her brother.

'You asshole, don't be a philosopher.' Krish sided with Rahul. 'I strongly believe Adi has some secrets in his closet. That's not fair. Let's fart it out.' Krish went overboard when he was excited.

We started the game.

It pointed at me. Dia got the first chance to dig out the truth.

'Tina, are you a virgin?' I hadn't expected that bombshell to drop, though I couldn't have expected anything saintly from Dia. She deserved to know the answer, being our sex guru. We had watched our first porn movie at Dia's house. She had taken us through the fairyland of kisses, sex, and orgasms. I knew everyone she had kissed and had sex with. However, my first kiss and my first sexual encounter remained buried deeply in my own world.

Adi looked at me curiously.

Was he scared?

'No, I am not,' I said. It was time to tell the truth.

We are friends. Friends forever. Friends never keep secrets.

The next question came from Krish. 'Is that bugger here?'

'You can't ask me another question. Wait till the bottle points at me again.'

'No way. You have to tell us now,' said Krish.

'Yes, he's here,' I said.

Dia got up and turned towards me.

'I can't believe this . . . I swear, Tina . . . You are such a bitch, you never told me.'

'It was a mistake which I am not proud of. We were both drunk . . .' Strangely enough, my voice choked even though I wanted to play it cool.

'Who is this asshole? Adi? Rahul? No, it can't be Adi or Rahul. Who is it?' Dia stared at me.

'Well . . .' My eyes met Adi's for a few seconds. Everyone's jaws dropped.

'*Maa ki* . . . Are you kidding me? Adi, you motherfucker.'

Rahul and Krish jumped on him. Dia forgot to react.

'When did this happen, Adi? You've dated half the planet! How could you?' Rahul asked.

Dia just continued sitting, wondering or regretting.

Minu looked blank. Adi had no secrets from her.

Adi sat there like a saint.

'Tina's memory is better,' he said. He opened a beer and sipped on it. Then he lay back on the cemented floor and watched the stars.

I looked at him.

It seemed like it was just another "fuck" from his happening sex life. I didn't like it at all, but I had learned to let it go.

Sensible girls move on.

Stupid girls spoil their lives over the past.

I am sensible.

I am bloody sensible.

CHAPTER 28

The First Time I Had Sex

2015

You must be wondering why all the important things in my life happen on Valentine's Day only. I must say, I always looked forward to this day more than I looked forward to my birthday or Christmas, or New Year, or Holi, or Eid, or any other important festival that's celebrated in our country for that matter. I believed it to be the most romantic day and celebrated it even when I never had a valentine. But after Adi came into my building and into my life, he was always a part of my Valentine's Day celebrations. And every celebration had its own chaos which resulted in everlasting memories.

Eleventh standard turned out to be an eventful year for us. Though I had been waiting for some years to be Adi's official girlfriend, the blessing was never bestowed upon me. Meanwhile, Dia got into a steady relationship with a boy named Kevin from our tuition class. It worked out well for her as she stopped chasing other boys and we stopped hearing her spicy stories. Kevin looked happy with Dia, and sometimes he would join us for our evening sessions of chit chat at our favourite coffee shop. That same year, Rahul realised that girls did not excite him anymore. After some evaluation and introspection, he told us that he thought he was gay and fantasised more about boys instead of girls. Our reaction to this revelation was as if an electric shock had run through our bodies. Then we took it upon ourselves to help Rahul through this difficult time. But for that, Rahul had to first know if at all his feelings for boys were real.

Our hunt for Rahul's boyfriend started in full swing. We decided to look outside the school campus to keep him away from unwanted scrutiny. We were clear we had to find a boy who didn't behave like he belonged to another planet. The online world came to help. Of course, it was me who spotted the potential dating partners for our friend. Adi and Krish decided to interview the five guys we shortlisted. And finally, we found Rahul a boyfriend—Anjan, a mass communication student from St. Xavier's College. He wasn't too excited about the interview session, but he didn't have much of a choice really. By the end of the interview, we all loved him. In the days to come, even Rahul looked happy, until he found out that Anjan had been dating another girl for a few years. He liked to call himself "fun-gay". It was Adi who kicked Anjan out, saying, 'Don't mess with our friend's feelings.' Anjan promised he would leave the girl. But Rahul could not forgive him.

'Once a cheater, always a cheater,' Adi underlined.

It shocked us to see how badly Rahul had been affected by this break-up. Adi had dated different girls all the time, but we had never seen him crying over his break ups. Dia believed in "fuck buddies" and never looked back at her ex-boyfriends after she had moved on to the next guy. Kevin was the first one she got seriously involved with, since she was heartbroken when Adi started to date others. But she wasn't stupid like me and always moved on to a new guy faster than a racing car. Rahul, however, remained stuck in his Devdas mode and decided to be single.

'Man, this is crazy! It sucks. Now I know what Tina talks about.' My sympathies were with Rahul, and his with me.

That same year, Rohit proposed to me. Dia advised me to be smart and get out of my dream world to face reality. My mom too, had taken an extra interest in Rohit, talking and chatting with him whenever she met him at my tennis practice.

'Rohit is a good guy, I think he likes you.' She would say this more times than needed.

One day, I broke the news about my decision to go out with Rohit on Valentine's Day to Mom. She looked excited, and even helped me dress up that day, as if I was getting ready to walk down the aisle. That was quite a welcome change from her lack of enthusiasm whenever I had speculated my possible dates with Adi in the past.

As Valentine's Day had come closer, I had wondered about Adi and his new Greek girlfriend, who was also working in his dad's next movie, and was three years older than him. Adi denied dating her every time we broached the subject, but she looked like a Barbie doll and was almost always all over him whenever we saw them together.

On Valentine's Day, for the first time in my life, I prepared to celebrate it with my official valentine, Rohit.

My friends—Dia with her boyfriend Kevin, Adi with his Greek girlfriend, and Krish, Rahul, and Minu as singles—planned to celebrate Vaentine's Day at RockS. Krish assumed he could dance with Minu.

Rohit had promised to pick me up from home and take me to RockS. My mom waited for him more anxiously than I did. But he didn't turn up and we couldn't reach his cell phone either.

Was there something called a "Valentine's Day Curse"?

But whether there was actually such a curse or not, I was a victim of it and ended up spending my Valentine's Day evening with Mom, Rajesh Khanna, and some popcorn.

Not much later, my phone rang—Adi. He let out a laugh when he heard about my date with Mr. Khanna. Half an hour later, Adi knocked on our door. He'd come to take me to RockS.

'Where is your Cleopatra incarnate?' I grumbled.

'She is there at RockS.'

That night we had fun. We sang the moon and fart song. We danced and we drank. I mentally thanked Rohit for ditching me. I had a wonderful night, save for a few glitches that happened due to Adi's rumoured girlfriend hovering around us like a shadow. Krish danced with Minu all evening, and I predicted that she would soon be dating Krish. It's always better to be with a friend than a stranger.

'That's gross, Tina, I don't love him,' Minu told me.

Next day at practice, I met Rohit, who was in a scary avatar—eyes swollen and face bruised.

'I fell in the bathroom. And I couldn't call you because I lost my phone too.' I didn't bother to comment or discuss the incident with him as I had had a better night.

And my date with Rohit ended as fast as it had started.

February 14, 2016

The unexpected twist in my life happened on Valentine's Day. Again. We were in the twelfth grade. A month earlier, Adi had started dating his childhood family friend Shruti, a girl from a privileged business family, who had done her early years of schooling in London and who spoke in a British accent.

Rahul found his lost love in another guy—Ram, shortened version of a much longer South Indian name, who worked in Bollywood and had a struggling but promising career as a director. Ram visited Krish's restaurant often. Whenever he came alone, he would only order a masala dosa, but he would try every delicacy on the menu when someone else was footing the bill. We hated him purely for being so inconsiderate, miserly, and selfish in every possible way. We wanted to find a better guy for Rahul, but Rahul decided to visit his middle-aged lover at his home, against our advice. Yes, love has no rules.

Dia and Kevin had their own plans while Adi, Krish, and I had planned a joint celebration.

In the evening, Krish, who was supposed to pick me up, dropped me a message: *Sorry, tied up. See you directly at RockS.*

Now I totally believed in the Valentine's Day Curse, and Mom too started to have apprehensions while dropping me.

A little after I got there, Adi came to RockS with Shruti. His parents adored Shruti, above all she had "class"—the same class Adi had spoken about years ago in that lift when I had first seen him. I could easily take a leap ten years ahead in time and see Shruti as Adi's wife, one who would attend all those filmy parties and press conferences. None of the other girls had fitted into Adi's life the way she did. It made me agitated, angry, and helpless even though I knew by now that Adi was going to be just a first-one-way-love confined to the pages of my diary and to my memories.

Meanwhile, Shruti had never expected or wanted us to intrude on her special night with Adi. 'We shouldn't bother Tina and Krish. Let's go somewhere else.' She pretended to be considerate. The worse part was that all my calls to Krish remained unanswered. I texted him: *Come fast before I fuck your happiness. Shruti is farting.*

Njoy. You will thank me later, he replied before switching his phone off. He must have found a girl in his restaurant, leaving me alone with the drama queen and a least bothered Adi. That wasn't cool.

'Let me go then, I don't want to spoil your night.' I deserved a Nobel Prize for generosity. Sinking in a bathtub and dying would have been easier than being so generous to Shruti.

'It's okay . . . Chill . . .' Adi didn't wait for Shruti's opinion. 'Krish will turn up in a while. Whenever he picks up a girl, he always gets kicked out in an hour.' I said nothing and sipped on my wine while Shruti held on to her champagne and continued to sulk.

'Let's sing the fart song,' Adi said.

Shruti refused to accompany Adi.

I sat there, confused.

Adi pulled me to the floor. We grabbed enough chorus singers and dancers on our way to the mike. When we returned to our seat an hour later, Shruti had left without telling us.

'I should have gone. I am sorry, yaar. Somehow, now I realise that I am a roadblock in your romance.'

Wow, Tina, what acting!

'At least you've realised it now.' Adi's mobile beeped.

Fuck you. Don't ever come back to me. You are the most insensitive person I have ever seen.

I read Shruti's generous compliment over Adi's shoulder, and hid my delight.

'This is worse than what I think about you.' I chuckled.

'Do you want to dance?' Adi asked instead of bothering about what we thought of him.

'Oh really? I thought you danced with only your girlfriends.'

'Then it's okay. Let's just eat something.'

'I mean . . . I don't mind . . .'

That was the first time we danced together. Just the two of us. Adi had always had one girl or the other with him on the dance floor. That night I realised one more thing—I looked funnier than an ass when I danced, if an ass could dance. I could shake my own ass in the bathroom or in my bed without a care, but I didn't want to embarrass Adi. If I had to drink enough to be out of my senses, it would have helped me a little.

'I am going to have a drink,' I announced, but Adi just pulled me towards him, then moved at a slower pace, holding me tight.

'It's okay, Tina. You dance fine.' How had he read my mind? His nose touched my ears. Had he just kissed me or was I hallucinating? I tilted my head and looked up at him. He smiled. What did that mean? I had no idea, yet I put my arms around him, moved with him, leaned on him. And I had the best dance one could ever have, just hearing his breath, feeling his warmth against me, and sensing his heart around me. The trance of unbelievable calmness, the silence in noise, the love in hate, the hope in despair, and the time in emptiness, which forced me to get lost in time, in reality, in him, in me. How long? I didn't check. My head rested on his chest, my tears slept, my anger slumbered. Adi got me back to the present.

'Let's have a drink.' We went back to our table. I kept my mouth shut for a change. The feeling that I had just experienced was so divine that I didn't want to disturb its life and rhythm, which still throbbed in my cells.

'Thank you, it was so good,' Adi said. Was he being sarcastic? Not likely. There was this strange calmness in him which I had never seen before. I was scared to look at him. Suddenly, he became someone whom I'd never known for all this while. I sat next to him with a weird heaviness and shyness in me, as if I had just met him. Time, however, flew by at the speed of light.

'I have to go to the washroom.' Adi accompanied me. Just before I stepped into the ladies toilet, he gifted me a kiss. The drink started to work on me, however, and the feeling of his lips on my right cheek remained real even when I went into the loo and emptied my bladder. I didn't forget to shake my ass inside the bathroom and check my boobs in the mirror and give them a push to make them look bigger. And I remembered, suddenly, an earlier occasion when we had all gone to see a live orchestra and how my boobs had failed me there royally.

It was one of my earlier outings with enemy-transformed-to-best-friend Adi. Now, Riha always wore sexy dresses, and I had started to believe that boys loved sexy girls with thrusting boobs, silky legs, and tattooed abdomens. That night, I wore a sexy tube top inside my shirt when I left home. Just before reaching the venue, I removed my shirt. The padding I had fitted inside my bra made it look fuller, like a *Baywatch* girl's, a little lesser maybe. My tube top ended just above my navel. I didn't have a tattoo like Riha did, but I made some heads turn even after beauty queen Riha had literally cemented herself onto Adi. I saw the amazed look on Adi's face when he saw me.

Instead of appreciating my makeover, he had bluntly said, 'You are looking like a slut now.'

What the hell?

His girlfriend wore shorter clothes whenever she went out with him. If she didn't look like a slut, how could I? I wanted to ask him this. Instead, my tongue melted with his insult.

Oh! I had been in the bathroom for a long time thinking about Adi. I rushed out.

Adi was still waiting for me outside the washroom section.

'I was about to enter and kick open the washroom door. We should go home now.' He brushed back my hair.

We left Adi's car behind at RockS and got into a taxi.

I sat close to Adi. He put his arms around me. I looked at him, he looked straight ahead. I muttered, 'Thank you for making my day so special . . .' Then my lips were on his. He wasn't cold, yet closed, but there. I stayed there, not knowing how this silly action of mine would change our equation. I decided to move away. At the same time, I felt Adi's tongue on my lips. I must say, that was my second kiss. My body experienced a sudden chill. Adi's warmth rained on me. Adi's kiss transported me to the stars the same way it had done years ago on that foggy night inside that cold tent in Panchgani.

Oh God, it's been ages, but it still tastes the same, feels the same . . .

What happened next outshone the fanciest of dreams locked in my diary. He bit my ear softly, which tickled me. I felt like I'd died and gone to heaven. I dropped onto him the way a leaf falls from a tree in the rain. Adi held me closer, his raised heartbeat sounded like a thunderstorm in my ears. I heard him clearly, it was as real as me and him.

'I love you, Tina . . .' His words sent a spasm through my chest, between my thighs, and then in my head. I wanted to die. I mean I would have happily died in his arms.

The voice of the driver telling us that we had reached, separated us.

We were outside my building. It was time to say good night.

'Are we home yet?' Adi looked outside doubtfully. This must also be the theory of relativity. We lost time, but I still floated in the air. I didn't want to leave him and go. The taxi driver looked at us through the rear view mirror, perhaps wondering about "kids these days".

‘Do you want to come home with me?’ Before I said yes to Adi’s suggestion, I sent a silent thanks up to Mother Mary. This wasn’t the first time I was going to stay back at his home, but today it felt special, even though it appeared ambiguous.

The ride to Adi’s house was like the calm before a storm. It’s true, great feelings are meant to be felt. I just heard his quietness. I felt his kiss, the gush, the wetness, the stolen love over and over until we tiptoed into Adi’s room.

The moment Adi latched the door, he hugged me as if he would never let me go. Was he going to apologise like he had in the past? That would be such a shame! In my confusion, I felt his bulging tool against my body. I had seen it only in the YouTube videos that Dia had showed me while she had explained to me how those videos had misguided her.

The kiss on my mouth lasted longer this time. Strangely, something moved over my body like fluid, sending tremors throughout my body, tingling me, warming me up, pleasuring me, and making me cry out. It was so divine to lie next to Adi and feel his naked body against mine. My hands ran over him, like they always did in my dreams. Adi kissed me on my neck, on my shoulder, and moved towards my breasts. I forgot to worry about the smallness of their size. He kissed them and took them into his mouth, one at a time. I felt a burning all over me, I couldn’t control the gasps of ecstasy coming out of me. I was a little scared, but the sensation took me to heaven. The passion I had always imagined I would feel when I would be with Adi, I was feeling it right now! All the moments I had spent with Adi in my thoughts turned real. The universal law of attraction and my prayers to Mother Mary in Mahim Church were coming true. That’s what I wanted to believe then. I held Adi tight, kissing him all over . . . I didn’t realise I had left marks on him. His huge manhood pressed against my body.

'Can I touch it?' Was I stupid to ask him that? But that's what I asked. It was his private part after all, and I didn't want to intrude without asking for his permission. Adi took my hand and guided me there. I touched him for the first time. It was hot. I thought it would turn to ashes in my hand.

'It's okay,' he said. I turned and looked down at the thing in my hand while his hand moved inside my panties. I felt a pool of wetness accumulating there. Did boys like that? Adi didn't behave as if he hated it. He moved down and kissed me there. Hell, that was something I had never anticipated and I could never ever have imagined, even in my wildest of dreams, the feeling it gave me. Why was I crying? Did every feeling, good or bad, end in tears? I felt the bliss, the closeness, and the longing for more wash over me. My mind slipped away, my hormones ran out of me, into him. I inhaled the scent of Adi, something I'd only imagined. Adi turned me towards him, and looking into my eyes he said, 'How could I have waited so long . . . I love you . . .'

I stared at his face until he kissed my eyes, then my neck, and then my breasts. Then his fingers went deeper into me.

'It hurts . . .' I whispered. Was it the pain or something else?

'I will do it slowly . . . Okay? . . . If it pains too much, let me know. I don't want to hurt you.'

It did hurt me. But I didn't stop him. Pain had always been with me since the day I had met him. For the first time now, however, the pain had a meaning, a purpose, and faith. I felt Adi's manhood finding a way inside me.

'Are you okay?' Adi was more concerned about me. I nodded. He moved up and down in a rhythmic manner as he eased himself into me. I screamed a little; it felt like something was cutting through me. Then Adi suddenly stopped, looked at me, and separated himself from me.

What the hell now? I was stunned.

What else could it be? He must have remembered his girlfriend. He would tell me now, Tina, I am sorry, we are just friends, please keep this between us.

I pulled a sheet over me and sat up, looking for my clothes.

I had never been so embarrassed.

Insulted.

And felt like an ass.

'Hey . . .' Adi tried to turn me towards him.

'Stop it, Adi. I know you are sorry. I am sorry too.'

I didn't want to look at him. Keeping my back to him, I tried pulling my dress over me, but I couldn't do it properly as I was literally shivering. Adi came up behind me and hugged me. My dress got stuck halfway down my head.

'What's wrong with you, Adi? Let me go.'

'Shhh . . . Just stand there.'

'I am not your doll . . . or your girlfriend . . .'

I pushed his hands away from me.

'You are not. You are much more than that.' He held me closer again.

'I see that. If possible, please help me put on this damn dress.' I was crying by now.

'Come here, Tina.' Adi took me back to his bed again. And instead of helping me wear it, he pulled the dress off again.

'I don't have any condom with me, that's all. So let me just hug you and sleep.'

'Is it because of that?' I couldn't believe that. 'You should be having them in hundreds.' I had always been jealous thinking about all those girls having such intimate moments with my Adi.

'Tina, you are still same, the same arrogant little girl who made me fall . . .' He looked into my eyes. My breath stopped.

'Fuck the condoms, Adi.' Saying that, I kissed him.

'Are you sure?' But I didn't hear him completely.

We were on the bed, rolling, kissing, as if this would be the first and the last time we would make love. I didn't scream again. Sometime later, something happened. The stars burst inside me, thrust out of me, and turned into a new star. I hugged Adi hard, fearing I would fly away with whatever had erupted out of me. My breath and my tears were a homage to Adi for giving me the most wonderful feeling I had ever experienced. And then it fell on me, the white fluid from Adi as he curved back with a moan, hugging me, and taking me along with him in his powerful hug. My breathing became deeper, quicker, and stronger, and a powerful sensation of love rose inside me. It was overwhelming. The sensation only became more intense as the seconds went by. I had no idea how much time had passed by. Finally, the sensations tingling all over my body slowly faded away and I calmed down in Adi's arms, on his chest. I was at peace, my heart, his heart, and the feeling of being loved was ecstatic. Then we remained there, holding each other. I kept my head on his shoulder, our sweat mixed together, and we became one in our body fluids while remaining two in our thoughts.

I hadn't said "I love you" to him since we had kissed in the pub. My tongue had said it a million times earlier. They are right, the strongest emotions are to be felt, not spoken in words.

And this is what had happened last Valentine's night.

Some would say I lost my virginity quite late, some might say it was too early, many would wonder what's wrong with our generation, but my mom didn't say anything because she failed to articulate her reaction. She just got up and dashed into the kitchen to wash the dishes and kept shouting out from there that she would talk to me later. She didn't call me Angel. The previous night, her daughter had had sex with her so-called enemy-turned-first-love-turned-best-friend, and had reached home at lunch hour that day, still hung over from the drinks and her first orgasm.

May 27, 2016

My friends, they were all ears.

I didn't tell them everything in detail. However, they were all flabbergasted knowing Adi and I had had sex.

'I had always wished Adi to be the first guy I had sex with. I don't regret it. Not then, not now,' I concluded, omitting the part that Adi was the only one I wanted to have sex with, ever.

'I guess you both should thank me.' Krish winked at me.

I remembered his text. Had he done it deliberately? Perhaps he had wanted to help me fulfil my most important wish. This was his redemption for what he had done in the past.

'Of course, thank you,' Adi said. Was that sarcasm or was it a genuine thank you? Adi could always confuse others like this.

'You should have thanked him a long time back,' Minu said without clarifying the statement for our benefit. The brother-sister duo could speak in riddles which nobody could understand.

'I am proud of you, sweet. Finally you did it, that too with Adi. How was it? Did you see heaven and hell together?' Dia almost bit my ears.

'Yes, I saw the universe too.' I closed my eyes. It was time to let go of everything, everything which had Adi in it.

Adi dropped his jacket over me. It was getting colder.

'I was thinking, did you really tell me what I thought I heard that day . . . Did you really mean it? I mean, I know you didn't mean it, as you told me . . .' I fumbled for words.

Adi lay next to me silently.

I waited for his answer. But Adi didn't say anything.

Then I said, 'Thank you, Adi. It gives me closure before I go.'

Adi continued staring at the stars. I heard my friends vaguely and I heard Adi's heartbeats next to me.

'Friends?' Finally, I uttered that word.

I had stopped believing the universe would help me get Adi's love. Grrr.

Reality sucks, but that's the reality.

'I will miss you, Tina . . . I know . . .' He put his hand under my head like a pillow and kept me close to him. I could stop my tears, but not my running nose.

'You will be okay without us. You are strong now.' Adi didn't look at me even now.

Did that mean I hadn't been strong earlier?

Adi was right though. Every small thing, even a breeze used to affect me. But I learned to conquer it all—my asthma, my allergies, and every fear I had, one by one, step by step, day by day. I learned to honour my actions. I learned to keep my word. I managed to handle extreme situations. I started to be happy for others, and above all, I learned to forget and let go of everything that hurt me, including Adi.

'Tina, you will soon be able to forgive too. I will be the happiest then,' Adi said. I forgave my friends, I forgave myself, I forgave Adi, but I still had to forgive one person—my dad. I could never forgive him. Never.

'Adi, it will be tough there without you. I am scared . . .'

'You will be fine, dear . . . I promise.'

This was Adi's second promise.

I closed my eyes.

I didn't want to see the colours of love around us.

Adi kissed me on my forehead without saying anything.

It had the promise of friendship.

It had the coldness of my lost love.

It had the tears of my loveless days.

It had the warmth our bodies had shared once.
It had the memories which would never fade away.
It was the ending of my first love.
And it was the beginning of a new life.

CHAPTER 29

The Butterfly Effect

May 28, 2016

There are twelve stages in a person's life. So far, we had successfully crossed six—pre-birth, birth, infancy, early childhood, middle childhood, and late childhood. We would be finishing the seventh one soon—adolescence. And every stage had its own chaos, beauty, and lessons.

The last days with Mom and my friends were eventful. In the mornings, I would get up with a heavy heart, possibly the same as someone on a death row. Mom and my friends tried to cheer me up. Instead of spending time with them, I went to tennis practice frequently in order to spend time away from them. I even tried to instigate a fight with Adi and Mom, thinking it would be easier to leave them in anger.

I failed.

On the morning of May 28, Adi took me to Mahim Church. This time, I stood next to him and just stared at Mother Mary while he prayed.

I know you didn't listen to my prayers. I want to believe you have a reason for that. I don't know what that is . . . but whatever it is, take care of Adi, take care of my mom, and my friends, take care of Ajit Uncle, take care of Miss Rose, my coach, and Rohit . . .

'The last time you prayed for nine weeks to be with Riha through all your seven births. But you guys broke up. You still believe in Mother Mary?' I asked Adi while returning from the church.

'Yes,' Adi said. I didn't ask him what he had prayed for then or now. Let that be his secret.

It was time for me to say goodbye. Mom tried hard to put up a brave front. But the more she tried, the more she cried. Ajit Uncle didn't stop her. I remembered what my mom had told me years ago—the right man will never ask you to change. I hugged both of them. My friends—Adi, Dia, Krish, Rahul, and Minu—stood around me like my guardian angels. There were tears, laughs, hugs, and a hope that we'd meet again, soon.

I saw Rohit in the distance, standing with a bunch of flowers in his hands—lilies this time. I ran and hugged him.

'Hope you will forgive me.'

'Do I have an option? Hope to see you on the courts soon.' Rohit smiled. It had shades of pain.

Adi clicked a selfie with all of us in it. He pulled Rohit in for the shot before he could go. I noticed that, for the first time, they both were not giving any attitude to each other. We all made faces for the photo, however, our eyes brimmed with tears. We hugged each other, and then, finally we all hugged together.

It was time to go. My heart sank, my eyes sobbed, and my feet froze. I turned to Mom. I wanted to ask her, 'Would you please let me stay?' but I didn't.

I hugged Adi for the last time.

I didn't say anything.

He didn't say anything.

Why was I thinking he felt the same pain that I felt?

Just because he stood wordless?

'I have to go.' I freed myself from Adi's hug. Adi had a gift for me. His favourite "I WIN" cap, which he had refused to ever part with in the past. He put it on my head. I stood there, my eyes closed, feeling him all around me.

'It's my favourite. It suits you now.' Our eyes locked. I saw his red eyes, my heart wept.

God, how would I live without this guardian angel?

Adi leaned towards me to gift me a peck on my cheek. Dia's camera flashed. I turned to her, and she winked at me with a thumbs up. Then she gave me and Adi a look, as if she was trying to say, 'You stupid girl . . . Don't just go like an idiot.'

I smiled at Adi, or was it a silent cry? I hugged him again.

He turned my face towards him.

'Tina, we all are here for you. If you need anything, just ask. We will be there . . . You are our princess . . .'

'I know . . .' I wanted to kiss him. No, I wanted him to kiss me. We were so close. Our noses and our hearts touched and felt each other. I leaned a little towards his lips, Adi moved closer . . . It was like a waiting game to see who would take it forward . . . I waited in anticipation . . . But Adi's eyes shifted away from mine. He pushed the cap off my head, just ruffled my hair, and kept it back. Then Adi turned around and walked back towards our friends, leaving me there. I still hoped that he would come back, hug me, and stop me from going. But he didn't.

All this nonsense happens only in the movies.

I walked ahead, leaving them all behind.

I didn't turn.

I was crying, crying, and crying.

Up in the sky, I cried, cried like I was the last surviving

human on this planet. The Russian sitting next to me checked on me with a concerned look, 'Is everything okay?'

'No, I am not okay.' I cried some more. He didn't know how to react and gave me a bottle of water.

'And I wouldn't be okay anytime soon. Maybe never,' I said.

I saw the clouds where I had floated with Adi for years.

I saw the twinkling stars which we had touched together.

I saw the rainbows we had parachuted to.

I saw us, walking away from each other.

I saw my future, I saw my reality, I closed my eyes, wishing for the memories to fade, just fade, not disappear.

The "I WIN" cap lay close to my chest, collecting my tears, feeling my heart, breathing my lungs, telling me the story of a boy who fell from the sky and a girl who fell from the moon, how she broke all her bones, buried her heart in the sea, and then learnt to walk again. She heard them saying,

'Memories are to be cherished.
Unsaid is meant to be heard.
Unheard is meant to be felt.
Love doesn't have any form.
Love defines nothing.
Love defines everything.
Love is unnamed.
Love is timeless.
Love is you. Love is us. Love is everything.'

And I saw the colours of love. This time, they had shades of white.

I smiled.

CHAPTER 30

My Life in Florida

2016-2017

We fall, but we learn to get up again. We cry, but we never drown in our own tears. We see the dead end, but then we walk back to find a new way. We feel hopeless, but we search for a reason to be alive. We feel alone, but still we see smiles around us. We get tired and we want to quit, but we don't because we do not quit, never, whatever happens, ever.

Yes, I didn't quit.

The first three months in the US seared me inside out. I cried in the night for hours. I longed for phone calls which we hardly had any access to and that helped me in some ways. I wanted to run back to my mom and my friends, and to Adi.

Months passed and even though the memories and the pain of missing them didn't go away, they faded enough to heal my sore wounds. I had learned to put bandages on my heart and wait for it to heal.

I had also made some friends at the institute. My coaches were strict but good, and I learned to find the purpose of being there, or possibly, of being there on this planet.

I religiously spent all my evenings at a nearby cafe. I'd sit with a cup of coffee and listen to music. Still, Adi always took away a good chunk of my time. Memories of him made me smile. They gave me a reason to be a better person, to share a smile, to understand others, and to be kind to others. He made me wet in my lonely nights. I didn't feel any guilt or shame about that. Some nights, I woke up feeling his hands around me. We spoke about once a month. We would discuss everything under the sun in those five minutes but not our lost love. After all, we were friends now. Sometimes, we asked about each other's love life. Somehow, he was never surprised to hear me say, 'Single, still single.' Adi said he'd gotten too busy with being an assistant director and hardly had any time to waste on girls. He even joked, 'Looks like my love life ended the day you left.'

'I didn't curse you, okay?' I laughed.

Dia, Krish, and Rahul waited for their own thirty seconds while Adi finished his time. Mostly, they ended up hearing me on the speaker. They had already made plans to visit me for Christmas.

'It's so nice to hear you laugh, Tina.' I know Adi missed me too. I never asked him or told him how much I missed him, since I had learned to live without him.

My mom and Ajit Uncle came to meet me on my birthday. That one day off was the only luxury I had gotten since I had joined the academy. Ajit Uncle left both Mom and me alone to have our girly time. We went to the same coffee shop where I had learned to heal my wounds. Mom was happy to see Nicky—the owner of the cafe who had become my friend.

'Are you okay? I hope Ajit Uncle is not troubling you.'

'He has been so kind and loving. Thank you for bringing him into my life.'

'Then what?

'Don't you want to know about Adi?'

'I've learned to live without Adi.'

'Well, Adi sent this for you. He hates your academy for not having phone access regularly.'

Oh, he had never told me that! Stupid.

'He is buttering you, Mom.' I put the gift packet in my bag. But Mom was expecting me to open it in front of her.

'Mom, it's private.'

'Don't be so mean, Angel. I am your mom and we are friends. You know what, I found it funny that Adi misses you now. I can see that.' Just imagine who said this! My mom who always said I lived in a dream world.

I felt like I had won a Wimbledon game. But I said, 'Oh, he was so used to me eating his brains out every day. That's why.'

Heights of self-control!

I spent the rest of the evening with my step-dad and mom. I still called him Ajit Uncle. When he asked me to pick anything I wanted as a birthday gift, I just smiled and said, 'Not now . . . I don't need anything.' Shopping was not my priority. The time I spent with them was worth much more than that.

I looked at them, and I could see them as proud parents of a kid soon.

'Mom, Ajit Uncle would love to have kids of his own. I know how much he loved Jai.' Mom stared at me. Her eyes turned red.

'We have you, Angel . . . That's what he said too.'

'But I would love to have a little sister or a little brother. I should have someone to cheer for me when I play tennis.' I stopped.

I had one more thing to do. I called up my dad.

'How are you, Dad?' He was speechless. Then I heard him sobbing.

'Dad, it's okay . . . It's just okay . . .'

He still didn't have any words.

'Happy birthday, Angel.'

'I am sorry, Dad . . . I hated you so much . . .'

'I am sorry too, Angel. I deserve it . . . But you should know, I wanted to come and meet you in the hospital. But I couldn't get any leave . . .'

'I believe you, Dad . . . I do . . .' I hadn't believed it back then.

'When I see the stars, I think of you, Angel. I fall asleep watching the stars . . .'

It was my time to cry silent tears.

'Dad, will you come and meet me? I still have another year to go before I can get leaves.'

'I will try . . . I want to . . . I will be there next year on your birthday . . . I promise.'

'How is . . . the little one?' I didn't even know his name.

'Nirmal is a doing great.'

'That's good to hear, Dad. I love you.'

'I love you, Angel. I never stopped loving you ever since I first saw your smile.'

'I know, Dad. Love never changes.'

I didn't say that only people change.

Back in the room, I stared at Adi's gift. What could it be? I had no idea. It was from Adi, so it could be anything, even a baby elephant! I was patient for another ten minutes. I did twenty push-ups. Then I went and sat on the commode, counting back from hundred.

Why the fuck was I testing myself?

It's okay, Tina. You still love him, that's okay. It's not a crime.

I ran out of the bathroom.

I opened it. And I saw . . . It was just an empty box. Yes, there was nothing inside.

I cried again. Were these happy tears? Were they the result of the realisation that without Adi I had been empty all along even though I had claimed to move on? Or was it a realisation of the fact that love is just empty or perhaps it is full even when it's empty? Is it that you don't need big gifts to make you happy or is it that just knowing someone thought of you is enough to make you cherish the moment?

It could mean cherishing the memories . . .

Or it could mean burying them as well . . .

It could be all of the above.

CHAPTER 31

A Twist in the Tale

2017

The months flew by without me noticing.

And some good things happened in between. Miss Rose got married and moved to New York. She came to meet me too. Sitting at my usual cafe, I told her it was my turn to offer her coffee and sandwiches. She still had the same warmth about her, along with a new glow added by the presence of a man who adored her. Of course, she deserved only the best. We discussed Adi and how I had mended my broken heart, and in fact, how he had helped me do it. Miss Rose held my hand.

'There is always someone up there watching out for us and giving us the best. So don't worry.' Yes, that was the best thing to believe in when our human efforts failed. Now, I could smile while looking back at all those mad days.

Rohit had started to play internationally. Adi once told me that he should have really taken his autograph. Rohit sent me an email saying he looked forward to playing doubles with me some day. That would be fun. He had fallen in love with a girl who got hit by his car while she'd been walking on the road, that too when she had been on the phone, finishing a break-up. He had taken her to the hospital first, and then to his heart. They looked cute together. Did I feel jealous? A little . . . I felt a little jealous whenever I saw people in love, even if they were someone my grandparents' age or my own mother.

Time passed, and before I knew it, Valentine's Day was here. I decided to celebrate it in spite of still being single. In the evening, I wore the best dress I had, picked up some red roses, and visited Nicky.

Nicky wasn't surprised to get the flowers from me and she handed over a big box of Belgium chocolates to me. I hugged her. It was good to have a sibling from another mother in a foreign land, or in any land for that matter. The balloons and the flowers in the cafe brought back memories of my stupid but golden days in the past.

I missed my friends.

I missed my time with Adi.

I missed our fart song.

I sat near the glass window and watched the much-in-love couples at the flower shop at the corner and inside the cafe. Love still existed, with all its madness. I had company too—my "I WIN" cap sat on the table. I promised myself then that I would let this cap go when I was ready for my second love. It was the only gift from Adi that remained with me. I had even parted with the bracelet Adi had given me, which I had taken care of for all these years like it was my magic genie. I had thrown it in the garden, near my academy, where I went sometimes. I had cried then. But later, I had felt better. Still, my mind wandered to what Adi's Valentine's Day plans must be. Would the whole gang go to RockS and sing the moon and fart song?

A cup of steaming hot coffee and a gift packet reached my table, bringing me back to the cold evening that was keeping me miles away from Adi. I sipped the coffee and opened the gift absentmindedly. The next moment, I screamed, the coffee mug fell from my hands, and broke. Nicky and her staff came running to me.

'Tina, are you okay? You've turned pale like a ghost.' Nicky asked one of her staff guys to get me a fresh coffee, while another one cleaned the area. My hands shivered, my breath stopped. I turned to Nicky and asked her, 'Nicky, who gave you this packet?'

'I don't know, Tina. It was left at the counter with a note saying it was for you. What's in there?' Nicky looked at the packet as if it could be a ticking time bomb. But all she saw inside was a diary with a faded cover.

'Jeez, you scared the hell out of me.' She smiled and playfully smacked me on my head before heading back to the counter.

But I didn't breathe. How could Nicky know that the diary in front of me was more dangerous than a nuclear bomb? Because it was the same one that I had lost in the eighth grade, the same one which had taken away my sleep and even my right to crap in peace. It was the same diary in which I had written about my crazy dreams, my star treks, and kisses and orgasms with Adi. This was the same diary which had made me a poet. It was where I had written my wishes and sent them to the universe and to the Gods above. Who could have had it all these years? Was it my mom who had given it to Nicky? She wouldn't have made my life hell by stealing it from my classroom, not unless she could come into the classroom as the wind or a ghost.

My lost diary, no, my found-again diary stared at me.

I picked it up and smelled it. It still had the smell of my tears, my dreams, my love, and my hopes. I opened the first page. On it I had written in red. Nah, not my blood, just red ink.

To whoever is reading it,

This is a private diary, so I request you to be a little civilised and not to read further. If you are curious, just know, I was alive, I fell in love, and I broke all my bones.

Time will tell if my first love is going to be my last love or just my first love. Whatever . . . I loved him without any reason and that made me a perfect human being in this imperfect world of this perfect universe.

I am grateful to be alive, to love, and hopefully, to be loved.

Soon or sooner, but not later.

-TG

I didn't say bye to Nicky or pay my bill. I just ran out of the coffee shop and stopped only when I reached the public garden some blocks away.

Due to the cold evening and it being Valentine's Day, the garden was relatively empty. I sat on a bench and opened the diary. My breathing became laboured and I even forgot the diary was my own. I turned the pages, one after another. How every thought about Adi had made me so happy, how his one look and smile had given me the world! Tears ran out of my eyes like a flood. I cried aloud for the last time. I would bury the diary under the palm tree in front of me. I would let go of the most beautiful and most painful days of my life.Then, I stopped at the last page.

TINA'S WISH LIST

~~*1- Get a telescope as a birthday gift from Dad.*~~

2- Have breakfast at Tiffany's.

~~*3- Find out that I am someone's secret crush.*~~

~~*4- No more rashes and asthma.*~~

~~*5- Fall and break all my bones. Where are you? Come fast and help me break them.*~~ ☺

~~*6- My boyfriend should have Rajesh Khanna's cute smile.*~~

~~*7- Getting a birthday wish from Shah Rukh Khan. I wouldn't mind a gift also. What would I tell him then? I have to wait*~~ ☹

~~*8- I want to celebrate all my Valentine's Days with Adi until I die. 2013, 2014, 2015, 2016,*~~ *2017*

~~*9- I want to have my first kiss with Adi.*~~

~~*10- I want to have sex for the first time with Adi when I am seventeen. Mom, sorry, eighteen would be too late.*~~

~~*11- I want to hear from Adi that he loves me and he will love me forever. Only me.*~~

~~*12- Break up of Adi and Riha.*~~

~~*13- Go to the Mahim Church with Adi for nine weeks.*~~

14- Name the stars—Adi loves Tina.

I had never struck off the wishes from the wish list except the first one. Who had done this? Who knew about my fulfilled wishes except my mom? I ran back to Nicky's. She winked at me as if she had been waiting for me.

'Nicky, please, you have to tell me who gave this to you. It's not funny, okay?'

'Go to your seat, and let me get a coffee for you.' Of course, the corner table from where I could see the flower shop and observe the hustle and bustle of the street outside had become my seat ever since I had visited the place for the first time.

I sat there, still staring at my wish list.

'I think it's yours.' A hand pushed my '"I WIN" cap which I had forgotten to take with me while storming out of the cafe earlier. Before I could say thanks, I saw a white card without an envelope under the cap. I read it.

Can I go to Tiffany's with you?

I looked up. A man in a jacket and a cap smiled down at me.

FUCK!

It was Adi!

I stared at him, knocked for a six. He just looked at me with his most charming smile.

'Adi, what the hell are you doing here?'

'I thought you don't own Florida and I am not a terrorist. They let me land.'

'Fuck you, Adi, you could have just told me. You gave me a heart attack. I hate you, you asshole.'

'Good, I don't give you a fart anymore . . . And Tina, would you mind being my valentine? I mean for life . . . I have waited so long for this day. You can think and tell me.'

Was I dreaming?

I cried out loudly enough to get everyone's attention until Adi came and hugged me. His lips were on my forehead.

'Shhh . . . Shhh . . . I am here,' he whispered in the same voice that I had kept on hearing when I had been unconscious in the hospital all those years ago. I wanted to ask him a million things, but instead, I pinched him on his hand, hard enough to make him jolt away from me for a moment.

'I was just checking if I am awake or not.'

'Stupid, don't you think you should be pinching yourself for that? Huh?'

'Idiot, no. It pains me when it pains you.'

'It pained me all these years just to be your shadow. Did you know that?' I turned to him and saw that his eyes were glistening.

'So you were the one who watched over me when nobody was there for me.' I remembered the Valentine's Day card and the birthday card I had found in the class. It had disappeared once I got back with my friends. My mom had once told me that that's what a first love or crush is like—it goes away as fast as it comes by.

My mom was wrong. Hiyyaa!

'I have watched over you ever since I saw you in that lift. I waited for this day like that butterfly waited for the rainbow in the summer.' My jaw dropped. I didn't touch the stars or see the butterfly on my own. It was Adi who took me there. Adi carried me and floated in the clouds. They were his tears that had fallen on my forehead, his lips that had touched my face. It was Adi who had asked me for forgiveness, it was Adi who had whispered into my ears that he loved me and would never leave me. I had been hearing him when I had been in the coma. Then why had he done everything to put me there?

'I know what you are thinking. But I hope you will forgive me for what I did.'

'Yes, I forgave you the day I forgave my dad.'

'I wanted you to learn by yourself why I did whatever I did. I have been waiting for this day since then.'

'I know. You did everything to make me stronger, to make me own up to my actions and words, to make me face the consequences, and to teach me to fall and walk again, to help me let go of things and to forgive, to be a better person, to love without reasons, to feel the pain of love, to know the joy of love, to help me to live without you, to prepare me for this day and every day ever to happen in our lives . . .' I stopped.

And I cried. Again. This time, they were tears of realisation.

'Thank you for making me believe in your Mother Mary. I asked for you, for this day, for all our days, all the time,' Adi said.

I saw the colours of love from him, in me. I jumped up and down in the cafe, in the middle of the road, in between the honking cars, while Adi just watched me with his wide eyes, with the most beautiful smile, one like Rajesh Khanna's, with open arms and an open heart.

We walked through the streets, hand in hand, listening to each other's thoughts. I remembered the same class where Adi had proposed to Riha and had said, 'I wanted to look into your eyes and say I am in you and you are in me,' while looking at the display of his phone where I was in the corner of the photograph, next to Riha. I heard him saying, 'I fell in love with you the moment I turned back and looked at you.' He was talking about the lift and me. The ass display fiasco had happened because Adi had feared Krish would fuck me as he had boasted. He wanted to keep Krish away from me by making him his best friend. And by making Krish check under my skirt, Adi had ensured that I would hate Krish. It was Adi who had stolen my diary. And then through all these years, he made sure he fulfilled my wishes one by one. I remembered how Adi had come to RockS on our first Valentine's Day with Riha and the photo he had uploaded which had me, even though he had pretended that he hadn't expected to see me there. It was Adi who had brought Shah Rukh Khan to RockS on my birthday, made him gift me his watch, click a photo with me, and upload it on Facebook. Adi kissing me under the stars at Table Top hadn't been a mistake. He hadn't come for Riha. His watching the stars with me that night hadn't been accidental either. He hadn't meant Riha when he had said that he had kissed his girlfriend and that the one he would marry was sitting with all of us. When he had asked me if I had enjoyed the kiss, he had meant our kiss, not Riha's brutality. Adi had never french-kissed Riha, and that's why she had chosen the dare and literally bitten my lip off in anger. When I had said that if I had to choose between Adi and Mom, I would choose Mom, I remembered his tears had fallen on me. It had definitely hurt him, but he had never said anything. When he had said, 'I wouldn't want anything to be erased from our lives. Nothing, not a thing,' he had meant every word of it. That's why Minu had said, 'You should have thanked Krish a long time back.' She had known all along that Adi loved me.

'You didn't come to the tent for Riha that night, right?' I asked.

Adi just smiled and wrapped his hands around me. We didn't need any words. Adi had visited the Mahim Church for nine weeks not for Riha, but for me. Adi knew all along that I LOV ADI was me. When I had said I wouldn't stalk him but would still love him, he had told me, 'I am looking forward to seeing you honouring your words. You better do that.' I had thought he was being sarcastic.

He was the one who had written the truth on that blackboard about I LOV ADI. He had let me win that fight in school, he had uploaded the audio clip to honour my actions. He hadn't expected me to slit my wrist and quit loving him and living. Every Valentine's Day, he made sure we were together, one way or another. When he had said, 'Once you learn to live without me, my girlfriend would remain with me forever,' that girlfriend was me. When I had worn skimpy clothes, he had said that I looked like a slut, but he never bothered when Riha did the same. Because he never cared about what she did; he cared about me. He came to the tennis match for me, but faked being not interested. It was not just me who followed him everywhere, he did it too, but without making it obvious. When he had said "I love you" to me while making love, it had been the truth. Later, he hurt my heart like a devil just to make sure that I leave Mumbai and focus on my career. This is what he had said—'When you learn to live without me, I will be there.' At Mahim Church, when he had said that he still believed in Mother Mary, he had meant it, because he hadn't asked for Riha, it was me he had asked for. The bracelet he had gifted to me—which now lay somewhere in the garden, and which I would dig out very soon—had been bought for me, not for Riha. That's why it fitted me perfectly. 'The day you left, looks like my love life ended,' hadn't been a joke either.

'Did you beat up Rohit on that Valentine's Day two years ago?'

Adi shrugged, but with a wink.

'I didn't want to, but he didn't leave me with much choice. He was in love with you. I believed nobody could love you more than me.' That's why they always avoided each other.

Would it have been great if I had known Adi loved me as much as I loved him? Probably not. I wouldn't have become the person I am today, I wouldn't have had the same experiences, and I wouldn't have been stronger.

The night was colder than all the other previous nights.

The winter clouds saw Adi next to me, his arms around me.

The chilly breeze around us knew Adi would keep me warm.

We walked towards the same bench in the garden where I had sat just a little while ago. The stars appeared in the sky for us. Adi looked up like an astronaut. He pointed up in the sky, showed me two stars twinkling for each other.

'That's Adi Loves Tina.' Adi then gave me a certificate with a map which marked these two stars. This is what I had muttered in one of my drunken sojourns. It was my dream.

'I don't have anything to give you.'

'You gave me your life . . . And you are my stupid girl.' We sat there silently, going back to those moments.

We loved each other when we fought.

We prayed for each other even when we hated each other.

'Adi, I just can't believe it. It's like a dream . . .' I said.

Adi put my hand in the pocket of his jacket. My hand closed upon something. I picked it up. It was the same bracelet that I had made for Adi with our names inscribed on a rice grain and it was the same one that I had put on the wrist of that guy from RockS, the one who had wanted to have sex with me. I could have never imagined he would have gotten it back from him or saved it for today.

'Happy Valentine's Day, my love.' Saying that Adi just looked at me as if we had met for the first time. I experienced the same shyness, the same restlessness, blushing, and gratitude that I had felt after the first time we had had sex.

I put the bracelet on Adi's wrist and kissed him.

Adi took my diary and struck off number eight and fourteen on my wish list.

'Tomorrow morning, we will strike off number two on the list—having breakfast at Tiffany's.' Adi pulled my nose. And I became silent.

'What? What's bothering you now?' Adi was curious.

'What will happen when you become a big movie star?'

'I waited so long for this day to tell you this—we will live in love and we will die in love. You have to trust me on this. Wherever I am, whatever I am, wherever you are, whoever you are . . . our love won't change, we won't change, I won't. This is a promise, Tina. And I never break my promises. You know that. I believed I had earned your trust by now. If not, I command it.'

'I am sorry, Adi. I didn't mean it that way . . . I was wondering . . .'

'It's okay, Tina. The best thing I love about you is you always pour your heart out. And I see what's in your heart before you even say it. Trust me, we are going to be fine. No, we are going to be great. I can't wait anymore.'

Adi always kept his word.

And I didn't want any Facebook guarantees anymore.

I didn't want the world to know Adi was mine.

And I would never be bothered about all those girls around him, not anymore. I know that we are meant to be together.

For some, their first love always remains their first love.

And for some, their first love becomes their last love.

We belonged to the second group.

I lay in Adi's lap, listening to our breaths singing in harmony, hearing the music of rain, the dancing of the wind, seeing the paintings of the stars, seeing us in the sky, in the stars, in the moon. It is true, if you truly wish for something, the universe will bring it to you even if it looks impossible.

'Tina, I see the colours of love . . . I always saw them when you were around . . .'

'What are the colours you see?' I asked.

Adi whispered the colours into my ears.

I smiled. He smiled.

And we sealed our first love with our lips, tongue, and heart.

Love Never Ends

"I am sorry ... didn't ... that way ... I was wondering."

"It's okay. [illegible] ... [illegible]"

[illegible] ... [illegible]

[illegible] ... [illegible]

... always kept his word.

And I didn't want [illegible] characters [illegible].

I didn't want the world to know [illegible] was him.

And I would never be [illegible]

But not anymore. I know that we are meant to be together.

[illegible] that true love always [illegible] first love

And the songs [illegible] become [illegible] love.

We belonged to [illegible]

[illegible]

[illegible]

[illegible]

[illegible] impossible.

[illegible]

[illegible]

"What [illegible]"

[illegible]

[illegible]

[illegible]

ACKNOWLEDGEMENTS

Every story has a story behind its birth. My earlier novels, *Goodbye Girl* and *Gone with the Bullet* had their own stories. So does *First Love.* I have been frequently asked why I write crime fiction that is too brutal which may inspire teenagers in a wrong way. What I can say is, no crime fiction writer writes a novel to inspire people to pick up a gun. However, I have always believed, and still believe that our right to get justice shouldn't be lost in translations which are merely a concept in our lifetime. I would like to use this opportunity to say that my crime stories are not to influence the readers in any wrong way. I also believe that readers are much smarter than the writers.

First Love is a dedication to the teenagers who read my books and to mothers who are worried about crime novels. Your mails, love, and support are overwhelming. Tina, this is for you and for your wonderful parents, Arjit Biswas and Sudarshana. You are the teen we are proud of. My gratitude to my teachers for being there for me then and now. My English teacher, Usha ma'am, I thank you. Thank you Agnes Jacob for being the inspiration for the character of Miss Rose in this book. She was there when I rebelled and was lost and troubled. Your never-ending friendship makes me wish for more teachers like you. Also, *First Love* has sprung out of my realisation about the importance of friends and family in our life.

You wouldn't have been holding this book without the support of my publisher, Gaurav Sabharwal. I would never forget that his belief in my stories made my journey as an author. I am extremely grateful to Shikha Sabharwal, publishing director of Fingerprint! Publishing, who made my dreams into reality. Every encouragement and support you showered upon me is beyond a thank you. A million thanks to my wonderful editors Pooja Dadwal and Garima Shukla for being the backbone of this book. Your guidance and faith in me made my days and inspired me to write better. Garima, I must say, I have hardly ever come across anyone who values time the way you do. You surprised me with every single call you made at exactly the scheduled time. Special thanks to Gayatri Goswami for her insightful suggestions and contributions which made a lot of difference to the book. Special thanks to everyone in Fingerprint! Publishing and Prakash Books.

My heartfelt thanks to Director Anurag Basu for his kind words about this book. I met you with this book during your busy schedule. Your encouragement and support is much more than I could ever dream of.

Ketan Sedani, as always, you were there through this journey. It means a lot and a big thank you. Arushi Chaudhary, thank you and hugs. Nida Razak, it's an honour to have you in the team. We are eagerly waiting to grab your books from the shelves very soon. Sameer Matai, love you for my pic.

Thank you, my friends, who know what friendship means. You inspire me.

And MYK, thank you. You know for what.

SHEEJA JOSE is the author of two bestselling crime thrillers—*Goodbye Girl* (2015) and *Gone with the Bullet* (2016). She was the creative director of some of the successful TV shows such as *Adalat* before she found her calling in writing. A fan of Tarantino and Christopher Nolen, she enjoys studying psychology and physics. She believes that the best learning happens by travelling and strangers are the best teachers.

Sheeja lives in Mumbai and is currently pursuing her Masters in literature.

To know more about and to connect with Sheeja Jose, contact her at:
sheejasthoughts@gmail.com
https://twitter.com/sheejasthoughts
https://www.facebook.com/sheeja.jose.96
https://www.facebook.com/Sheeja-Jose-302087689998420
Insta: authorsheejajose